DEATH IN TRAVELERS REST

J. A. Thompson

JACOB ALLEN
PUBLISHING

An Imprint of Kingdom Knight Productions, LLC

To Amanda, my love and my muse

CHAPTER ONE

"Whoa, whoa, whoa. Whatcha doing there, Blake?" asked Mr. Turner.

Blake froze with his book halfway inside his backpack and looked up at Mr. Turner through strands of his long, brown bangs.

"Putting my stuff away?" Hoping that his hoodie and hair masked his embarrassment, Blake tried to sound more annoyed than busted.

"I didn't hear the bell ring." Looking around to the rest of the class, Mr. Turner asked, "Did anyone else hear the bell ring?"

The rest of the eighth-grade English class responded to their teacher with an assortment of smirks and eye rolls, except for a couple of wannabe teacher's pets who called out, "No, we sure didn't."

"Come on, Mr. T. There's less than five minutes left of class."

"That's five minutes you could spend reveling in Ray Bradbury's brilliant dystopian novel, *Fahrenheit 451,* and answering my study guide questions."

Blake responded with his best deadpan look before returning the book to his desk and muttering, "I wish the government would burn *this* book."

A soft, digital beep sounded. A mad scramble ensued, with books and folders stuffed into bags and slung onto shoulders.

Blake gave Mr. Turner a "see-I-told-you" look, palms up. Mr. Turner gave him a sly grin before raising his voice over the hubbub. "Don't forget, if you didn't finish your study guide questions in class, then the rest are homework."

Great, Blake thought. *Another missing homework assignment for my mom to complain about.* School took up enough of his day. No way was he going to let homework cut into his video game and streaming time.

"Man, I finished those questions twenty minutes ago," boasted Frankie, a lanky kid with dark, chin-length straight hair parted down the middle. The dork was wearing his oversized Mexican national team jersey again, along with baggy, sagging jeans which forced him to shuffle as he made his way to the door.

Mr. Turner responded in the tone that kept you guessing whether he was mocking or being sincere. "I know, Frankie, you *always* finish early."

"Bye, Mr. Turner."

"Bye, Jessica."

"See you tomorrow, Mr. T."

"See you tomorrow, Devontae."

Blake wished they would just shut up and walk through the door so he could get to lunch. He was starving.

Hoi, a tiny Asian chick with long black hair and small oval glasses, paused near the doorway, holding up the line. With a determined expression, she turned back to face the teacher.

"Mr. Turner, will you be at our volleyball match after school today?"

A few of the other girls in class, also on the volleyball team, slowed their exit, creating even more of a bottleneck as they waited for Mr. Turner's response.

"Uh, yeah, I hope to. 4:30, right? I can probably stick around after school that long and catch a set or two. I expect you to kick some butt if I do, though."

Hoi blushed and looked down. "We'll try our best."

And with that, the dam of stupid girls in front of Blake burst, allowing him and the rest of the class to flow down to lunch.

JONAS TURNER TURNED back to his desk, shaking his head. He tried to attend as many school functions as he could to support his students, but he knew he had to be careful with middle-school girls.

He didn't have movie-star good looks, but he could probably pass for "ruggedly handsome" status, as long as the person judging was far enough away and squinting. Between his imposing height at 6'4" and his athletic build earned from years of playing sports, Jonas attracted more than his fair share of middle school crushes. Usually, his friendly yet business-like approach and extreme caution in one-on-one interactions deterred his female students from being too forward. He could only remember two occasions when students had been so brazen that he'd had to recruit fellow female teachers to intervene on his behalf.

Jonas was in his sixth year of teaching at Plainview Middle School. He had applied to this poverty-stricken school straight out of college with the mindset that these kids needed him more than the kids on the other side of the tracks. His time here had been a rollercoaster, though. The school was a revolving door for teachers and principals. He was already the longest tenured teacher in the English department, and this year marked the fourth time in six years that a new head principal had taken the helm.

On top of all the personnel changes and fluctuating administrative expectations, the school had recently moved into an abandoned high school while their old, dilapidated building was renovated into a new, state-of-the-art facility. The old premises provided plenty of space and nicer sporting facilities, but all the critters that made the school their home had been difficult to eradicate. The frequent occurrence of mouse droppings and occasional sightings of the furry little beasts were bad enough, but what really bothered the staff were the snake incidents.

Jonas himself had experienced two of the worst encounters. Once while he'd been explaining a new poetry unit, a six-foot black snake had slithered through a hole in a ceiling tile and hung halfway out, directly above two female students. Jonas had tried hard to calmly convince the two girls to leave their seats and go stand by the door without causing a panic. But, thinking they were in trouble for no good reason, the girls had got an attitude and demanded to know why. As he began to explain that a snake was dangling over their heads, it had dropped like a heavy leather belt onto their desks.

It still amazed him that no one had got hurt in the mad stampede towards the door. Or suffered permanent hearing loss from the two girls' ear-splitting screams.

Jonas wasn't exactly afraid of nonvenomous snakes, but that didn't mean he was eager to pick one up—especially a six-foot monster that was freaking out as it struggled to find traction on the smooth laminate flooring. He'd decided to let maintenance handle it, but by the time they arrived, it had made its way to the air conditioning unit and crawled inside, never to be seen again. Which didn't make anyone happy. It took some serious coaxing to convince his students to return to class.

The other incident was less dramatic, but more concerning. Standing outside his classroom to greet incoming students, Jonas had looked down and noticed a tiny snake curled up a few feet from his room. At first, he'd thought one of his students was playing a joke on him by planting a rubber snake by his door. But as he reached down to pick it up, there was a slight rattle of the tail. It was real.

He'd called maintenance again and warned his fellow teachers not to let students down his end of the hallway. Ms. Agnew, the eighth-grade science teacher from his team, had identified the snake as a baby eastern diamondback rattlesnake and insisted that they scoop it into a jar and release it back into the wild.

Initially Jonas had been okay with the plan, but after doing a little research the next day and finding out that baby rattlesnakes have even more venom in their bites than grown ones, he'd regretted the decision. He paid a lot more attention to his surroundings now.

With an obligatory check of the floor on either side of his room, he closed his classroom door and headed towards the cafeteria.

His room was at the end of a long hallway in a building on the back side of the school grounds. With long, powerful strides, he speed-walked past the sea of blue lockers mounted on either side of the hallway.

Jonas moved quickly everywhere he went. He was naturally impatient and hated wasting time. If it weren't for the complication of startling people, he would sprint from place to place. He still did, on occasion, if a parking lot looked empty enough. But he kept that to a minimum after he'd noticed several different people clutching at their heart or wallet when he ran by.

As he sped by the second-to-last room on his right, he

heard a commotion in what should have been an empty classroom. It sounded like one of the big, black-topped science desks being moved across the room. Jonas stopped, backpedaled a few paces and peeked inside to see if Ms. Agnew needed help moving it.

What he saw was an all-out brawl between two students. The tussle had cleared out a space of about fifteen feet, with the monstrous desks scattered in all directions. The student with his back to Jonas had tightly pulled cornrows and a muscular build. He was clearly getting the better of the fight. Powerful punches kept connecting with the other boy's face, while the flailing return blows looked more like feeble attempts at self-protection.

Jonas rushed into the room. "Stop! Stop! What are you doing?"

The boys gave no indication they'd heard. They continued to throw wild haymakers, so Jonas moved in behind the bigger student. As the boy reared back for another swing, he snatched him up in his arms and twisted the boy away in one swift motion. Conscientiously keeping his body between the two combatants so neither one could get in a sucker punch, he carried the bigger kid towards the exit.

"Get off me! Let me go! I ain't playin' with you, you better put me down."

"Calm down. It's over. I'm going to put you down, but we're going straight to the principal's office," Jonas told him.

"Yeah, whatever." The boy shouted over his shoulder, "This isn't over. I'll see you after school."

Jonas put him back on the ground in the hallway, but he kept both hands firmly on the kid's shoulders. In a voice that was calm but carried a hint of malice, Jonas bent his head and spoke in the boy's ear.

"No, this is over. You will not hit that boy again. If I have to follow you around this school and keep track of your every movement, I will. But we're not going to tolerate that kind of violence. So let it go."

"Whatever, man. Just get your hands off me."

Jonas dropped one of his hands, but kept the other firmly on a shoulder as he came up beside the boy. "What's your name?"

He looked away.

"I asked you for your name."

"Zeke."

"Ok, Zeke, I'm going to hand you over to Assistant Principal Bryant." Jonas opened the door to the tiny office, where a broad-shouldered black man was peering over reading glasses at some paperwork. Principal Bryant looked every bit the middle-aged former defensive lineman that he was. He was an intimidating presence unless he was smiling, and he wasn't smiling now.

"You again." Principal Bryant broke off his death stare at Zeke long enough to look Jonas's way. "What did he do now?"

"I found him bashing another student's face in down the hallway. I need to run back there and deal with that one. Is he good with you?"

Principal Bryant's eyes shifted back to Zeke. "Yeah, I'll take care of him. Bring me the other one when you're ready."

"Will do."

Jonas spun around and jogged back to the science room. He half expected to find the room empty, but the boy was standing by the sink near the back of the room, facing the wall.

"Hey, are you ok?"

The boy didn't answer or look in his direction. Jonas walked up behind him and gently turned him around.

He was surprised to see it was one of his own students—in the blur, he hadn't registered the familiar face. To be fair, the kid's face was barely recognizable. One eye had swollen shut, his whole face was puffy, and blood was leaking from a busted nose and split lip.

"Davontae, what happened? What were you guys fighting about?"

Davontae looked away, still trembling from the adrenaline spike.

"Tell me what happened. If he attacked you for no good reason, I'll make sure he never does it again."

Davontae set his mouth and shook his head. "I ain't no snitch."

The comment hung between them as Jonas debated the pros and cons of pushing the issue. It was unlikely he could convince Devontae to tell him what had really happened. He was also aware that if Devontae got labeled as a snitch, life could become even harder for him. So he simply put a hand on his shoulder.

"I know you're not a snitch. You tell Principal Bryant whatever you want to tell him. Just remember this: I'm here for you if you need me. If you want to talk about anything—and I mean anything—just say the word. If you need help, I will find a way to help you. Heck, if you want me to, I'll even show you some sweet dance moves so you can snag you a girlfriend."

Devontae rolled his one eye and started to laugh, but it quickly turned into a deep, chest-heaving sob. Jonas squeezed his shoulder a little harder and told him it would be okay, but a dam had clearly broken. Jonas pulled him into a hug and let him cry it out.

After a minute, Devontae pushed away sheepishly and turned back to the sink. Jonas pulled a couple of paper towels from the dispenser.

"Here, take these. Crying is the body's way of healing. Everyone does it. Once you wipe away the blood around your mouth, I need to take you to Principal Bryant's office."

Devontae turned towards Jonas and made brief eye contact before looking back to the ground. "Thanks, Mr. T."

Jonas glanced down at his watch as he walked through the cafeteria doors. Lunch was almost over, but he hoped the food lines were still open so he could grab a plate to eat during his next class.

As he rushed past the teachers' table on his right, Dave, the math teacher from the other eighth-grade team, called out. "Hey, Jonas, did you have a little mishap with a ketchup packet? You've got it everywhere, buddy."

Jonas looked down at his light blue button-down shirt that now had red streaks all over it. "Ah, man, I must have got some of Devontae's blood on me."

Ms. Agnew sat up in alarm. "*Blood?* What happened? Is Devontae okay?"

"He'll be okay, but his face is pretty busted up. He and some kid named Zeke were going at it. In your room, actually. Your desks are scattered all over the place."

Ms. Agnew's eyes narrowed as she looked down at his shirt. "Did you step in and break up *another* fight?"

Jonas's face flushed. He looked away.

"Are you kidding me, Jonas? Are you trying to get suspended? You know district policy forbids teachers from getting involved in an ongoing fight. I know you know this, because you were right in the middle of the huge brawl last semester that led to the emergency staff meeting to remind everyone of the district's hands-off policy."

Last semester two eighth graders who were old enough to be high school sophomores had gotten into a gang-related altercation in the cafeteria. The one who always wore a shade of blue was 6'4" and 250lbs. The other student, who usually wore a bright red T-shirt, was average height for an eighth grader, but was about as muscle-bound as any middle-schooler Jonas had encountered.

When they'd started throwing punches, they'd cleared out everything in a twenty-foot radius, with nearby teachers pulling students away from the danger zone. Jonas had wanted to step in right away, but even he was leery of getting between those two.

But as the two gladiators seemed to be wearing down, a handful of teachers closed in. As soon as they took a step back from one another, Jonas snatched the boy in the red T-shirt from behind, twisted him away, and started marching him to the other side of the cafeteria while five or six other teachers circled the blue-clad giant and tried to restrain him.

Unfortunately, they weren't successful. The man-child was like a raging bull that only had eyes for his red target. He plowed through the teachers holding him and anyone else standing in his way. As cries of "Look out!" filled the room, Jonas managed to duck under a right hook and roll to the side; the behemoth of a student came crashing down on the student in red.

Jonas had hopped up, jumped on top of the two boys, and done his best to pin them down so they couldn't get a good punch in. That's how they'd stayed until the cops finally arrived to haul both kids to juvenile detention.

Remarkably, no one had been seriously hurt, but a few teachers and students had been left with bruises, and the district had sent a memo expressing its displeasure at the handling of the situation.

All eyes from the teacher table were now on Jonas, but he wasn't ready to back down.

"Look, I'm not going to let some kid get pummeled while I stand back and watch. By the time I called the resource officer and he made his way over from across the campus, Devontae could have been seriously injured. And, frankly, even allowing one more punch was one too many. If they want to suspend me for breaking up a fight, then they'll just have to suspend me."

Some teachers nodded in understanding, while others shook their heads. The bell rang, signaling the end of lunch. Jonas glanced toward the line and wondered if he could talk his way into getting a plate still. He figured his odds were pretty good, since he was on good terms with the lunch ladies, and they always talked about needing to fatten him up.

"What are you going to do about that shirt?"

Jonas turned back to Ms. Agnew and shrugged. "What *can* I do about it? I don't have a spare."

Mrs. Nichols, the math teacher across the hall from him, spoke up. "Just run back home and grab a new one. You don't live far. I can bounce between our rooms and keep the peace until you get back."

"Are you sure?"

"Yes, yes, just go."

"Yes, go, we've got you covered," chimed in Ms. Agnew. "You can't go around looking like a victim from a horror film. Besides, it's not sanitary. Go home and change."

"Okay. I'll be back as soon as I can."

Jonas drove like he walked—as fast as he could without scaring people or attracting law enforcement. His GPS said it was ten minutes to his house, but he usually pulled into his driveway in eight minutes or less.

He and his wife, Jessica, had just moved into a nice subdivision four months ago. If it had been up to him, he would have happily stayed in their two-bedroom-one-bath starter home until they paid it off. He was easily content and tended to be more of a saver than a spender.

But his wife had hated their neighborhood. She'd told

Jonas that she wouldn't even consider having kids while living on a street sandwiched by two trailer parks and a mere quarter mile from railroad tracks. It drove her crazy that Jonas couldn't even hear the trains go by. They were like white noise to him.

Wanting to do whatever it took to convince his wife to start raising kids, he'd agreed to move somewhere more upscale. They didn't have to go far. Just a few miles north of the rundown neighborhoods of West Greenville, where Plainview Middle School sat, was the quaint little town of Travelers Rest. Between his salary as a teacher and Jessica's as a physical therapist, they were able to afford the mortgage of the smallest model in a posh new neighborhood called White Meadow. Jonas still felt like an imposter surrounded by so many luxury homes and cars, but he had to admit he enjoyed living there. Neighbors were friendly, walkways felt safe, and a large pool was within walking distance.

The only downside was the hyper-vigilant HOA. The middle-aged white women in the neighborhood did not mess around when it came to enforcing rules. If you failed to mow your lawn at least once every two weeks, then you could expect a notice in your mailbox. Changing the color of your fence without submitting a form and waiting for approval was an automatic fine. Just last month an emergency HOA meeting had been called to put a stop to the few neighbors trying to lobby for solar panel installations. They'd been deemed too ugly and detrimental to house values.

Knowing that speeding through the neighborhood could launch a hundred angry Facebook posts on the neighborhood community page, Jonas slowed way down after turning left into his subdivision. Feeling the pressure to return to class as soon as possible, he leapt from his car as soon as he put it into park. Racing to the doorway, he unlocked the deadbolt and doorknob.

His ranch-style house had an open-floor plan. After passing the small laundry room on the left and the short hallway to the right with the guest bedrooms, the home opened to a kitchen, dining room, and living room with no dividing walls. The only room on the left side of the house was the bonus room with all Jonas's books.

The master bedroom was in the back-right corner of the house, down a short hallway shooting off from the living room. In his rush, Jonas barely had time to register that it was odd to find its door closed. He and his wife always left it open unless they had company over.

When he swung the door open, he jolted to a stop. Something was in his bed.

Jonas's conscious mind couldn't register what he was looking at, but his subconscious mind did. He felt the hairs on his arms rise; a cold sense of dread made his stomach clench. As he tried to make sense of what he was seeing, it was as if the room tilted to the right.

He closed his eyes tight and leaned against the doorframe, trying to regain his equilibrium. The blood rushing to his head was loud in his ears. Thinking about the sound of his own blood pumping in his veins made something click. Jonas opened his eyes and turned to the bed again.

There was blood everywhere. It was all over the woman in his bed, all over the comforter, and all over the wall above the bed.

The woman was lying on her back with her face turned towards the far wall. Her hair, matted with blood, covered her face. She was wearing black lingerie, and from the middle of her low-cut outfit, the handle of a knife was sticking straight up. The blade was buried so deep that only a quarter of an inch separated the handle from her skin.

When Jonas looked down at her bare legs, which had somehow escaped most of the blood spray, a sense of familiarity brought on another adrenaline spike. He knew his wife was at work. He had kissed her goodbye when she'd left that morning in her scrubs. And she never wore lingerie. She complained at how quickly he always took it off, so she hadn't worn any in years.

But these bare legs looked just like his wife's.

Trying his best to avoid the blood spatter, Jonas crawled onto the top corner of the bed and leaned over the body. Propping himself up with his right arm, he slowly took his left hand and pulled back the bloody hair from the woman's face.

It was Jessica.

"No, God, oh please, God, no!" Jonas's eyes darted over her body and the bed, still trying to take in what he was seeing, but none of it made sense. He turned back to his wife's bloody face. "Jessica, can you hear me? Please wake up. Oh, please don't be dead."

Her eyes were open and lifeless. Despite that, Jonas frantically felt her neck for a pulse. At the same time, he bent his head down to her mouth and listened for a breath.

He couldn't find evidence of either. Her body wasn't stiff, but it was cold to the touch.

Jonas dropped off the side of the bed, grabbed his head with both hands, and buried his face in the mattress. "God, please save my wife. There's nothing you can't do. Please bring her back to life. I don't want to live this life without her. Take my life if you have to, not hers. Please, Lord, please."

He looked up, tears streaming down his face. His wife lay just as still as before. He hadn't expected to see her sit up, but it sure felt better to bury his head in his hands and hold on to an ounce of hope than to look up at the nightmare before him.

He wanted to collapse to the floor and pretend this was some horrible dream, but something inside him clawed its way through the numbness fogging up his brain. With the sleeve of his dress shirt, Jonas roughly wiped away his tears and pulled out his phone.

For the first time in his life, he dialed 911.

CHAPTER TWO

Officer Olivia Selman killed the lights and siren of her patrol car and checked her rearview mirror one last time. It appeared that she had achieved her goal. After two near-collisions as she wove around vehicles and blew through intersections, she'd managed to be the first responder on the scene.

It wasn't often that dispatch alerted local law enforcement of a possible homicide in Travelers Rest, a small town outside the mid-sized town of Greenville, South Carolina. The reason she had pursued a degree in Criminology and then joined the police force right out of college was her desire to prevent and solve violent crimes such as rape, armed robbery, and murder. But her first four years had been spent pulling over drunk drivers, breaking up domestic disputes, and hauling in a variety of drug abusers.

She worried about a smile creeping onto her face in her excitement, so she narrowed her eyes and pressed her lips together as she made her way to the front door.

Tall hydrangea bushes with massive light green buds

bordered the three steps to the porch. As she approached the first step, movement behind the bush on the right froze her in place. A tall, skinny man in khakis and a light blue button-down shirt slowly rose to his feet. There were red stains on his chest.

Olivia placed her hand on her gun. "Who are you?"

"Jonas Turner. I'm the one who called 911."

"Why did you conceal yourself behind that bush?"

The man looked to the road and scanned the sidewalk. "We have a lot of dog walkers in this neighborhood, and I wasn't in the mood to wave hello."

"What happened here?"

"I don't know. I came home from work and found my wife stabbed to death. There's blood all over our bedroom. I have no idea how something like this could happen, or *who* could do something like this."

The man was remarkably calm. It was hard to tell if it was due to shock, unusual inner strength—or a more sinister explanation.

"Are you sure she's dead?"

"Yes, I'm sure."

"Is there anyone else in the house?"

"I don't think so. I didn't see or hear anyone."

The wail of distant sirens getting louder by the second told Olivia EMS was on the way. She knew other responders wouldn't be far behind. "I'm going to clear the house. You stay out here and let the EMTs know I'll be back to let them in as soon as possible."

The man nodded as she slipped inside the door. There was a hallway to her right and a small laundry room to her left. After a quick glance inside the laundry room, she methodically cleared the hall closet, the bathroom, and the two bedrooms connected to the hallway, including both closets.

She proceeded to the large space that made up the kitchen, dining room, and living room. It was easy to clear; there was little to hide behind in the rooms. After a quick check of a spare room to the right of the kitchen, she made her way to the large sliding glass door that led to a small porch on the backside of the dining room. A quick glance registered a grill, a small round table with four chairs, and some gardening tools, but no signs of life.

Olivia had neither seen nor felt a presence in the house so far, but that changed as she approached the last hallway. Her skin crawled and her heart raced as she stepped into the master bedroom. She struggled to tear her eyes away from the crime scene on the bed, but she knew the importance of finishing the job of clearing the house.

With fast, fluid movements, she opened the door to the master bathroom and checked the toilet room, shower, and walk-in closet for a possible intruder.

The only presence she could see or feel was the woman lying on the bed. Turning back to the bedroom, Olivia paused in front of the large mirror above the double sink vanity. She looked hard into her own eyes. Then she closed them and took in a big breath, letting it out slowly.

"You can do this," she whispered. "Just focus on the facts."

Stepping back into the bedroom, she finally allowed herself to focus on the scene before her. The man outside hadn't been kidding. There was blood everywhere. Her eyes followed the spatter up the wall above the headboard. The arterial spray reached all the way to the nine-foot-ceiling.

She looked back down at the knife sticking out of the victim's chest. It appeared to be driven directly into the heart, but the killer's last thrust had been only one of many. Olivia bent over for a closer look, but a wave of nausea hit her fast and hard. Her hand shot to her mouth and nose and she ran back into the bathroom, barely making it to the toilet before she spewed chunks of her burger-and-fry combo from lunch.

She quickly wiped the toilet rim clean and flushed the toilet, hoping no one would be able to tell that someone had thrown up. Washing her hands, she stared daggers at her reflection.

She wasn't sure if it was the mutilated flesh or the pungent odor of copper from all the blood that had set her off, but she was determined to take a closer look at the body and surrounding area. Pinching her nose closed, she returned to the victim and once again examined her up close. With all the blood covering the body it was hard to tell just how many stab wounds there were, but she would guess there were about two dozen cuts to her chest, neck, and arms.

This wasn't a murder of opportunity or a dispute that had gotten out of hand. This was a rage-killing with extreme overkill.

Although blood had either soaked or spattered most of the bed, there was a triangle of body and bedspread that was largely unblemished, starting from the woman's thighs and extending to the foot of the bed. Olivia moved to the base of the bed and took in the body from that angle, trying to picture how the murder had taken place.

The killer must have been on top of the victim, pinning her down while thrusting the knife down again and again. As wounds began to open, blood had sprayed in every direction except for down, because the killer had been in the way. They must have been drenched in blood. Olivia needed to find those bloody clothes before they were destroyed. She glanced in the direction of the master closet and thought about the laundry room.

Unfortunately, she needed to get back to the front door to let the EMTs in so they could call the death and notify the coroner. She would have to look for the bloody clothes later. But before she let in other responders, she wanted one good look at the victim's face.

She pulled out her flashlight and pointed it at the dark hardwood floor to make sure she wasn't stepping in any blood as she eased to the far side of the bed. She stopped moving as soon as the beam hit the floor. There were blood smears all over the three feet of space separating the bed and the far wall. And in the center of one smear was a near-perfect shoe print. A very large shoe print, with tread resembling a pair of sneakers.

Olivia looked up into the vacant eyes of the woman in the bed.

"You deserved better than this. I know it's small consolation, but I promise you, we will find your killer. And he will pay for what he did to you."

SHE OPENED THE door to find two EMTs bending over the husband, taking his blood pressure, though they grabbed their bags and sprang to their feet as soon as they heard the door open. They were both young and fit. The only discernible difference between the two was that one had reddish-brown hair while the other's was jet-black.

"You guys are cleared to go in and check the body. The victim is most certainly deceased, though, and this is a murder investigation. Move the body as little as possible, and do your best to avoid the blood spatter on the floor and bed."

"Yes, ma'am," they both chimed as they rushed inside.

"Stay away from the far side of the bed," she called after them.

"Why do they need to stay away from the far side of the bed?"

Olivia turned around and faced the husband, looking him up and down. "What did you say your name was again?"

"Jonas Turner."

"Mr. Turner, did I hear you correctly that you came home from work to find your wife like this?"

"Yes, that's correct."

"Where do you work?"

"I'm a teacher at Plainview Middle School."

Olivia arched an eyebrow. "Is it common for a teacher to come home in the middle of the day?"

The man's face flushed, and he looked down. "No, it's very unusual. I can't remember the last time I came home during the school day, but I got some blood on my shirt today, so I came here to change."

Olivia's eyes dropped to the red smears all over his chest. "Are you saying that the blood on your shirt is not your wife's? You got blood on your shirt before you came home to find your wife covered in blood on your bed?"

The man's face got a shade redder. He turned his head to the right, then the left, and then back to the right in quick, agitated movements as he spoke.

"Yes, it's not my wife's blood. It's not my blood. I broke up a fight at school today, and one of the students had a busted nose and lip. I got some of his blood on me. The reason I came home was to change my shirt. I know it's a strange coincidence, but this blood on my shirt and my being home in the middle of the day have nothing to do with my wife's murder. We need to figure out who did this."

Olivia fixed him with a penetrating stare, mulling over the guy's story and willing him to keep talking.

"Officer Selman, can I have a moment of your time?"

Olivia looked over her shoulder to find Officer Roger Mullins standing a polite distance behind her.

You couldn't help but think of the word 'round' when looking at Roger. His torso formed an almost perfect circle, topped by a round face and glasses with thick, round lenses. Olivia wasn't sure how he passed the fitness test each year, but other than that, she was glad to have him working in her precinct. He was diligent and trustworthy. But at the moment, his timing sucked.

She turned back to the husband. "Stay right here. I'll be right back." Taking four quick, long strides towards Roger, she did her best to keep the frustration out of her voice. "What do you need, Roger?"

"I was just wondering what you wanted me to do while we waited for the lead detective to arrive."

Olivia looked around and waved a hand in the general direction of the neighborhood. "You know what to do. Put some crime scene tape around the yard. Keep the neighbors away. Ask them if they saw anything this morning. I need to get back to interviewing the victim's husband." She started to turn.

"Um, Officer Selman?"

Olivia turned back, answering through clenched teeth. "What, *Officer Mullins*?"

"Did you hear who was assigned to this homicide investigation?"

"No. I was too busy clearing the house and securing the crime scene. Who did they give it to?"

"Detective Vogel."

Olivia closed her eyes and took a deep breath. She'd known the Criminal Investigations Division for Greenville County would have to assign a homicide detective to this case, but she had hoped that it wouldn't happen immediately. And that it wouldn't be Detective Vogel. He had a reputation for two things—closing cases quickly and busting balls. He preferred to work alone and demanded everyone do things his way. It was the worst possible assignment for her involvement in the case. This might be her only chance to interview the husband.

She looked up as two more patrol cars parked near the house. There would probably be many more within the next hour. Homicide investigations were like flames to a moth for police officers. She turned back to Roger.

"Could you make sure we get some crime tape up and have any arriving officers help with interviewing the neighbors? I have a few more questions for the husband."

"Are you sure that's a good idea?"

"Just take care of the crime tape and neighbors, Roger. Let me worry about me."

The husband was standing in the same spot as before, looking in her direction. Olivia walked straight up to him and began the line of questioning weighing heaviest on her mind.

"Do you often wear tennis shoes to work?"

They both glanced down at his shoes.

Sounding puzzled, he replied, "I wear these running shoes everywhere."

"Everywhere?"

"Yeah, pretty much. Not to weddings or funerals, I guess, but just about everywhere else. I have bad feet. Too many years of wearing cleats wore the pads of my feet down to the bone, so now I wear the most comfortable shoes I can at all times."

Olivia stared hard into the man's eyes. They were a mixture of bright green and slate blue, and they returned her gaze without blinking or shifting. She didn't read guilt in them, but the circumstances told her there was a high probability that she was staring down a murderer.

"Did you touch the body after you came home to find your wife in this condition?"

"No, I didn't do anything to the body." He stopped talking abruptly, as if something had just hit him. "Wait, no, I did touch her hair—and her neck when I checked for a pulse."

"Why did you touch her hair?"

The man's eyes took on a thousand-yard stare. His words came out much quieter this time. "I wasn't sure it was my wife. Her hair was covering her face, so I couldn't tell for sure. But it was her. I listened for a breath and checked her pulse, but she was already gone. I knew she was gone."

Olivia felt a pang in her chest. Clenching her teeth, she chided herself for being moved by his words, whether true or not. This was not the time for empathy. She needed information. "Did you go to the far side of the bed to check her pulse?"

His eyes came back into focus and met hers. "No. I crawled onto the corner of the bed nearest the door because it had the least amount of blood. I tried my best not to contaminate the crime scene. Why do you ask?"

"So you never stepped foot on the far side of the bed for any reason once you came home from work?"

His voice rose a couple of notches in intensity. "No, I never stepped foot on the far side of the bed. That's her side of the bed. I rarely step foot on that side, period, let alone today, when I came home to find my wife murdered. Why do you keep asking about the far side of the bed? What did you find over there?"

A car door slammed behind them. Turning together, they watched a man with thick, gray hair and a weathered face wearing aviator glasses and a dark suit rapidly approach from a black Ford Explorer.

Detective Vogel.

He stopped two feet from Olivia and the husband, looking back and forth between them as a muscle twitched in his firmly clamped jaw. Without a word, he went around them, took off his sunglasses, and opened the front door. Before stepping inside, he turned his head slightly to the side.

"Officer, a word," he said, and then proceeded into the house.

Olivia turned to the husband. "Stay right here."

As she followed Detective Vogel into the house, the two

EMTs headed out. They paused momentarily when they saw her, and the one with reddish-brown hair spoke up.

"You were right, there were no signs of life. We've alerted dispatch to send the coroner out."

Olivia nodded, and the guys filed past her.

She found Detective Vogel standing in the open expanse of the kitchen and living room, still with his back to her, holding his hands behind him. Once she was within a couple of feet, he spun around and fixed her with a hard stare.

"What is your name?"

"Olivia Selman."

"Was that the husband you were talking to, Officer Selman?"

"Yes."

"The husband of the murdered woman in the next room?"

"Yes."

"So you were questioning the prime suspect in a murder investigation?"

Olivia felt a rush of heat to her face, but she didn't give him the satisfaction of looking away. "I was gathering information for the sake of the investigation. I don't know that he is the prime suspect."

Vogel feigned enthusiasm as he broke into a big, mean smile. "Oh, so you've already uncovered another suspect, have you? Who does the husband think did this?"

"He doesn't know."

"Well, then, who do *you* think did this? Did you find some strong evidence to point to someone other than the husband?"

This time Olivia couldn't hold his gaze. Looking at the floor, she spoke through gritted teeth. "I don't have another suspect yet. I just meant that I'm not sure he's the one responsible."

"Well, I'm not *sure*, either. Right now he's just a suspect.

But since he's the only person we know that's been in
the house, and he's the only person we know so far that
might have a motive to kill, that makes him our *primary*
suspect." Vogel leaned forward and threw his hands out
dramatically. "From now on, I'm the one who interviews
potential suspects. Initial responses to questions are
everything to an investigation. Every careless word they
speak, every mannerism and facial tic, is a gold mine. I need
that information. I hope you have a good memory, Officer,
because I need every single detail written down in your
report."

Olivia looked up into Vogel's eyes. "I do, and I will. You
will have every word spoken and every mannerism displayed
documented in my report."

This time he was the one who broke off his gaze, turning
his head toward the bedroom. With a hand stretched out in
that direction, he prompted her. "Okay, then lead the way.
Show me what we've got."

Olivia walked into the bedroom and took a position at the
foot of the bed, where she could watch Vogel's reaction to the
scene without the fear of stepping in evidence.

His eyes were drawn to the blood spray on the wall
and ceiling, just as hers had been. He looked down to the
hardwood floors and took careful steps as he approached the
bed. Bending at the waist, hands behind his back, he peered
closely at the woman's chest.

"It looks like a kitchen knife. Have you checked to see if
there's a set of knives in the kitchen missing a blade?"

"No, I haven't gotten that far yet. I mostly just secured the
scene before you arrived."

Vogel didn't respond. He appeared engrossed in his
examination of the many wounds on the woman's chest
and neck. When he turned his head in Olivia's direction, he
appeared surprised she was still standing there.

"Well, are you going to check to see if this knife matches a set in the kitchen?"

"Yes, sorry, I'll do that now."

Embarrassed, she rushed out of the room and swept her eyes over the kitchen counter. There was a block of knives by the stove. Three were missing.

She looked closely at the handles without touching them; they appeared identical to the handle sticking out of the woman's chest. Next she peered into the sink in the middle of the large granite island. There were a few bowls and spoons, but no knives.

Grabbing a paper towel, she gently opened the dishwasher. There in the silverware rack were two more knives with the black handle and three silver dots. With the one embedded in the body in the next room, the complete set was accounted for.

Olivia returned to the bedroom to find Vogel staring at the bright white section of bedspread under the woman's bare legs.

"It's a knife from the set in the kitchen."

He looked up and nodded slowly. "Yep, and this was a very personal killing with extreme overkill. The killer jumped on top of the victim and stabbed her at least thirty to forty times. Many more than was needed to get the job done." Standing up straight, he backed away from the bed, still looking at the body. "Where is the husband supposed to have been during all this?"

"He's a teacher at a nearby middle school. He says he came home from work to find his wife this way."

Vogel raised his eyebrows, put his hands in his pockets, and rocked back on his heels. "He's a middle school teacher? And, what?" He nodded towards the body. "He just comes home in the middle of the day for a little afternoon delight? It seems highly unusual for a teacher to leave school grounds in the middle of the day for a little nookie."

Olivia frowned and rested her hands on her utility belt. "He said he came home to change his shirt, which had gotten blood on it from a student altercation. I got the impression that he was surprised to find his wife at home."

"What?" Vogel's face became animated as he took his hands out of his pockets and directed both of them towards the body. "You're telling me that the husband came home from work unexpectedly, and he was surprised to find his wife at home? Surprised to find her half naked wearing a sexy little outfit?" He shook his head dramatically. "It's not looking good for your secondary suspect, Officer Selman. Not good at all."

Already annoyed by his jibe, Olivia knew that what she was about to say would only make the husband look worse, but she wanted credit for the vital piece of evidence she'd found. "I need to show you something on the far side of the bed."

Switching on her flashlight, she moved to shine the beam directly on the shoe print in the middle of the smears of blood on the far side of the bed.

Vogel stood beside her, leaning forward. "The husband looked pretty tall out there. Does he have big feet, too?"

"Yes. And he's wearing running shoes. He also claimed he never stepped foot on this side of the bed."

"Hmm. It appears our husband has some explaining to do."

"Should we go back out and ask him a few more questions?"

Vogel chuckled. "We, huh?" He eyed her up and down. "As long as you don't step on my interrogation, I'll let you sit in and listen, but it's not going to happen here. We're done letting this guy feel like he's in control of the situation."

He spun and headed towards the door as he continued

talking. "Take him to your precinct and put him in the interview room for me. I want to walk the house with the crime scene technician and make sure he's documenting everything he needs to document."

Olivia hustled after him. "But we're not arresting him, right? What if he doesn't want to go to the precinct?"

"Convince him."

"Should I have him meet me down there so he doesn't think he's being arrested?"

Vogel stopped on the front porch and turned back to her as she came up beside him. "No, we need to have a look inside his car, and we want to keep him on his toes. Don't cuff him, but tell him we need to take him to the precinct to record an official statement. Don't treat it like an option. Just do it."

Jonas watched as the man in the suit and the female officer spoke in low tones on his front porch. He couldn't make out what they were saying, but they seemed at odds about something.

While they were inside his house, he had walked down to the street and leaned against the guy's black Ford Explorer. It made him at least a little less conspicuous to the growing throng of neighbors gawking at his house.

Now the man in the suit was headed towards a different SUV that had pulled up a few minutes ago. The female officer swept the front yard with a quick side-to-side turn of her head before spotting Jonas up against the SUV. He stood up straight as she slowly made her way to him.

A thousand different questions had come to mind while he waited, but when she stopped a couple of feet in front of him, all he could think to blurt out was, "Have you found anything?"

The officer pursed her lips, seeming to mull over how to

respond.

Jonas filled in the pregnant pause with rapid-fire follow-up questions. "Do you have any idea who might have done this? Or why they did it? Anything pointing in one direction or another?"

"It's too early in the collection of evidence to say." The officer paused again, and her face tightened into a harder look. "I assure you, we will find out who did this. But right now, I need you to come with me downtown so I can get an official statement."

"Oh, okay, sure, I can do that. I might need some of these cars to move so I can back out of my driveway."

"That won't be necessary. I'll drive you down."

The officer turned and started walking towards her patrol car. Jonas scrambled after her.

"Wait, how will I get back home?"

She opened the back door of her patrol car and motioned for him to get inside. "I'll make sure you get home when we're done."

Jonas looked down into the back seat and then back up at the officer. "You want me to get in the back?"

"Yes."

"I'm not under arrest, am I?"

"No, I'm just transporting you to the station. We're discouraged from having civilians sit up front. It's a security risk. Just hop in, and we'll go get that statement."

Jonas's face flushed. He willed himself not to look around at all the eyes he felt on him as he ducked his head to climb into the patrol car. The officer closed the door and made her way to the driver's seat. Starting the vehicle, she did something with a box on her console, and the siren let out a quick "whoop" sound as she did a U-turn on his street.

He couldn't help himself; as they passed his nearest neighbors, he looked out the window to see who was watching him leave. Every other house they passed had a stay-at-home mom or a retiree standing on the front lawn, craning their neck to get a glimpse. Within the hour, the whole neighborhood would know he'd been hauled away in the back of a patrol car.

"I'm going to have to move," he muttered.

The officer looked up at him in her rear view mirror.

He kicked himself for saying it out loud. What was wrong with him? Was he in shock? Why was he worrying about what his neighbors thought? This was no time for morbid humor.

Jessica had been murdered. Her last moments of life had been terrifying and brutal. That should be his focus. He forced himself to think of that and what she must have endured.

The wave of grief his guilt demanded hit him like a tidal wave. The inside corner of his eyes burned, and his vision began to blur. Images of Jessica's bloody body and blank stare started attacking his mind, drowning out all other thoughts. He grabbed his head with both hands and rested his elbows on his knees, rocking rapidly, trying to will the images out of his mind.

"Are you okay back there?"

Jonas stopped rocking and, without looking up, responded in as steady a voice as he could muster. "Yes, I'm fine."

He sensed her gaze for a few more seconds, but she said nothing else.

He didn't think he could do this. Not thinking about Jessica's death made him feel heartless. Thinking about her death turned him into a basket case. He began praying silently.

Lord, please help me. Give me the strength to see this through. Help me bring Jessica's killer to justice. Give me the supernatural peace you promise to those who turn to you. Oh God, please help me.

The pit in his stomach was still there, but as he exhaled, his shoulder and neck muscles relaxed. His mind took on a new sense of calm clarity.

Cautiously, he allowed his mind to resume its effort in pulling together the details of his wife's death. But it was like putting together a puzzle with half the pieces missing. So many of the circumstances surrounding her death made no sense to him. And try as he might to push it to the side, there was one puzzle piece he kept picking up and turning over, unable to see how it could possibly fit.

Why was Jessica wearing that little black negligee?

CHAPTER THREE

The chaos of after-school dismissal was in full bloom. Little islands crowded the breezeway; most students had already gravitated towards their clique. Annoying sixth graders were running around the various groups, trying to peg each other with paper balls.

Blake cranked up the volume in his earbuds and kept his head down as he navigated his way past the car riders and around a large group of Hispanic kids. Next was a little group of the most popular eighth-grade girls, which he planned to give a wide berth. But as he was scooting sideways between them and the camo wearers, one of the sixth graders running for his life from a paper ball plowed into his back, knocking him into the circle of popular girls.

Blake put his hands up to soften the impact, but the result was more like a two-handed shove to the back of a girl named Monica. She whipped around, snarling in disgust when she saw who'd pushed her. If "shrivel up and die" had a face, this was it.

She started yelling at him, but he couldn't hear her over

the screaming lyrics of his heavy metal music. Judging by his limited ability to read lips, it was something about him being a freak. At least, he hoped that was the word she used.

Blake looked around for the sixth grader who'd knocked him over to redirect some of this blame, but he was nowhere to be found. He resigned himself to mumbling an apology while backing away.

Walking much quicker this time, he made his way to bus station number three. He hated his bus. It made no sense that of the seven bus routes, number three was always the last to leave. He just wanted to be home, in his room, watching YouTube and playing video games. Away from stupid people.

Someone was looking at him. He glanced to his right, where a group of guys from the basketball team were hanging out. The one named Cameron seemed to be saying something to him. Blake started moving in the opposite direction, pretending he hadn't seen.

The machine-gun-like rhythm of drums and guitars in his ears came to an abrupt stop.

Cameron held Blake's earbud in his hand. "What are you listening to?"

"Nothing. Give me back my earbud."

"Obviously, you're listening to something, since you can't even hear me talking to you. Is it girly music? Is that why you don't want me to listen to it?"

Blake clenched his jaw and stared daggers as Cameron slipped the earbud into his ear.

The moment it was in, Cameron's eyes widened in shock and confusion; he tilted his head to the right, as if his body was trying to escape the sound. "What the hell *is* this?"

"Bloodywood."

Cameron looked at Blake like he had a second head growing out of his neck. "Bloody wood? Is that the name of the song or the band?"

"The band. It's a heavy metal band from India. Now give me back my earbud."

Cameron tossed it back. "Dang, Blake, that's some real psycho stuff right there. You better not go and shoot up our school."

Blake rolled his eyes and turned away, but Cameron grabbed him by the arm.

"Come on, man, you know I'm just playin' wit' you. But for real, though, where is that girlfriend of yours?"

"I don't have a girlfriend."

"Don't play dumb with me. You know who I'm talking about. That cute little blonde that you're always chillin' with. What's her name again?"

After a few moments of sullen silence, Blake responded. "Ari."

Cameron's face lit up. "Yeah, Ari, that's it. I wouldn't mind getting to know her a little better. Where has she been lately?"

"I don't know."

Blake did know, but he wasn't about to tell Cameron. It was none of his business. Ari had been with her mom in the hospital the last few days. He wasn't exactly sure what was wrong with her mom, but it must be pretty serious. Normally, he and Ari would hang out at least three or four times a week and text religiously. This week he had only received a few cryptic texts. He missed his best friend.

Cameron kept talking, but Blake was done. He walked towards the bus loading area where the teachers congregated, knowing that Cameron and his buddies wouldn't follow him there.

He was about to reinsert his earbud when he heard one of his teachers talking about Mr. Turner. He knew Mr. T. had been absent the second half of the day, because all his afternoon classes had had extra students from Mr. T's classes. Teachers were always splitting up their classes among the other classrooms when they couldn't find a sub.

It was rare for Mr. T. to do it, though. He'd looked perfectly healthy in third period, so it seemed strange for him to leave school in the afternoon without getting a sub. Crazy rumors about him beating up a kid were already circulating among the students.

Blake inched up behind Ms. Agnew and Mrs. Nichols to listen more closely.

"How do you not even call?" asked Ms. Agnew.

Mrs. Nichols shook her head slowly. "I know. It's completely unlike him. I hope he didn't get in a wreck."

Ms. Agnew frowned and responded under her breath. "Unless he *was* in a serious accident, you would think he would at least call and let someone know what's going on. I got stuck with Isaiah and Anthony in my class twice today. Twice. Once is more than enough with those two knuckleheads."

Dr. Fell, a middle-aged woman with short brown hair who was Plainview's newest head principal, approached the loading area with her clipboard.

Ms. Agnew waved her over. "Dr. Fell, have you heard from Mr. Turner yet?"

Dr. Fell nodded slightly and looked around before moving in closer. "Yes, he called in about an hour ago."

"Really?" Ms. Agnew said with excitement. "What did he say?"

Dr. Fell moved in even closer and whispered something to the two teachers that Blake couldn't make out. Their reaction to whatever she said was immediate and extreme—both teachers gasped and covered their mouths.

Mrs. Nichols bowed her head and started to tear up. Ms. Agnew dropped her hand from her mouth to her heart and asked, "How?"

Dr. Fell shook her head. "I don't know the details yet, but

he's definitely not coming in tomorrow. Could you ladies make sure his emergency lesson plans are ready and on his desk for the sub tomorrow? And let's just keep this between us right now."

Both teachers nodded as Dr. Fell turned and walked away.

Blake's mind was spinning. What news could have caused that kind of reaction? Mr. T. often gave him a hard time for being a slacker, but he was one of the few teachers Blake actually liked. He hoped everything was okay.

THREE HOURS.

Three hours of doing nothing but staring at dingy, off-white walls. Arms crossed, sitting on a cheap metal folding chair, Jonas shifted his gaze to the camera mounted in the upper corner of the room. He hoped someone was watching and picking up on the malevolence he was directing at the camera lens.

The first hour had been a battle between grief and disbelief. He kept hoping he would wake up from this nightmare, but the part of him that knew he was awake kept breaking down in chest-heaving sobs.

The second hour was when anger started to seep in, along with a thousand questions. By hour three, the anger had become all-consuming. He pictured himself flinging open the door and raging at all the incompetent cops keeping him in this tiny, twelve-by-eight-foot interrogation room for hours on end.

He would start with that female officer. Jonas couldn't figure her out. She'd brought him here to take a statement, but she had yet to take it. She'd been plenty happy to ask him all kinds of questions at his house. Now that he was in the interrogation room, there was no interrogation.

She had popped her head in a few times and asked him if

he was okay, but she'd refused to answer any of his questions. *What is going on with the investigation? Why aren't you taking my statement? What is taking so long?* "I don't know. I don't know. I don't know." She seemed as clueless as he was.

Maybe they only kept her on the department's payroll because of her looks, or to help them reach some kind of diversity quota. He imagined a minority woman would look good on paper among the sea of white men that made up the Travelers Rest police force.

He would be afraid to guess her ethnicity, but something about the shape of her face and her naturally darker skin tone and hair color made him think of South America. Brazilian or Venezuelan, perhaps? The only feature that made him second guess that conclusion was her eyes. Big, bright green, almond shaped eyes.

Regardless of how or why, she was weirdly attractive for a cop. He didn't want a good-looking cop. He wanted a competent, knowledgeable cop who knew how to run an investigation. Someone had brutally murdered his wife, and the only police response he was seeing was someone periodically popping in and asking, "Are you okay?"

Jonas slammed his hands down on the desk and pushed himself to his feet. He began to pace the room, even though that meant pivoting in the opposite direction every three steps.

As he paced, he stared down at his stockinged feet. They had taken his shoes, dress shirt, and phone when they'd brought him in. He felt stupid in his tight white undershirt, khakis, and thin brown dress socks. He understood why they'd taken his shirt, since it had bloodstains on it. But he couldn't figure out why they'd wanted his shoes. And taking his phone was just annoying. The wait wouldn't have been so unbearable if he had been able to play some games or scroll social media to take his mind off this unmitigated disaster.

Fortunately, they had let him call the school when he'd gotten to the precinct. He had completely forgotten about his classes until he was in the back seat of the police cruiser. Principal Fell's gruffness had transformed into cooperation the moment he'd mentioned his wife's death, despite the scarcity of details he'd offered.

He needed to call his parents, but they lived in Arizona, and there was nothing they could do for him at the moment. Jonas had decided to shield them from the news until he had more time to talk with them.

Jessica's parents had died in a car accident when she was a freshman in college. She didn't have any siblings and wasn't all that close to any of her extended family. He had only her work friends and church friends to notify, but he needed to do it soon to avoid them finding out through news outlets or social media.

Having his church family find out was what he dreaded the most. It had to happen, if for no other reason than to find a replacement for the Sunday school class he taught. But as soon as the church found out, he would be flooded with calls, texts, and acts of service. He would be loaded down with casseroles and gift cards and words of encouragement. He loved his church and their generous responses to those in need, but right now he didn't think he could handle it. If he opened his heart to their empathy, he would turn into a blubbering mess. Right now, he needed to be strong.

Jonas sat back down and resumed staring at the door, willing it to open with some news of progress.

CHAPTER FOUR

O livia, could you please stop doing that? I can't concentrate."

Olivia looked over to see Roger leaning around his computer screen, looking at her over the round, black-framed glasses that had slid down his nose.

Lost in her own thoughts, it took her a moment to register what he was talking about, but she finally noticed the loud squeaking her chair was making as her left leg rapidly bounced up and down. "Sorry. Are you almost done with your report? I'd like to look it over."

"I hope to be done soon, as long as I can focus."

Olivia had uploaded hers two hours ago. She had also printed out a hard copy in case Vogel wanted to see it right away, but he had yet to return.

The wait was killing her. Her mind kept going back to the crime scene and all the information she could be gathering as opposed to the nothing she was doing by babysitting the husband.

She felt bad about making the guy wait so long. The

reception she received each time she popped in to check on him was getting frostier and frostier. What was taking Vogel so long?

Hearing a car door slam, she sprang out of her seat and walked over to the widow near the front entrance for what felt like the hundredth time. But it was just Officer Holcombe leading an old, shaggy man with stained, loose-fitting clothes into the precinct.

She opened the door for them and nodded to Holcombe as he passed before craning her neck down the street for any sign of Vogel. With no black SUV in sight, she returned to her desk.

Her printed report was lying on the floor in three different places near her chair. What rude idiot had knocked it off her desk and not bothered to pick it up? She bent over at the waist to scoop the papers up without getting any of the floor's disgusting grime on her pants.

"Mmm, mmm, mmm, that's a view I could get used to."

Olivia spun around like she had just been poked with a cattle prod. She snarled through her teeth. "Did you knock my papers on the floor?"

Officer Grady continued to leer at her with his tiny yellow teeth and thin lips. Wanting to smack the twinkle out of his blue eyes, Olivia strode forward to within three inches of his chest. She couldn't care less if he was a head taller and outweighed her by fifty pounds of muscle, or that he'd spent six years in combat as a marine. "Keep your hands off my stuff. The next time you make a remark about my body, I'm going to rip off your balls and shove them down your throat."

For a split second, the smile left Grady's lips and his eyes went hard. But then his face resumed its smug insolence. "Those are big words for a little lady. If you want to touch my junk so bad, all you have to do is ask politely."

Without another look in her direction, he strolled slowly

away.

Olivia envisioned pulling out her gun and emptying a clip into him. She could feel everyone in the room looking at her, which made her face even hotter than it already was. Staring straight ahead, she made a beeline for the bathroom.

Taking a handful of water from the sink, Olivia splashed it over her face to cover up the fact that a couple of tears had seeped out. She hated her tears. Tears were for sadness and pain, and she never cried when she was sad or in pain. Why were her tear ducts always triggered by a combination of anger and embarrassment? It was infuriating.

She yanked two paper towels out of the dispenser and wiped off her face. Then, with both hands on the sink, she stared hard into her own eyes. "Why are you so weak? Why did you let him get to you?"

She stood up and took in her entire physique. Her looks had always attracted attention. In high school and college, a few modeling agents had approached her with offers. One in particular had hounded her for months.

"Your face has perfect symmetry," he'd said. "Those beautiful almond-shaped eyes and that caramel skin tone give you an exotic look that advertisement agencies would go crazy for. And with those curves—you could make a lot of money modeling, honey."

Olivia liked the way she looked, but she didn't want to be known for her looks. She wanted to make a difference. She wanted to do something that would have a lasting impact.

Her goal was to become a detective who kept murderers and rapists off the streets. But it was nearly impossible to become a detective without first becoming a patrol officer. Her current job was just a stepping-stone to the job she wanted.

She turned sideways and assessed her profile in the mirror. She wore a tight-fitting sports bra and pants two sizes too big in an effort to minimize her curves. But she couldn't hide them altogether, and she was the subject of lewd comments on a regular basis. It was expected from the delinquents she engaged with in the community, and their words rarely fazed her. When the sexual harassment came from her own team—that's when it hurt. They were supposed to have her back.

Grady's leering face floated back into her mind's eye. She turned the image into a fantasy where she throat-punched him and then kicked him in the face while he was hunched over.

A gentle knock on the door broke her out of her reverie. "Olivia?"

"What do you need, Roger?"

"Detective Vogel is back. He's looking for you."

Of course he is. The moment I go to the bathroom, he shows up and is wondering where I am. Throwing away the paper towels, Olivia swung open the door and marched back into the office area as Roger scrambled out of her way.

She spotted Vogel at her desk. He was sitting on the edge of it, reading her report, but he looked up as she approached. "There you are." He held up the report. "This is good work. Very detailed, just how I like it. Are you still interested in joining me for the interrogation?"

"Yes, absolutely." She also wanted to know what had taken so long and what Vogel had found, though she struggled to come up with a tactful way to find out. She settled on, "Did you find anything else of significance in the house?"

Vogel shrugged. "It was less about what we found than what we didn't find."

"What didn't you find?"

"Any sign of forced entry, for one." Vogel stood up. "Or any indication that a robbery took place. There was a laptop and some nice jewelry sitting in plain sight, not to mention forty dollars in cash just sitting on the dresser."

Olivia stated the obvious conclusion. "So the attack was likely personal in nature."

"Correct." Vogel held up a plastic evidence bag from on the desk beside him. "And this is the key to finding out who might have had a personal motive to kill our victim."

She could tell by the shape and size that the bag contained a phone.

"We found it under the victim's pillow. Remarkably, it managed to avoid any blood contamination, so we went ahead and processed it for fingerprints, and it has now been cleared to be used for data retrieval.

"Now, we could get a search warrant and ship the phone off to a digital forensics lab to gain access, but that process can take weeks, months, even years. I would much rather gain access to the data immediately. So, our goal is to convince Mr. Turner to let us search his wife's phone."

Olivia nodded her understanding.

"Remember, let me do the talking. If you have something really important to add, text it to me. Interrogations have a rhythm and flow. You have to know when to press and when to let up. Momentum is everything when it comes to convincing a suspect to confess something they wouldn't confess with a lawyer present. Do you understand?"

"Yes, I understand."

"All right then. Let's go rattle Mr. Turner's cage."

CHAPTER FIVE

L ord, please give me the strength and patience I need to endure this well."

Jonas's grief and anger had given way to exhaustion. No longer containing the energy to pace the room or rage at his circumstances, he sat with his head buried in his arms on the desk.

Closing his eyes for what felt like a long second, he was startled by the sound of someone clearing his throat. He looked up to find the detective from the crime scene and the female officer staring at him with quizzical expressions on their faces.

"Sorry to disturb your slumber, but I was hoping we could discuss your wife's murder, if that's okay with you."

The detective's words had a tinge of sarcasm that pissed Jonas off. Suddenly wide awake, he bit down on the side of his tongue to stop himself from spewing the first few responses that came to mind. "I've been ready and willing to have this conversation for the last four hours. So, yes, I would be more than happy to *finally* start talking about my wife's murder."

The detective pulled out a digital recorder and placed it on the table as he and the officer sat down opposite Jonas. "My name is Detective Vogel. I believe you already know Officer Selman here. As we get started, you should know this about me, Mr. Turner. I'm not one to beat around the bush. So, let's get right to it. How did your wife end up with your kitchen knife sticking out of her chest?"

The question hit Jonas like a punch in the face. He was momentarily struck dumb by both its bluntness and the shocking revelation that the murder weapon had been a knife from his kitchen.

His words came out quiet and strained. "I have no idea."

"No idea, huh? You can't think of a single person who might want to kill your wife?"

"No." Jonas responded with more force this time. "This wasn't someone who knew her. Everyone loved her. It had to be something else."

"Like what? What do you think happened here?"

He had thought of little else since he'd found his wife bleeding in his bed, but he could only come up with one plausible scenario. "I think someone must have broken into the house to see what they could steal. They probably thought no one was home, but when they stumbled into my wife..." Jonas's voice tailed off as he slowly shook his head. "I don't know if she tried to fight them off, or they just killed her because she could ID them, but that's the only explanation I can come up with."

"So a home invasion gone bad, huh?"

Vogel and Selman made eye contact with one another and seemed to share some unspoken thought, but Jonas didn't have long to guess what the look meant before Vogel threw out another question.

"Where were you when your wife was being stabbed to

death?"

Not there to protect her, Jonas thought. "I was teaching. I'm an English teacher at Plainview Middle School."

"A teacher? Do you only work half a day? What were you doing home at noon?"

Jonas glanced at Officer Selman. "I teach full time, but as I shared earlier, I got some blood on my shirt while breaking up a fight at school, so I came home during lunch to change."

Vogel looked both amused and incredulous. "So you got someone's blood all over you at school, which is why you were home to find your wife's blood all over your bedroom. That's a crazy turn of events."

He continued to stare at Jonas in disbelief, as if he was expecting some kind of further explanation, but Jonas sat stone still, waiting for the next question.

"Does your wife not work?"

"Yes, she works. She's a physical therapist at Elite Physical Therapy."

"But she had the day off today?"

Jonas shifted in his seat and looked away for a moment before returning Vogel's gaze. "No, not that I'm aware of."

Vogel's eyebrows lifted in exaggerated fashion. "Not that you're aware of? Do you guys not talk about those kinds of things? Was she still in bed when you left for school this morning?"

Jonas felt the rush of blood to his face. He fixed his eyes on a discoloration on the wall a couple of feet above Vogel's head. "Jessica left for work before I did. She had to be at work by seven, so I know she went into work today. I guess she came home for lunch."

"Lunch, huh? Did she often go home to eat lunch?"

"No, but it happened on occasion."

Vogel leaned back in his seat and tipped it backwards as he laced his fingers behind his head. He shared a conspiratorial look with Officer Selman before focusing back on Jonas. "You know, your wife didn't look like she was dressed for lunch. She looked like she was dressed for a little afternoon delight. The question is, was she dressed that way for you, or for someone else?"

Jonas bolted up from his chair with fists clenched at his side.

The sudden movement startled Vogel and caused him tip back in his chair far enough to lose his balance. He waved his arms wildly, trying to counteract his imminent fall; Officer Selman reached out and pushed down on the front corner of his seat, returning all four chair legs to the floor.

"Don't talk about my wife that way." There was steel in Jonas's voice and more than a little menace in his posture.

A flustered Vogel looked intimidated for a moment, but after an awkward pause, he appeared to remember that he was the one with a gun and shot to his feet. With one hand on his service piece, he snarled, "Sit your butt down. If you so much as flinch in my direction again, I'll have you chained to this desk. Do you understand me?"

For five long seconds, Jonas stared him down without blinking or acknowledging Vogel's words. But then he unclenched his fists, retrieved the chair that had skidded back against the wall in his sudden rise, and sat back down with arms folded across his chest.

Vogel sat, too, and continued in a softer tone. "Look, I'm sorry if my question upset you, but it's a fact that your wife was killed while wearing a racy negligee. That seems like a significant detail. One we need to get to the bottom of. Do you have any idea why she would be dressed that way?"

This detail had plagued Jonas's mind for the last five hours, but why Jessica had been wearing that outfit was still a complete mystery to him. He offered his best guess with little conviction. "She must have been trying on something she had just bought to make sure it fit right."

"So you weren't familiar with this particular outfit?"

"No."

"Did she often buy sexy outfits to spice up your sex life?"

Even though she had yet to utter a word, Jonas was acutely aware of Officer Selman's piercing green eyes on him. He glanced her way, then back at Vogel, before resting his eyes on the initials "C.S." scratched into the edge of the table. "Not that often."

"But it did happen? When would you say was the last time she modeled a new negligee for you?"

Jonas had asked himself this same question already. He couldn't remember a time she had worn such an outfit since their first year of marriage, but he didn't want to admit that to Vogel. "I'm not sure."

A knowing smile tugged at the corner of Vogel's face. He stared into Jonas's eyes like he was reading his mind. Jonas expected to be grilled further on the topic, but Vogel's next question surprised him again.

"Which door did you come home through?"

"The front door."

"Was it locked?"

"Yes, it was locked. I remember unlocking both the door handle and the deadbolt when I came in."

"Was the garage door open when you came home?"

"No, it was closed."

"Why didn't you enter through the garage?"

"The garage isn't big enough for both of our cars. At least not with all our junk in there. I let Jessica park in the garage, so I usually don't bother with opening and closing the garage door."

"What about the back door?"

"What about it?"

"Do you ever use it to enter the house?"

Jonas's eyebrows knitted in confusion. "You mean the sliding glass door for our back porch?"

"Yep, that one."

"No, that one stays locked, and you can't unlock it from the outside."

"It stays locked? You never go in or out that door?"

"The only time we go in and out that door is to do a little yard work or use the grill, and we haven't done either recently."

"When was the last time, specifically?"

Jonas rubbed his forehead, trying to remember. "I don't know, maybe two weekends ago. Why do you ask?"

"And it stays locked unless you're grilling out or working in the backyard?"

"Yes, Jessica is... was a stickler for making sure all doors were locked before we left the house and before we went to bed. She would even put a little metal bar in the track of the sliding glass door because she was afraid someone could jimmy the lock. I'm sure that door was locked when we left the house this morning."

Detective Vogel and Officer Selman shared an interested look.

"Did my wife's killer leave through that back door?"

Vogel rubbed his chin and stared off for about eight seconds before responding. "We don't know for certain that the murderer left through that door, but what we *can* say, with hundred percent certainty, is that we found that door unlocked. The metal bar you mentioned was lying beside the door, outside of the track."

Jonas lifted his hands off the table, palms up, wordlessly communicating the question, *What more proof do you need?*

Vogel leaned forward in his chair. "What interests me more than how the killer left the house is how the killer got *into* the house in the first place. If the back door was always locked, as you claim, and the front door was locked, and the garage door was closed, how'd the killer get inside?"

Jonas responded with more confidence than he felt. "Someone must have broken in."

"How?" asked Vogel.

"I don't know. I'm guessing through a window. I don't know if they broke a window or if we accidentally left a window open, or what."

"There are absolutely no signs of forced entry." Vogel ticked off the evidence on his fingers. "No broken windows. No unlocked windows. No damage to any doors or windows. Not even any sign of disturbed dust or footprints inside or outside any window. Either your wife let the killer in, or he had a key. There are no other explanations."

Jonas leaned forward in his seat and held the sides of his head as he stared between his legs at the floor. This wasn't making any sense. Jessica would never answer the door while wearing a negligee. He racked his brain for a plausible scenario.

"Turner!"

Jonas looked up at Vogel, who had apparently asked him a question.

"Did you hear me? Who else has a key to your house?"

Jonas shook his head. "No one. Jessica and I had the only keys."

"No spares?"

"Yeah, we kept a hidden key in a hanging basket on our back porch, but that was only for emergencies. We were the only two who knew about it."

Vogel turned to Selman. "Make sure the crime scene tech locates that key. I want to know if it appears to have been used recently, and then I want it fingerprinted."

Selman nodded her understanding.

Vogel turned his attention back to Turner. "Would this

spare key open the back door?"

"No, the back door is just a simple sliding glass door with no keyhole. Like I said before, it can only be locked and unlocked from the inside. The spare key is for the front door."

Officer Selman's eyes had been a constant, penetrating presence throughout the questioning, so Jonas noticed their absence almost immediately. She was looking down now, doing something with her hands below the table. Years of experience busting teens with cell phones made it obvious to him that she was texting.

Vogel drew his attention. "Can you think of anyone in your circle of family and friends who your wife would have opened the door for?"

Jonas tried to take the question seriously, but it seemed ridiculous. Jessica would have been horrified to open the door to her best girl friend in such an outfit.

Now Vogel was fumbling underneath the table with his right hand too. He was obviously trying to be sneaky about looking at something on his phone. Then he sat up straight and made eye contact. Jonas braced for another question.

"Do you have one of those video doorbells? The ones that capture audio and video of anyone who approaches the front door?"

Jonas's mouth went dry. He had forgotten all about the doorbell camera. He had never used the app himself, but he had seen some of the videos captured on his wife's phone. It showed the whole street in clear detail. A video of his wife's killer might be at his fingertips. "Yes, we have a doorbell camera. I don't have the app on my phone, but my wife does."

Vogel leaned over, grabbed something off the floor, and slid it onto the table. "On this phone?"

Inside a thick plastic bag was the purple case with metallic gold butterflies of Jessica's phone.

"Do you know her passcode?" asked Vogel.

"Yes."

Vogel pulled the bag closer to his side of the table and slid the phone out. "All right, well, what is it?"

Jonas had a moment of hesitation. It seemed wrong to open Jessica's personal life to this jerk of a detective who didn't love her or care about her. There was also the daunting reality that the identity of his wife's killer could be on the other side of this locked screen. It made his chest flutter and his breath quicken.

"1-1-4-4-7-7."

Holding the phone with both hands, Vogel hit the screen with his left thumb several times and then stopped. After a quick glance up at Jonas, he made the same motions with his thumb again, only much slower and more deliberately this time. With a look of disgust, he put the phone back on the table, turned it around, and slid it over to Jonas.

"Are you lying to us, or do you really not know your wife's passcode?"

Jonas looked down at the locked screen. He extended his left index finger and carefully pressed 1-1-4-4-7-7. Nothing happened.

"That's always been her passcode," he said quietly.

"Well, it's not now," Vogel said as he snatched up the phone and threw it back in the evidence bag. "Let me tell you what I think, Mr. Turner. I think *you* killed your wife."

The words hit him like a cement block.

"No." The word came out in a hoarse whisper.

"I think you found out she had a lover, and you killed her in a jealous rage. You saw her in that little sexy outfit, and you lost your mind. You grabbed a knife from your kitchen and went to town on her, stabbing her again, and again, and again!"

Jonas slammed his hands down on the table. "No! I would never hurt her." He jammed his left index finger into the table with each word. "I. did. not. do. this. I *found* her dead in my bed."

"Okay, then, prove it." Vogel leaned forward, getting into Jonas's face. "Take a lie detector test. Show us that you're telling the truth."

Still seeing red, Jonas spoke through gritted teeth. "I would be happy to. Hook me up right now. I have nothing to hide."

Vogel gave a sardonic grin as he stood up. He nodded at the doorway to Selman, and they both shuffled to the exit. Before pulling the door closed, he looked back at Jonas. "Just sit tight. We'll have you hooked up to that polygraph machine before you know it." And with that, he closed the door.

Jonas stared at the closed door for a few seconds, still breathing hard. Once the adrenaline spike tapered, exhaustion rolled in like a London fog. He laid his forehead down on the cold, metal table and let his arms dangle at his side.

How can this be happening? What am I going to do? It was all too much in too short a time. He didn't want to think about it anymore. Instead, he thought of Psalm 23. He began to repeat it to himself over and over again as he waited.

Olivia glanced at her watch as she followed Vogel back to the office area. 7 p.m. She would kill for a fajita burrito from El Tejano's about now, but she wasn't about to ask for a dinner break as long as Vogel was giving her access to the case.

"How are we going to give this guy a polygraph? We don't have anyone trained at this precinct."

Vogel snorted. "Yeah, I figured as much. I'll make a call to the guy at the Greenville precinct."

"Do you think you can get him here tonight?"

"He better get here tonight. He's on call 24/7. That's just

the nature of the job." After he pulled out his phone, he paused and turned around, looking her in the eyes. "That was good work in there."

"Good work? All I did was sit there."

Vogel wagged a finger at her. "Don't underestimate the power of a silent interrogation partner. Two people are always more intimidating to a witness than one. Especially when one of the two are pinning the suspect down with a killer stare and not saying a word. You definitely made him uncomfortable."

He sat on a corner of a desk and started tapping on his phone with his thumb, but then paused again and looked up at Olivia. "Yeah, you had him squirming." Letting out a sudden laugh, Vogel slapped his leg. "Forget a penny. I bet that guy would have paid a hundred dollars to know what you were thinking."

Olivia smirked despite herself. She still wasn't convinced that her presence had made much of a difference.

"But the really 'great work' I was referring to was the question you texted about the doorbell camera. That was brilliant. It would have never crossed my mind to ask that. It was the perfect way to convince him to open his wife's phone. It's too bad he didn't know her passcode."

Olivia nodded. "Yeah, he seemed pretty confident that he knew it, like she had always had the same code. I think you may be right about the wife having a lover. A sudden change to a longtime passcode is a common indicator of an affair."

"Oh, there's no doubt there's another man involved. She wasn't just randomly trying on sexy outfits. And you saw how defensive he was. He knows. He doesn't want to admit it, but he knows." Vogel reached into his jacket pocket and pulled out the evidence bag with the victim's phone. "The frustrating part is that everything we need to know might be right here on this phone, but we'll be lucky to see any of it before summer hits."

Olivia started to say something, but then thought better of it. Vogel noticed and looked at her with raised eyebrows.

She shook her head. "Nothing. Never mind."

"Come on, Selman, spit it out. What are you thinking?"

"What if—" She looked around the office to make sure no one could overhear them. "What if we were to take the phone to the morgue and see if we can get the phone to open with the facial recognition feature?"

Vogel's eyes got big for a moment, and then he tilted his head back and let out a deep, full-bodied laugh. "I knew I liked you, Selman. You've got one devious mind. Do you think it will work?"

Olivia gave a slight shrug. "I have no idea, but I think it's worth a shot."

Vogel stood up and handed her the evidence. "Let's give it a try, then. I'm going to call my polygraph guy and start on some of this paperwork. If you're able to get into the phone, change the passcode to 1-1-1-1-1-1 and bring it back here immediately."

"You want *me* to take it over? Do I need to sign it out somewhere?"

"Don't worry about all that. I'm running this investigation, and I'm giving you permission to handle the phone in an effort to access its contents. You're covered." Before walking away, he leaned in and patted her on the shoulder. "But let's just keep this between you and me."

For several moments, Olivia stood there alone in the middle of the office, holding the evidence bag. She was not excited about the prospect of going to the morgue by herself. It wasn't the dead bodies that bothered her—it was the thought of being hung out to dry if this plan broke some kind of law. But the allure of finding out what was on the phone was too difficult to resist. With a brisk pace, she headed for the exit and out into the warm spring evening.

CHAPTER SIX

S on of a—" Blake slammed his controller down on the bed and snatched up his pillow to scream expletives into. He couldn't afford to have his mom hear his potty mouth again. It would probably mean another week of no devices.

Normally, he was a stud at all first-person shooter games. The friends he had made online were always begging him to play. But tonight, if they handed out an award for "Biggest Scrub", he would win hand's down. He had been the first or second person killed on his team in every mission.

His phone lit up and vibrated with an incoming text. He leaned over and read the screen.

Dillon: Dude, why are you sucking? Get your crap together.

What a prick. He carried their team most nights. How about cutting him some slack? Blake tossed the phone back on the bed. He should have never given that guy his phone number. He was probably some 28-year-old loser sitting in his mother's basement—but the guy wasn't wrong.

Why *was* he sucking?

Probably because he couldn't stop thinking about Ari. He was really starting to worry. Was her mom still in the hospital? Or was Ari mad at him? He couldn't think of a reason why she would be, but she had never ghosted him for this long.

His phone lit up with another text. He grabbed it expecting it to be Dillon again, but hoping it was Ari.

Frankie: Did you hear about Mr. T?

Blake raised an eyebrow. He and Frankie shared a few classes and got along fine, but they rarely texted. Blake had heard several different rumors about Mr. T. that afternoon, but he was in no mood for guessing games.

Blake: No. What's up?

Frankie: Mr. T's wife was murdered.

Blake felt the skin on his arms goosepimple. Murdered? Gangbangers got murdered, not teachers or their wives.

Frankie: The cops think Mr. T killed her.

What? Blake frowned. *There's no way. Mr. T. would never do that.*

Blake: How do you know that?

He stared at the screen, waiting for a reply.

Frankie: Langston's dad is a cop. He said they have all kinds of evidence proving he did it. I think he's already in jail.

Blake squeezed his phone and looked up at the familiar walls of his room, grasping for confirmation that this was really happening and not some twisted figment of his imagination. How could Mr. Turner be a murderer? He was always talking about God and doing the right thing. Had something made him snap, or was all that God talk just a mask for psycho tendencies?

His phone vibrated again.

Ari: Hey

Blake stared at the text, hardly able to believe his eyes. She had finally texted him back. He quickly thumbed a response.

Blake: Hey. Are you ok?

Ari: Not really

His thumbs hovered over the screen as he debated what to say back. More than anything he wanted to make sure she wasn't mad at him, but he didn't want to seem like a needy loser. If she was upset over her mom's sickness or if she'd gotten in another fight with her dad, then he wanted to be there for her. He decided to text back the safest question he could think of.

Blake: How's your mom?

Ari: Dead

Blake's right hand went to his forehead. Boy, he knew Ari had a dark sense of humor, but this was *dark*, dark.

Blake: That's not funny.

She texted back in less than five seconds.

Ari: I'm not joking.

Blake's skin prickled; his breaths came in short, labored gasps. The rest of him felt frozen. How could Ari's mom be dead? She was young, like younger than his mom. And Ari had never mentioned any kind of previous health problems.

He wanted to ask what had happened, but he already felt like crap for assuming she was joking. He had no idea how to respond. How do you console a friend who'd just lost her mom? He couldn't imagine losing his. He would probably want to crawl into a hole and die.

It sounded lame, but he texted back the only words he could think to say.

Blake: I'm so sorry. I don't even know what to say. If there's anything I can do for you, just say the word.

It didn't take long for his screen to light up again.

Ari: Can I come over?

She often came over after school. Even though she lived in a much nicer neighborhood on the other side of town, she rode the bus home with him two or three times a week and made her parents come pick her up. But she had never visited at night.

Blake: Tonight?

Ari: Ya. I really need to talk.

Blake didn't see his mom saying yes, but he didn't want to let Ari down. Especially when her mom had just died.

Blake: Ok. How will you get here?

Ari: Don't worry about it. And don't worry about your mom. She won't even know I was there. Just make sure your window is unlocked.

Blake: Ok

Oh man. If his mom found out about this, he was screwed. His heart was racing so fast he could feel the pulse throbbing in his neck. He hadn't taken one step in the last two hours, but he felt like he had just run a marathon. He flopped back on his bed and stared at the ceiling, trying to calm down.

What the hell was going on? How could his best friend's mom and favorite teacher's wife die on the same day? Death had never impacted him before today, unless you counted his grandfather from Michigan whom he had only visited a few times.

And now Ari was coming over to sneak into his room past his bedtime. The thought both thrilled him and terrified him.

This might go down as the craziest night of his life.

Olivia surveyed the front entrance of the morgue, contemplating how she wanted to handle this. Should she just admit her desire to use the victim's face to open the phone, or should she try to get it done without the coroner's awareness?

She had no pull as a traffic cop. She didn't know this coroner well, either. They had only crossed paths twice. Once when a car had pulled out in front of a motorcycle, and another time when a teen had lost control of his car on a curve and rolled it down an embankment.

He'd been nice enough to her on those occasions, but he was stereotypically weird. With his thinning brown hair, pale skin, and silver-framed glasses with big square lenses, he *looked* like he belonged in a morgue. She knew she was being unfair because it was his job, but the guy seemed way too comfortable with dead bodies.

She decided to go with the sneaky route. She didn't want to risk the coroner saying no. Taking the phone out of the evidence bag, she stuck it in her back pocket and headed for the door.

A young, round-faced black woman with lots of long, curly hair was sitting behind the receptionist desk. She broke into a big grin when Olivia approached, and her voice was oddly perky for a night receptionist at the morgue. "Hi there, how can I help you?"

"I need a quick look at a body that was brought in this afternoon."

The woman popped out of her seat. "Okay, honey, I'll go see if Mr. Davis can make himself available to you. You just have a seat, and I'll be right back."

She was gone in a flash, leaving Olivia with nothing to do but stand at the desk and take in the room's sparse decorations. Within two minutes, the woman bounced back into the room trailed by Mr. Davis, the coroner.

"Officer Selman, to what do I owe the pleasure?"

He remembered her name. She wasn't sure if that was a good thing or a bad thing.

"Detective Vogel asked me to come down here and take a look at the body that was brought in today. Jessica Turner. We're working together on the investigation into her death."

Mr. Davis tilted his head to the side, the eyes behind the big lenses filled with a mixture of curiosity and confusion.

"Why did he want you to see the body? What are you looking for?"

Olivia put her hands on her utility belt and began rocking on her heels. "Well, we have a theory about how she might have been killed, and we just want to check it out really quick."

Mr. Davis looked amused."You don't think it was the forty-seven stab wounds to her body?"

Forty-seven. Wow, that was way more than she had suspected. The killer had absolutely snapped.

Olivia scrambled. "We're aware she was stabbed to death, but we have some theories we're working on about why. Since you've identified each of her stab wounds already, does that mean you've completed the autopsy?"

"No, no, I have only done a preliminary examination. I couldn't help but count the number of incisions while doing so. It wasn't easy to pin down the exact number of cuts with how much overlap there was." For a couple of seconds Mr. Davis seemed lost in the moment, but he shook himself and resumed eye contact with Olivia. "I'm intrigued by these theories you have about what got Mrs. Turner killed. What exactly do you hope to see on the body?"

Olivia squeezed harder on her utility belt and forced herself to stop rocking. "I'm afraid I'm not at liberty to disclose that information at this time. They're just theories at this point, and I do not have permission to float them about."

The receptionist hadn't returned to her desk. She remained by Mr. Davis's side, listening to the conversation with rapt attention. The two of them exchanged looks, skepticism written all over their faces, as Olivia fought to keep the knots in her stomach from affecting her calm demeanor.

But in the end, Mr. Davis merely shrugged and said, "Okay, well, follow me this way. I'll take you to the body."

He led her down a long corridor and into a sterile room that had a strong chemical smell. As she took in the instruments on the counter, Mr. Davis walked directly over to the table in the middle of the room and pulled off the white sheet covering Jessica Turner's body.

Jessica's wide-open eyes drew Olivia's attention, and she found them difficult to ignore as she examined the rest of the body. Despite the many wounds, seeing the body without the blood-drenched teddy on made it even more apparent how attractive Jessica had been. Could someone have attacked her out of lust or obsession? It was another possibility to consider.

"Was there any sign of sexual assault in your preliminary examination?"

The coroner clasped his hands behind his back and seemed to consider the question carefully. "I didn't find any evidence of trauma to the pelvic region, but not all sexual assaults cause obvious physical trauma. There was evidence that she had engaged in sexual intercourse recently, but if I had to guess, I would say it occurred at least twenty-four hours ago. We'll know more once the forensics lab runs their tests."

Olivia looked back down at the body, honing in on the chaotically bunched wounds to the upper chest. "So, did the killer just keep stabbing the body long after the victim was dead?"

The coroner pulled out a latex glove and put it on as he moved closer to the body. He pointed out various cuts as he spoke. "Actually, most of these wounds are fairly superficial. Only four or five penetrated deeply enough that death was certain."

She tried to make sense of this new information. Why were so many of the wounds shallow? Had the victim been able to fight off her attacker well enough to make most of the cuts nonlethal? If so, that might tell them something about the attacker. He couldn't have been very big or strong.

Or there could be another explanation. Maybe the superficial wounds were a result of hesitancy. Perhaps the attacker had been conflicted about wanting to kill her. The husband could fit into that category. *He comes home, suspects his wife is cheating and starts attacking her, but deep down he doesn't want to kill her.* That would work.

"Is there anything else I can point out for you, Officer Selman?"

The words snapped her out of her musings. She had almost forgotten what she was here to do. Olivia walked around to the other side of the table, putting herself on the opposite side to Mr. Davis. She slipped the victim's phone out of her back pocket, keeping it below the table. She bent over, pretending to look more closely at the victim's face. "Do you have any more of those latex gloves?"

To her disappointment, Mr. Davis simply reached into his pocket and handed her a pair. She grabbed them with her left hand, careful to keep the phone in her right hand below the table.

She looked at the cart of instruments right behind Mr. Davis. "What do you use those clippers for?"

The moment the coroner turned his head she tapped on the phone, swiped up, and held it screen-down a foot above the victim's face.

"Those are my rib shears. I use them…"

Olivia flipped the phone the other way when she heard Mr. Davis's voice trail off. She pretended to take a picture.

"…for opening chest cavities. What are you doing with that phone, Officer Selman?"

"I just wanted to get a couple of pictures for Detective Vogel."

"I take professional-quality pictures of every part and angle of the body. If you wanted a picture, all you had to do was ask."

"Yeah, I know, but Detective Vogel wanted these right away. Just trying to pin down a suspect as soon as possible."

Mr. Davis's face set into a firm frown. "I could upload pictures and make them available to your precinct in the time it would take you to drive here and back. There's really no reason to rely on cell phone images."

Olivia edged towards the door, speaking in her most contrite voice. "Wow, I didn't realize the turnaround was so quick. That's impressive. I'm so sorry to have wasted your time. I really appreciate you going out of your way like this. I'll go ahead and get out of your hair now."

Her heart was racing as she power-walked down the corridor. Nearly getting caught by the coroner was only partly to blame for her increased heart rate. The bigger contributing factor was what she'd seen when she flipped the phone around.

The screen was unlocked.

Tapping on the phone every few seconds all the way to her patrol car, Olivia climbed inside and shut the door. She went into the phone's settings and tried changing the password like Vogel had asked, but she needed the original passcode to change the code.

She cursed under her breath. If the screen locked again, they would lose out on this information for at least another week or two. And that was assuming a judge would sign off on a warrant. She imagined coming back here and asking for permission to see the body again. There was no way. She would look like an idiot and might get into serious trouble.

But she couldn't tap on this screen every ten seconds all night long. Maybe there was an option to keep the screen unlocked. She went back into settings and clicked on "Display". The phone was set to auto-lock after one minute. She clicked on that feature and saw the options "30 seconds, 1 minute, 2 minutes, 5 minutes, Never".

She smiled as she hit "Never". Now all she had to do was keep it charged, and she wouldn't need to open it again.

No longer paranoid about being locked out, she searched for the app with the video footage from the doorbell camera. Luckily, it was a brand she recognized, so she found it quickly. Olivia opened it and searched for today's videos.

Apparently, the camera recorded every movement. Even before all the emergency personnel had arrived, the app had captured over thirty videos. It would take too long to look through all of them. She placed the phone down and put her keys into the ignition.

Before turning the car on, a thought struck her, and she looked back down at the phone. If the killer was someone the victim had known, then there was a good chance they had talked recently. There could be evidence of an argument or a threatening text right at her fingertips.

Snatching the phone back up, she opened the text-messaging app and scanned the most recent ones. The last text Jessica had received was from someone named "Dee". It was simply a thumbs-up emoji.

Dee appeared to be the only person she'd texted that morning. Olivia opened the thread to see what Dee had been responding to.

She almost dropped the phone when she read the message.

Jessica: The back door is open. I'm ready for you to have your way with me.

It ended with a winking, kissy-face emoji.

This was huge. Dee wasn't a girl friend. Or, at least, not a regular girl friend. Dee was a *lover*. Olivia held in her hand concrete evidence that the unlocked back door and sexy outfit were due to an affair.

Olivia scrolled down to read the text exchange from the beginning of that morning.

Dee: I need to see you.

Jessica: Oh, we're talking again now, huh? It's about time. When do you want to meet up?

Dee: Now

Jessica: Now? You're crazy. I'm at work, silly. I might be able to get away tonight. We could get a hotel.

Dee: I don't want to wait. I want you now. Tell them you're sick and let me come over.

Jessica: Where was all this passion the last few days? Ok. I'll try to get Tamera to cover my appointments until after lunch.

Jessica: Ok, we're all set. Give me about an hour. I have a little surprise for you.

Dee: I've got a little surprise for you too. See you soon!

Jessica: Here's a little sneak preview for you

The text included an image of Jessica in the black teddy, posing seductively. The text thread ended with the following messages:

Dee: I can't wait to have my way with you while you're wearing that outfit!

Jessica: The back door is open. I'm ready for you to have your way with me.

Winking, kissy-face emoji.

Thumbs-up emoji.

The suspect pool had dwindled to two: it was either the husband or the lover. They had the husband. They needed to find this lover. Olivia scrolled further up the thread to see if there were any more picture exchanges. A picture of their suspect would be ideal.

It didn't take long for her to come across confirmation that Dee was male. Olivia felt her cheeks get hot as she looked away from some of the images he'd sent Jessica. Unfortunately, she had yet to see a face. Finally, a selfie with the two of them in some kind of bar showed up in the thread.

Dee was a good-looking white male with dark brown hair. She would guess he was in his early to mid-forties.

"Gotcha," she whispered as she set the phone down on her console. They should be able to trace the phone number to an address within the hour.

Things were really moving now. Olivia couldn't wipe the grin off her face as she peeled out of the parking lot and sped back to the precinct.

CHAPTER SEVEN

Only a skeleton crew remained in the precinct at this late hour. Olivia sipped the last of her soda as she proofread her latest report. Vogel had been impressed with what she'd found, despite the fact that Dee's phone number had turned out to be connected to a generic, pre-paid cell phone. It would be difficult, if not impossible, to track down. Especially if Dee had paid for it in cash.

At least they had messages and videos to piece together. Vogel and Olivia had sat side by side at her desk to watch all the doorbell camera videos leading up to the murder. It hadn't taken as long as she'd expected. Most of the clips prior to Mr. Turner's arrival home were less than ten seconds long. A passing car would activate the camera, and then it would shut back down a few seconds later. The only other events of note were the occasional dog-walker or mom with a stroller. No one had approached the front door of the home until Jonas Turner ran up the steps and opened the door with his key.

The time stamp read 12:22:56 when Turner entered the house. The next video began at 12:31:14. It showed Turner pacing the front porch for a couple of minutes and eventually sitting down on the left side of the porch with his head between knees.

According to the call center, Turner had called 911 at 12:28. That meant if Turner was the killer, his stumbling upon the affair, the ensuing altercation, and the decision to call 911 had to have taken place within the span of about five minutes.

Olivia had expressed her concerns about Turner being able to commit the murder in such a short timeframe, but Vogel had merely shrugged and said, "How long does it take to stab someone a bunch of times?" He'd proceeded to demonstrate how quickly he could stab downwards with an imaginary knife. Olivia still had her doubts.

When the polygraph expert arrived, Vogel had told her to go get something to eat while the husband did the test. She would have loved to listen in, but her body was craving food, so she hadn't put up much of a fight.

The polygraph test was taking a long time. She kept eyeing the door to the interrogation room, wishing she had refused the suggestion to go eat. Of course, it was easier to think that way now that she had a full stomach.

She got up to throw the trash away from her Bojangles two-piece meal just as Vogel reentered the office area. He didn't look happy.

"How did it go?"

Vogel put his hands in his pockets and gave a slight shrug. "Inconclusive. I know we've got our man, but it was hard to tell from the test."

"Why are you so sure it's the husband and not the lover?"

Vogel pulled his hands out of his pockets and held them palms up. "Where's the motive? He's coming over for a good time. It's the husband who is being wronged. This is a crime of passion, and who is more passionate than a jilted spouse?

The knife, the shoe print—everything points towards the husband. We'll wait until all the evidence is processed, but I'm telling you, this is our guy."

"But we're still going to track down the lover, right?"

"Sure, sure, we'll track down the lover. He might be our best witness in this case. Let's find out where he bought that phone and see if we can track it down. And let's question some of her close friends. She might have told at least one of them about her affair." Vogel looked down at his watch and ran a hand through his hair. "But this stuff will have to wait until tomorrow. Let's call it a night and get some sleep. Can you take Mr. Turner back to his house to retrieve his car? Make sure he understands that he'll have to make other living arrangements for the near future, since his house is a crime scene, and don't let him touch anything other than a few pairs of clothes and the bare essentials."

"Yes, sir. What time do you want to meet back up in the morning?"

Vogel handed her his card as he gathered his stuff to leave. "I'll pop in at some point tomorrow, but don't wait for me. Start talking to neighbors and coworkers and see what you can find out. Call me if you stumble across anything significant."

He had been heading towards the exit as he talked. At the door, he turned back. "Remember, don't let the husband touch anything. I'm telling you, this is our guy."

Olivia nodded and turned towards the interrogation room. She was not looking forward to the ride back to Mr. Turner's house. It had been almost nine hours since she'd first placed him in that room. Their reunion was bound to be frigid.

ABOUT AN HOUR after Jonas had left the precinct, he slid a plastic card into the slot of a heavy metal door and pulled it back out. At the sound of the click, he pulled down the lever and swung the door open. Turning on the lights revealed two full-sized beds covered in matching coral comforters. A small lamp adorned each nightstand.

On the nearest nightstand, the clock read 12:48. He dropped his duffle bag of clothes and toiletries on the first bed and headed to the bathroom. He needed sleep, but he needed a shower more.

He spun the single shower handle to its hottest setting and began peeling off his clothes. Taking a moment to look at himself in the mirror, he concluded that he looked how he felt. Like crap. Grabbing a small bar of soap and the little container of shampoo, he stepped behind the wispy plastic curtain and let the water scald his skin.

If only he could wash away his memories like the dirt and grime.

He had been alone with his thoughts for most of the day but had made little progress in making sense of anything. Every time he tried to imagine what might have led to Jessica's death, the image of her pale face and lifeless eyes chased away every other thought. That moment where he'd brushed aside her bloody hair to reveal her identity had been imprinted so deeply in his mind that every other thought tumbled headlong into the impression of her dead face.

After lathering his entire body with the bar of soap, Jonas bumped the shower handle down a quarter of a turn. No way his front could handle the blistering heat his back had endured.

To avoid mental pictures of the murder scene, he focused on replaying his conversations in the interrogation room. He realized now that he should have asked for a lawyer. He had nothing to hide, and he didn't want to appear guilty, but there was no doubt they were treating him like the prime suspect. You don't take the shirt, shoes, and phone of a grieving husband, or hook him up to a polygraph machine, unless you suspect foul play.

Thinking about his time in that tiny room churned up the fear he had tried to suppress all evening. The fear that Jessica had been cheating on him. The thought seemed ridiculous. He knew his wife. She would never cheat on him. She was always talking about how much she loved him and how happy she was. They were good Christians who loved God and were active in the church. People like that don't cheat.

But the number of odd circumstances that he couldn't explain were mounting. The outfit she'd had on when she was killed made no sense. He hadn't seen her wear one like that in years. Her being home during the day was also weird. Jessica always ate out for lunch. How much she spent on eating out for lunch had been a source of contention in their marriage, and he couldn't remember the last time she'd driven home for food.

Then there was her phone. When had she changed her password? *Why* would she change it? Did she have something to hide after all?

If so, then who? All of their close friends were married church friends. Surely they weren't a threat. Could she have met someone at the gym where they worked out? Was there a coworker or patient who'd charmed her off her feet? The more he thought about it, the more the dread in his chest spread. There were so many parts of her day that he had no idea about.

Jonas braced both hands on the showerhead wall and put his head directly into the nozzle, hoping the sound of the water beating down on his skull would drown out his newfound suspicions.

They didn't.

He shut off the water and grabbed a towel from the rack, vigorously drying off his body, trying to focus on the task and not his thoughts. Catching sight of his own worried face, he threw his towel at the mirror and walked back into the main room.

The clock read 1:37. Just seeing the late hour triggered an exhaustion that made him weak in the knees. Jonas staggered over to the bed with his duffle bag, pulled out a pair of boxers, and put them on. He knew he needed to brush his teeth, but he couldn't muster the energy to do it. Sliding the duffle bag off the bed, he peeled back the covers and crawled underneath, letting out a full-bodied sigh as his head hit the bed.

The moment he closed his eyes, he saw Jessica's lifeless face staring back at him.

CHAPTER EIGHT

A distant rumble of a diesel engine. The barking of a dog a few houses down. The steady ticking of her watch on the nightstand. This was what Olivia heard as she stared at the ceiling in the predawn light. Despite the late night, she had been wide-awake since 5:30 a.m. She desperately wanted to go back to sleep, but she could not stop thinking about all the leads she wanted to follow.

The crime scene was calling her name. Now that everything was pictured and documented, she would have free rein to roam the house and try to piece together the evidence. Then there were all the neighbors she needed to interview. A handful of officers had already been tasked with asking nearby neighbors a few questions, and she would read their reports first, but she was sure they hadn't asked all the questions she would ask.

Had they thought to ask about video surveillance footage like Turner's doorbell camera? If not, there could be a crucial piece of footage out there just waiting to be discovered.

But it was the phone that had her staring at the ceiling.

She was paranoid about it going to the locked screen again. It was a treasure trove of information that she couldn't afford to lose. Besides offering clear video evidence of Turner's arrival home and damning text messages revealing an affair, it would also be an invaluable source for tracking down Jessica Turner's friends and family.

She needed to get back to that phone. Olivia threw off her covers and made her way to the bathroom for a quick shower.

THE ENTIRE FRONT yard was marked off with bright yellow crime scene tape. There also appeared to be some kind of seal on the front door. Unless they'd failed to lock the back door, there was no way to slip inside and look around without the cops knowing.

Jonas would have loved to see what they had marked off or taken out of the house so he had an idea of where the evidence was leading them, but the risk of getting caught was too high. He already looked guilty enough.

He spun around, taking his hands out of his pockets as he crossed the street and walked up his neighbor's driveway. It was early, a little before 6:30 a.m., but he knew Billy would be up. He always left the house by 7:15 on weekdays in order to take his two boys to school before heading to his current construction job site.

Jonas rang the doorbell and stepped back to the edge of the porch. Twenty seconds later Billy opened the door, a bit of wariness in his voice and mannerisms as opposed to his typically cheerful demeanor.

"Hey, Jonas, is everything all right?"

"Hey, Billy, sorry to bug you so early in the morning. I don't know if you heard about what happened yesterday, but I was hoping you might be able to help me get some answers."

Billy looked back over his shoulder and shooed one of

his boys away before stepping outside and closing the door behind him. "So, it's true, then? Someone murdered your wife?"

"Yes. It's true."

"Man, I am so sorry. I saw all the police cars in front of your house when I came home from work. And an officer came by and asked a few questions, but even then, I had a hard time believing what everyone in the neighborhood was saying." Billy shook his head and stared up the street before looking back at Jonas in earnest. "What can I do to help?"

"Is your doorbell camera still working?"

"Yeah, I use it all the time. Do you think there's something on the footage that will help you figure out what happened?"

"I'm hoping so."

"I thought you guys had one, too."

"We do, but all the videos go to Jessica's phone, and it's locked. The police haven't been able to open it yet to see the footage. But I'm betting your camera's footage will be even better. We should be able to see anyone that approaches my house or parks nearby."

Billy glanced at his watch as he pulled out his phone. "I don't know how much time I have. I've got to get my boys to school."

"I know. I'm sorry I'm holding you up, but I don't think this will take long. We don't need to look at the footage together. If you can just send the videos to my phone, then I can get out of your hair and look at them later."

Billy stared intently at his phone, tapped the screen a few times, and began scrolling. "There are a lot of videos from yesterday. You want them all?"

"I think the only ones I really need are the ones between when I left for work yesterday and when I arrived home around 12:30."

Swiping and tapping a little slower now, Billy held

his phone less than six inches from his face, the screen illuminating his features. "Okay, I think I found them. There's not too, too many, and most of them are short. Let me see if I can figure out how to do this."

Jonas put his hands back in his pockets and watched a car go down the street. He felt the urge to fill the silence with some kind of small talk, but he didn't want to distract Billy from his task. After another thirty seconds of awkward silence, he began humming a nameless tune.

"Okay, see if you're starting to get them."

Jonas felt his phone vibrate as he pulled it out of his pocket. When he unlocked the screen, he could see video after video popping up for him to accept. After a couple of minutes, he had them all. "Thanks, Billy, I really appreciate it."

"Sure thing, Jonas. I'm really sorry about your wife. If there's anything else I can do for you, just let me know."

"Thank you. That means a lot to me."

Once Billy stepped back inside, Jonas spun around and jogged back across the street.

"Please, Olivia. You have got to stop."

Olivia stilled her left leg as Roger lumbered out of his seat to give her the evil eye over their computer screens.

"You are killing me with that squeaking chair."

She shook the ice in her empty cup at him. "What do you expect when you load me up with donuts and mocha frappuccinos?"

"How was I supposed to know you already bought yourself a mocha frappuccino this morning? You could have given the second to someone else. And no one was putting a gun to your head to eat two donuts."

"I'm not going to not eat donuts. Especially when you bring

in my favorite kind. This is on you."

Roger brought donuts to work every Friday. He picked them up from a specialty shop in downtown Travelers Rest, and the maple-glazed bacon-sprinkled ones were to die for. Olivia didn't care if police officers and donuts were cliché. She would gladly stuff her face with these donuts even if a news crew were filming.

She had arrived a little after seven and spent the first two hours looking through the victim's phone. She'd started by taking a closer look at the doorbell camera footage directly after the husband called 911, hoping to pick up on some kind of tell while watching him sit on his front porch.

But nothing stood out, before or after first responders began to arrive. You could argue that he was a bit more stoic than one would expect, but that could just as easily be due to shock. She didn't sense a guilty vibe.

The text messages had been much more interesting. In fact, they were so valuable as evidence that she had decided to screenshot the entire "Dee" thread, page by page, and send the pictures to her own phone for fear of losing them. It had taken a while, but not as long as she'd expected. Although the thread went back almost ten months, there weren't many texts before the last month or so. It was obvious that Jessica Turner had been careful to delete the most incriminating evidence of their exchanges early on, but had grown increasingly brazen as the months went by.

The last three weeks took longer to screenshot than the previous nine months combined. All the graphic texts and images were found within that final three-week period. Olivia still had a hard time looking over those without blushing, and she was careful to look around the office every few seconds to make sure no one walked up on her while she was reading them.

Maybe there was something she wasn't seeing, but most

of the thread seemed relatively useless to the case, except to prove there had been an affair. But the last week of messages had all kinds of potential.

They started off with Jessica sending Dee a racy picture. He didn't respond right away, so she sent a follow-up text.

Jessica: Don't you like what you see?

He finally responded hours later.

Dee: Sorry it's been a little crazy this week. You're looking good baby girl.

Jessica: When are we getting together this week?

Dee: This week might be tough. I'll let you know.

Jessica: You know you can't wait that long to have your way with me.

Dee: lol you're probably right.

After that, Jessica had sent a few more late-night texts, but Dee had failed to respond to any of them. There was complete silence from his end for over sixty hours before he texted Jessica the morning of her death, asking to meet up at her house.

Something had been off between the two lovers the week before the murder, and Olivia had a strong feeling the explanation was the key to solving this case.

The only way to get the answers she needed was to find Dee, and the way to find Dee was through Jessica's contacts, which was why she had exported the contacts list to her own phone. Now all she needed to do was track down phone numbers and addresses with some Internet-stalking, something at which she excelled.

Within twenty minutes, she had home and work phone numbers, along with home and work addresses, for two of Jessica's most contacted numbers. Olivia had just typed the third name on her list into the search bar when a hand reached out and grabbed Jessica's phone from her desk.

"What do we have here? Is this that murdered chick from

yesterday?"

Olivia spun out of her seat and tried to snatch the phone back, but Grady blocked her with his left arm as he held the phone away from her with his right.

"Give me back my phone, Grady. Now. I'm not playing with you."

"Your phone? This doesn't look like you in the background picture. It looks like the girl from the crime scene photos. She's kind of hot. You find any nudes on this thing?"

Olivia tried to knock Grady's arm to the side and lunge for the phone, but he was too strong and warded her off easily. She could see that he'd opened the photos app and was starting to scroll through Jessica's pictures.

The lecherous look on his face, combined with the humiliation of being held back like a child, made Olivia snap, abandoning all inhibitions. She grabbed his left arm with both hands, using it as an anchor, and put all her body weight behind a kick to the back of Grady's left knee. It buckled immediately, tipping Grady back to an almost horizontal position. Olivia used his backwards momentum to slam him down to the ground. His shoulders hit first, but his head was a close second as it bounced off the ground with an audible thud.

She pulled the phone from his loosened grip and glanced at the screen as she took a few steps back in anticipation of his retaliatory response. The screen was locked. The idiot had locked the screen in their scuffle. She wanted to kick him again.

Grady's eyes were struggling to focus as he staggered to his feet like a punch-drunk boxer. A guttural sound escaped his lips. "Oh, you're a dead woman."

He took a shaky step towards her, but Roger and two other officers, Stevens and Braddock, stepped between them.

"Get your fat whale body out of my way."

Roger looked back at Grady with a matter-of-fact expression. "You shouldn't have grabbed evidence off Officer Selman's desk. She might have overreacted a little, but it's over now. Just let it go."

"Like hell I will," Grady snarled, glaring at Olivia.

Stevens stepped closer and spoke in a low voice. "What's your play here, Grady? Are you going to hit a woman? In a room full of cops? You only have two reasonable options. One, you can report her for kicking you and throwing you to the ground. Although, I've got to be honest with you, I don't think that will go well for you. It might cause you more harm than good. Or you can take option two, and just let it go."

Grady stepped forward and glared at Stevens, their faces less than five inches from one another. Then he stepped towards Roger, giving him the same menacing stare. Finally, he fixed his gaze on Olivia. He didn't say a word, but what his face communicated was clear. This wasn't over.

A couple more officers started inching closer, but with a sudden movement Grady pivoted in the opposite direction, pushing past Stevens and straight out the front entrance.

"Why is everyone standing around?"

The room turned as one towards the sound of Chief Duncan's gruff voice and then dispersed in varied directions, each man latching onto the closest task to make himself look busy.

Chief Duncan turned his bulldog face to rest his hooded eyes on Olivia, the only one still frozen in place. "Aren't you in the middle of a murder investigation? You're not going to find witnesses and evidence in this office."

"Yes, sir, I was just about to head back to the crime scene and canvass the neighborhood for leads."

"You do that."

Olivia hauled butt to the exit. Just before she pushed the door open, she looked back towards her desk, remembering the addresses she had written down for the two friends on Jessica's contact list. Chief Duncan was still scowling across the office a few feet from it.

Screw it. She would track those two down later. There was a crime scene calling her name.

CHAPTER NINE

This day had sucked. Most days at school sucked, but this one was sucking worse than usual. Blake's bus had been late to school, again, which meant he didn't get to eat breakfast in the cafeteria. Breakfast was dropped off to his first-period class for him and two other late bus-riders, but as soon as he received his, Dominick turned around and said, "Hey man, let me get that."

Blake knew if he refused, Dominick would just put more pressure on him and make "fat boy" comments. He would rather go hungry than put up with that crap again.

Then, to top off the morning, Mr. T.'s sub was the crazy old cat lady, Mrs. Hoffman. Known for screaming at students who dared to talk in her class, she expected absolute silence all period long, which was pretty much impossible for his classmates.

Halfway through third period, someone threw a paper ball that hit her in the head. Mrs. Hoffman lost her mind. For five minutes straight, she got into students' faces and screamed threats about suspension and expulsion.

Lucas finally piped up and said, "I saw Blake throw it," which meant that Lucas had probably thrown it. But after a couple of Lucas's friends chimed in and agreed with him, Blake became the focus of the screaming and was marched to Assistant Principal Bryant's office with a referral.

Mr. Bryant had been pretty cool about it, though. When Blake told him his version of events, Mr. Bryant simply shook his head and dropped the referral in the trashcan. The move was such a clear sign of support that Blake had been emboldened to ask, "Mr. Bryant, why does Plainview use someone like Mrs. Hoffman to sub? I mean, she's a certified psycho."

With a sad smile, Mr. Bryant had been surprisingly transparent about the situation. "It's not easy to find subs who will work at Plainview. There are a lot of schools in the district that have much easier classrooms to manage. Sometimes, we have to take what we can get. Unfortunately, Mrs. Hoffman only has two tools in her tool belt: yelling and writing referrals." He'd shrugged apologetically. "I know it's not ideal, Blake, but it is what it is. All I ask is that you continue to do your best not to be part of the problem. And I'll be sure to have a talk with our friend Lucas."

Mr. Bryant had let Blake stay in his office for the rest of third period, and now he was part of the throng headed to lunch. The discomfort in his stomach grew the closer he got to the lunchroom. As hungry as he was, he knew his stomach pain wasn't triggered by the smell of pizza.

Of all the things that had made this day suck, the biggest contributing factor, by far, was his relationship with Ari. Last night had been a disaster. Ari had needed a friend who would listen to her and comfort her, and he had botched it. Completely unprepared for the things she'd said to him and tried to do with him, Blake had freaked out. As a result, Ari had left his house pissed and refused to respond to any of his texts this morning. Dark clouds were forming over his head, and he was bracing for possible thunder, lightning, and hail.

Seventh graders ate lunch right before eighth graders, and most days, Ari lingered around long enough to say hi to Blake before she left. He wasn't sure which would stress him out more: seeing her waiting for him, or not seeing her at all.

He craned his neck around the head of the six-foot Sasquatch of a student in front of him and saw, to his tremendous relief, that Ari's class had completely cleared out from its table. He headed towards the nearest cafeteria line, trying to convince himself that his relief was due to wanting to talk things through at a better time, not because he didn't want to see her at all.

As he approached the end of the line, he glanced towards the row of trashcans where a few seventh graders were still throwing away food. There was Ari, hood down and long blonde hair flowing, which was a rare sight. She was smiling, which was an even rarer sight. And she was talking to Cameron, which he had never seen her do.

For the briefest moment, she turned her head in his direction and their eyes locked. Her eyes seemed to communicate a book's worth of information, but it was in a language he couldn't read. Then she put her arm on Cameron's shoulder, broke into a big smile, and said something that looked like, "Call me."

"Go, Blake, what are you waiting for?"

Blake glanced back at an annoyed Esteban and shuffled forward to close the gap in the line. But as he watched Ari exit the cafeteria, he realized he wasn't hungry. He left the line and walked to the far end of his class's assigned seating area, sat down, and buried his face in his arms.

BILLY'S VIDEOS HAD revealed nothing. Nothing for indicating

who might have killed Jonas's wife, at least. No one had parked near their house. No one had approached their front door or side windows. The only people to even pass by the house were a mother with a stroller and a couple of early-morning walkers whom he knew walked the neighborhood daily.

The only video clip that interested him at all was the one where Jessica arrived home. It showed her entering their remote-controlled garage at 10:37. That was awfully early for lunch. The timing bothered him. He had put a reminder in his phone to swing by Jessica's workplace and talk to Tamera, her closest work friend. Maybe something had happened at work that had forced her to return home.

While the videos had largely been a bust, they did confirm one important detail. Whoever killed Jessica had not only entered through the back door, but they'd also approached from the back of the house and stayed out of sight. That wouldn't have been easy to do.

Everyone in their neighborhood had a fenced-in backyard, and everyone on Jonas's side of the street had a yard that backed up to a densely wooded area with a creek. The only opening in the woods was a retention pond with a steep slope that was located behind the houses to the left of his backyard, the ones that led to the entrance of the neighborhood.

The only way to get into his backyard was to hop a series of fences, hike through the woods, or navigate the steeply graded slope between the fence line and the retention pond. Who would go through all that trouble? Had the killer approached their house with the intent to kill? Who would target his wife like that?

It made no sense.

His mind ran through every scenario he could think of. All the ones involving someone hiking through the woods seemed too far-fetched. The most plausible ones involved someone parking up the street and skirting the property line by the retention pond.

He decided to knock on every door that backed up to the pond and see if they'd seen someone walking behind their fence line. For once, he hoped his hyper-vigilant neighborhood would work in his favor.

Olivia pulled over to the curb in an almost identical spot to the day before. Having gotten the green light from Vogel to break the seal and have a look around, she ducked a string of yellow crime scene tape and headed towards the front door. She stopped short at the steps—the front porch triggered images of all the doorbell videos she had watched.

She glanced at her watch. 10:58. Twenty-four hours earlier, Jessica had just arrived home to prepare for her lover. This was the time of day everything had gone down.

Olivia turned around, scanning the nearby homes up and across the street. Who had been home at this time yesterday? The next couple of hours would be the ideal time to knock on doors and talk to potential witnesses. The inside would have to wait.

Crossing back over the driveway, past the garage, she peered down the side of the house. Like in most new neighborhoods, there wasn't much space between houses. Maybe twenty feet, max. A decorative stone path led to a four-foot stained wooden fence. Had Jessica's lover taken this path to access the backdoor, knowing he would be safely out of view of the front porch camera? Or was there a better way? She walked down the path and let herself into the backyard.

The yard was graded so there was a gentle slope, higher on the left and lower on the right. Olivia had a clear view of all the different fences to the right as soon as she stepped into the yard. Only the two closest were visible to her left until she reached the back of the fence. There she could see the fence line of every home backing up to the retention pond. The rest of the land behind the yard appeared to be a thick wooded area with blackberry bushes and briars throughout.

There was little chance Jessica's lover had come trudging through those woods. The retention pond had a steep slope with tall grass, but she could imagine a guy approaching from that direction if he stayed close to the fence line, especially if he was paranoid about being seen.

Looking around, she mulled over other possibilities.

Nothing else seemed likely. The lover had simply taken the stone path to the backyard, or he had circumvented the neighborhood by way of the retention pond and then hopped the fence. Either way, he would have to pass by the houses that backed up to the retention pond. She would start with those neighbors.

Jonas glanced back down the street at the yellow crime scene tape eyesore that was his house as he made his way up the steps. He pushed the doorbell—the seventh one he had tried. No one had been home at the first two houses. An older couple had invited him in for coffee at the third house, but they hadn't seen anything and exchanged bewildered looks when he asked if they had any video surveillance.

The fourth house was opened by an IT specialist named Ron who worked from home. He hadn't spotted anything unusual yesterday, but he'd willingly shared the doorbell camera footage he had. The videos hadn't revealed any new cars or neighborhood walkers.

No one had been home at the fifth house.

Last and least, a young mom with an infant on her shoulder had answered the door at the sixth house, and promptly shut it in his face as soon as he explained who he was.

Just as he was about to push the doorbell of the seventh house one more time, he heard the clank of a deadbolt unlocking and an older woman with short gray hair opened the door. "Yes, can I help you?"

"Hi, I don't believe we've met yet. My name is Jonas, and I live down the street. I'm sure you're probably aware of what happened to my wife yesterday." Jonas paused when the woman's face creased in confusion. "Were you here when all the police cars and emergency vehicles showed up yesterday?"

"Yes, I heard them go by, and looked out the front door to see what all the commotion was about, but I'm afraid I don't know much more about it than that. I'm not one to stick my nose in other people's business, and I was in the middle of planting flowers in my backyard."

"You were working in your backyard yesterday?"

"Yes, most of the morning and early afternoon."

"Did you happen to see anyone walking past your back fence yesterday?"

"As a matter of fact, I did. Well, he wasn't exactly walking. More like running, right along the edge of my fence."

Jonas's heart started racing. His mouth couldn't keep up with the questions popping into his mind.

"Which way—what was—did you recognize him?"

Olivia side-stepped through the front door, eager to move on. "Thank you, thank you, I really appreciate your time."

"Are you sure you don't want to take a couple of cookies for the road?"

"I've had too many already, really, thank you. Take care."

Wow, sweet couple, but they could talk your ear off—and, unfortunately, they hadn't had anything useful to share towards her investigation.

Olivia turned right at the sidewalk to get to the next house up from the Turners' residence when she noticed a man talking to an older woman a few houses further up the street. She stopped in her tracks when she recognized him, then grabbed her gun holster to keep it from bouncing as she jogged towards them.

The woman noticed her first and stopped talking, which caused Turner to follow her gaze. When he saw her, he took a few steps in her direction and waved her over.

"What are you doing?" she demanded.

"You've got to hear this," he blurted out. "I think this lady saw my wife's killer leaving my house."

"What are you talking about? Did she reach out to you to tell you this?"

"What? No, we've never met before today, but I've been knocking on doors all morning to see if any of my neighbors saw something suspicious."

"What doors have you knocked on?"

Turner waved his hand in the direction of his house. "Just the ones up this side of the street. Come on, you need to listen to what she has to say."

His body language kept trying to get Olivia to follow him up the steps of the old lady's home, but she stayed where she was, near the street.

He noticed the look on her face and returned to her side, this time with a much more subdued demeanor. "What?"

"Why are you knocking on your neighbors' doors? That's our job. I know you don't want to hear this, but you are still a suspect. You can't go around interfering in our investigation."

"Yeah, well, after last night, I wasn't convinced there would *be* any further investigation. It sounded like the only suspect you were looking into was me. And since I didn't kill my wife, I figured someone should start looking for who did."

His tone was pissing her off, but he wasn't completely

wrong. She looked back at the woman, who was still standing in her front door. "Why did you start with these neighbors? Why not your neighbors down the street or across the street?"

"I had to start somewhere. Why not these?"

The way he said it was almost natural, but not quite. Something about the inflection gave her the impression he was holding back. She gave him her most penetrating stare, intent on waiting him out.

After a shrug and about twenty seconds of fidgeting, Turner sighed. "Look, I have a theory that the killer got to my back door by hopping the fence from the backside of the subdivision. If I'm right, then he would have had to pass by all the houses on this side of the street. Or cut between them."

"How do you know this?"

"My neighbor across the street has a doorbell camera. He let me have the footage from yesterday morning. No one approached the house from the time I left for work to the time I arrived home. Not even close. So either the killer hopped a series of fences, traveling through people's backyards, or he came from behind the subdivision. The woods are pretty thick behind the houses down the street, so I figured I would start with the ones in this direction." He gave her a triumphant look. "And it turns out, I was right. This lady saw someone. So can we please go talk to her and follow up on this?"

Olivia glanced up at the woman still standing at the door, who had an amused look on her face. Olivia wasn't excited about conducting the interview with the prime suspect by her side, but convincing him to leave would probably be more trouble than it was worth. Maybe if he saw her taking this lead seriously he would back down a little and let them handle the investigation.

"All right, let's go talk with her. But let me do the talking. You just sit there and listen. Understood?"

Turner dipped his head in acknowledgment. "Understood."

CHAPTER TEN

Can I make you two a cup of tea?"

Olivia and Turner said "No thank you" in unison as they took a seat on opposite ends of an ornate white couch.

Pulling out her phone, Olivia asked, "Would you mind if I recorded this conversation? It's easier than taking notes."

"Sure, that's no problem at all."

"Thank you, Mrs....?"

"McCormick, but please, just call me Jane."

"Okay, Jane, Mr. Turner here tells me you think you may have seen his wife's killer. Is this true?"

Jane's face drained of color; her hand went to her chest. "Killer? That man killed someone?"

Olivia turned towards Jonas Turner in disbelief.

He leaned her way and whispered theatrically, "I hadn't got that far yet."

She shook her head and started over. "Jane, Mr. Turner's wife was murdered yesterday in their home. At this time, we have not identified the killer. We have reason to believe he might have passed by your house on his way to and from the murder. If you saw anyone pass by yesterday morning or early afternoon, we need to know."

Jane looked at Turner, eyes filling with tears. "You poor, poor boy. I am so sorry for the loss of your wife. I can't even imagine what you are going through."

Turner nodded and appeared to be holding back tears himself. Olivia could tell he was biting down on the inside of his cheek.

Jane shifted her gaze to Olivia. "I didn't realize we were looking for a murderer. We have the occasional car break-in, or something lifted out of an unattended garage, but nothing like a murder. It's scary to think that he ran by my fence just a couple of yards from where I was planting flowers."

"So you were outside, in your backyard, when he passed by?"

"Yes, I was putting some zinnias in my flower bed out back when I heard a commotion behind Dave and Julie's house. That's the young couple next door with the new baby boy. As soon as I looked up, a man in a black hoodie went rushing by."

"Approximately what time was that?"

"Oh, I don't know. I never wear my watch in the garden. I remember stopping for lunch a little while after that. If I had to guess, I would say around 11:30, maybe."

"Okay, some time before noon, around 11:30, you saw a man run past your back fence. Was this man familiar to you?"

"It happened so fast, I'm not sure I would have recognized him even if I knew him, but, no, he did not strike me as familiar."

"And he was wearing a black hoodie?"

"Yes."

"What about his pants?"

"It looked like he had on blue jeans. They were dark colored, though, almost as dark as the hoodie."

"Were there any distinguishing features on the clothing? A

brand name or image on the hoodie, or holes in the jeans?"

Jane looked down for a few seconds, but when she looked up, she shook her head with confidence. "No, the hoodie was solid black, and I didn't see any holes in the jeans."

"What about his face? What features stood out?"

"I'm afraid I didn't get a good look at his face. It was kind of a blur, and the hoodie was pulled tight, covering most of it."

Olivia gave that some thought. It had been a relatively warm day yesterday. Wearing a hoodie pulled tight on such a day was an obvious attempt at concealment. "Ma'am, this is really important. Anything you can remember would be a huge help."

Jane nodded. She turned in the direction of the back door, then stared at a spot on the floor for almost a minute. When she finally swiveled back in Olivia's direction, her words were hesitant. "I can't recall any specific facial features, but I remember thinking he was Hispanic at the time."

"Hispanic? Why Hispanic?"

"I don't know. It might be because the only people I've ever seen back there were Hispanic. The neighborhood has a landscaping crew come out twice a year to maintain the land around the retention pond, and the whole crew is Hispanic. And most of them are kind of short, like the guy who ran by."

Olivia mentally kicked herself for not asking about the guy's height already. "He was short? How short are we talking? 5'5", 5'6"?"

"Oh, I don't know. I've never been good at judging height. It was hard to tell because he was kind of crouching down as he ran by, but his head barely cleared my four-foot fence."

Olivia made a mental note to find out which crew did the neighborhood landscaping. She wished there was a way to pin down the man's ethnicity. If he really was Hispanic, finding the landscaping crew would need to be a priority. "I know you didn't get a good look at his face, but what about his hands? I can't imagine them being in his pockets while he tried to navigate the slope behind your fence line."

Olivia watched Jane's face closely as she made an effort to remember. Her eyes narrowed and two creases formed between her brows, but then her eyes went wide and her mouth opened in the shape of an "O".

"He was wearing gloves. That's the other reason I thought it was one of the landscapers. He was wearing work gloves, you know, the thick kind you would wear while working in the yard."

"They were thick? Do you remember what color?"

"Yes, they were yellow. At least, that was their original color. They looked pretty dingy and stained. They were far from new-looking."

Olivia felt Turner look her way. She glanced at him and nodded subtly to let him know she recognized the significance of Jane's statement.

"You say the gloves looked dirty or stained. Do you think it's possible that they were stained with blood?"

Jane gasped and shot a hand to her mouth. "Blood? Was your wife killed in a brutal fashion?"

Turner nodded slowly. "She was stabbed. Several times. The killer must have been covered in blood. With dark clothing, it might be hard to tell, but the blood would show up on yellow gloves."

"I wish I could say for sure, but he went by so fast, and his hands were in shadow behind the fence. I was only getting quick glimpses of them through the one-inch spaces between the slats in my fence, so it was hard to tell." Jane wrung her hands, glancing back and forth between her visitors on the couch, before adding in a shaky voice, "But I guess what I assumed was dirt and grime could have been... blood."

Jonas was the first one out the door. He waited at the bottom of the steps as Officer Selman thanked Jane for her time and gave her a card in case she remembered anything else.

As soon as the officer made her way down the steps, he pounced. "What do you think?"

"It was interesting."

When she didn't offer more, Jonas pressed. "Interesting? You don't think this was the guy? Who else would run, crouched down, behind the neighborhood fence line? Why would he wear a hoodie pulled tight around his face in the middle of a sunny spring day? And his gloves were stained. This is definitely our guy."

Officer Selman looked at him with an amused smile tugging at the corner of her lips. "Maybe. It's probably worth following up on. Do you know who the neighborhood uses for landscaping?"

"No, but I know where at least two of the HOA board members live, and I'm sure they could tell you."

"Okay, that'll work. Here's one of my cards. Text me their names and addresses, and I will follow up with them. I will also talk to the other neighbors on this street leading to the entrance and see if anyone else saw this man running by. Maybe we'll get lucky and find someone who saw him leave the back area and get into a vehicle."

"I would be happy to help with that. Do you want to knock on doors together, or split up to save time?"

Selman shook her head. "I don't think that's a good idea. I appreciate you leading me to Jane. She's a valuable witness. But from this point on, it would be best if you leave the police work to us."

Jonas was about to protest when Officer Selman's phone rang. She held a finger up and turned away. "This is Selman.

Uh huh. Talking to neighbors around the crime scene. Uh huh. Okay. I can probably be there in about fifteen minutes. Okay. Bye."

She turned back to Jonas. "I have to take off. I'll finish canvasing this side of the street later. Promise me you won't do it yourself."

Jonas struggled to keep his frustration in check. "Why? Why can't I help? I know this neighborhood and the way it works better than you do. Why not let me help you find leads?"

Selman looked exasperated and antsy to leave. "You're still a suspect. Anything you do to involve yourself in the investigation taints it. If we have questions, we will come to you and ask them. Just sit tight and let us do our jobs, okay?"

"You'll follow up on this guy that ran by Jane's house?"

"Yes. I will come back and interview the other neighbors. Text me the names and addresses of the HOA members, and I will track down the guys on the landscaping crew. I have this under control."

"Okay."

"Okay, you'll stop investigating this case?"

"I'll stop. For now."

Selman let out a visible sigh and gave him a look like he was being obstinate, but she didn't say anything else. Instead, she spun around and hustled back to her patrol car.

Jonas was watching her semi-jogging down the sidewalk when he felt his phone vibrate in his front right pocket. Pulling it out, he saw that the caller ID read "Mom". His heart sank as a sudden sense of dread spread through his chest. He had planned on calling his parents that morning, but the need to get to Billy's house so early and all the ensuing conversations with neighbors had pushed it out of his mind.

Now, they were calling him at a time they knew he was normally in class teaching. They must have seen something on social media. This was going to be a brutal conversation.

He started walking back to his car as he answered his phone. "Hi, Mom."

CHAPTER ELEVEN

Olivia was well familiar with the Greenville County Detention Center on McGee Street, but this was the first time she had been in the wing containing the forensics lab. She found Vogel standing at a glass-covered reception area.

When he noticed her behind him, he turned around and gave her a big smile. "Hey, you made pretty good time. You ready to hear what these CSI guys have to say about our crime scene?"

"Absolutely."

Vogel turned back towards the glass. "Donna, could you let Cory know we're here and ready to see what he's found?"

The woman gave him a brief nod and picked up her phone as she pressed one of the line extensions.

"How are we getting results back already? I thought it would be days, if not weeks, before we heard anything."

"I pulled some strings and convinced the powers that be to make our crime scene evidence the lab's top priority. It wasn't too hard. We don't have many murders in this county, and this one is going to be all over the news. A pretty young white woman, living in a nice neighborhood, gets brutally stabbed to death in her own home? People are going to want answers. Especially when the number one suspect is teaching some of their children." Waving a hand in the general direction of a nearby hallway, Vogel went on, "I've worked with Cory on a number of cases over the years, and I asked him to call me as soon as he found anything significant. We won't get any DNA results yet. Those tests are done in a lab across town and will take a couple of days to a couple of weeks to process. But I got a call about an hour ago to come down here, so they must have found something interesting in their fingerprint or shoe print analysis."

A short man with close-cropped sandy blond hair wearing clear-framed glasses with square lenses appeared out of the hallway. "Detective Vogel, thank you for stopping by."

"Hey, Cory, this is Officer Selman. She's working with me on the case."

The man blushed and gave Olivia an awkward smile as he extended his hand. "Nice to meet you. Thank you for stopping by."

"Thank you for having me."

Vogel slapped Cory on the back. "This guy is the lab supervisor and our top forensic print analyst. Forensic labs all over the Southeast consult this guy for his shoe print analysis skills."

Cory looked relatively young to be the lab supervisor. Olivia would guess he was in his late twenties, maybe early thirties. Vogel's flattery caused more blushing and a big, goofy grin that he tried to hide by heading down the hallway and beckoning for them to follow.

They entered an office that would have seemed spacious if not for all the tables, equipment, and paperwork lining every wall. Cory directed them to a table at the back that was covered in crime scene photos, along with the pair of running shoes they'd confiscated from Jonas Turner.

"Obviously, we have a lot of evidence still to process, but, as you requested, we began by analyzing the murder weapon and the bloody shoe print left at the crime scene. Do you want the good news first, or the bad?"

Vogel looked up from the table of evidence and put his hands in his pockets. "I'm a bad-news-first kind of guy. Always. So let's have it."

Cory reached out and grabbed the pair of running shoes. "The bad news is, these shoes did not make the bloody shoe print found at the crime scene."

"What? Are you serious?" Vogel picked up one of the photos of the bloody print and looked back and forth between the image and the soles of the shoes in Cory's hand. "They look the same to me."

"It's the same basic tread pattern. It's the same size and brand—a Mizuno Wave Sky, size 14. But the bloody print reveals evidence of wear and tear that these shoes could not possibly replicate."

He reached out with his empty hand and pointed out different sections on the bloody print image with his pinkie finger. "We are looking for a shoe with extreme wear across the front sole and around the edges, and a significant tear in the heel." Cory put down the left shoe and held up the right one for them to examine more closely. "As you can see, these shoes are relatively new with little wear to the tread. Not only that, but we found no trace of blood on these shoes. It's nearly impossible to remove all traces of blood from every crevice of a shoe, even with a thorough cleaning, and these shoes show no evidence of having been cleaned recently."

Vogel shifted his incredulous look in Olivia's direction. "So what are we saying here? That there's some other suspect running around out there with the same big-ass feet and the same affinity for these fancy running shoes? That's not possible. What's going on here?"

She had been thinking the same thing, but another possibility dawned on her. "Have we catalogued or processed any other shoes in Turner's closet? Maybe he has an older pair of running shoes?"

"We have pictures of the soles of every shoe we located in the house." Cory pulled a folder from a rack on a nearby desk and opened it wide on the table, fanning a few of the photographs. "A quick glance was sufficient to eliminate any of these as potential matches. There was only one other pair of running shoes in the mix, and they were New Balances, not Mizunos. The tread patterns are completely different."

The three of them stared at the photos on the table, willing a solution to present itself.

"He must have stashed them somewhere," Olivia offered. "If Turner did it, he wouldn't just leave his bloody shoes in the closet. At the very least he would try to throw them away, but if they're not in the trash bin, then we need to search every crevice and crawl space in that house. We know he didn't leave the house, so they've got to be there somewhere."

Vogel nodded along. "That's good, you're right, he must have stashed them somewhere in the house. I want you to head back there after this and try to locate them." He glanced at his watch. "I have an interview with News Channel 4 in about an hour, but I'll meet up with you afterwards if I can."

"You're giving an interview on this case already?"

"Yeah, I'm racking up some big brownie points with one of the reporters at News 4. What can I say? A murder like this one is big news, and it's good to have the media owe you favors." Vogel shifted his focus back to the lab supervisor. "All right, Cory, you promised me some good news too. What did you find that's going to make me happy?"

Cory held a hand towards the kitchen knife lying on the table. "The good news is that we were able to recover a partial thumbprint from the murder weapon. It was located on the right side of the handle at the very top, near the blade. And it is an identical match to Jonas Turner's left thumbprint."

Vogel clapped his hands together and looked Olivia's way. "We've got him holding the murder weapon, Selman."

She continued staring at the knife, picturing how she'd first come across it, buried in Jessica Turner's chest. "You didn't find any other prints on the knife?"

"No, the rest of the blade was too smeared with blood."

"How soon will you be able to tell whether any blood on the knife is from the attacker?"

"That's a great question, Officer Selman. In a frenzied knife attack such as this one, where the blade is drenched in blood, it's common for the blade to slip and cut the attacker. Honestly, it would be unusual for that not to happen with so many violent thrusts, which is why we ran a basic ABO test on several samples from the knife's handle to determine blood type.

"We were hoping to find two different kinds, but so far we've only found one that matches the victim. It's possible that the attacker has the same blood type as the victim. It's also possible that we'll find a secondary blood type in the other samples we've collected, but I'm less optimistic now. Either way, we'll know for sure in a week or two when we get a complete DNA profile back from the lab."

Vogel glanced at his watch and then shifted his gaze rapidly between Olivia and Cory. "All right, anything else?"

"We found one other piece of evidence while examining the knife, which may prove valuable." Cory picked up a clear plastic tube from the table and held it up for them to see. "We extracted this from the crevice where the blade meets the handle."

It was a thick fiber that had been splayed wide. On one side it was dark red, and on the other it was yellow.

"It was soaked in blood, but I opened it up and spread it flat so you can see the original composition better. It's a coarse yellow fiber that we're having trouble matching to any of the clothing or bedding connected to the crime scene. With luck, it's something we can match to the assailant's clothing."

Olivia's heartbeat pulsed in her ears as she examined the fiber. "With so few prints on the blade and no secondary source of blood, do you think it's likely that the killer was wearing gloves while stabbing the victim so many times?"

Cory looked down at the knife handle, but he appeared to be seeing something else. "That would certainly explain the absence of the attacker's blood. It might also explain the unusual blood residue pattern on the handle itself. The smears were atypical for a bare palm grab, but after finding the thumbprint, I didn't give them much more thought. I suppose it's likely that the thumbprint and the smears were left by different grabs of the knife."

Vogel's face settled into a grimace that said both "Where did *that* come from?" and "What are you doing?".

Olivia kept talking as if she hadn't seen the look. "You might want to try matching that fiber with a pair of work gloves. It kind of looks like that coarse yellow leather that's common in those types of gloves."

"Okay, what do you know that you're not telling me, Selman?" Vogel looked down at his watch. "Dang it, Cory, I've got to get to this interview. I really appreciate you taking the time to give us this update. I know you have a lot more work to do, so we'll get out of your hair, but if you find anything else significant, give me a call right away."

He had Olivia halfway to the door, prodding her along with a hand on her back, before Cory had the time to respond, "Will do."

Vogel leaned in to Olivia's ear. "And maybe on the way back to our cars, you can enlighten me on how you came up with this brilliant killer-in-work-gloves theory of yours." He said it jovially enough, but there was an edge to his voice.

As soon as they exited the room, Olivia rushed to explain herself, trying to make eye contact to ensure he was picking up on her sincerity. "When you called me, I had just stepped out of an interview with one of the victim's neighbors. Around 11:30 yesterday afternoon, this woman was gardening in her backyard when a man in a black hoodie ran past the outside of her fence. He had his hood pulled tight around his face, he was crouched down like he was trying to stay out of sight, and he was in the no-man's-land area around the retention pond."

Vogel maintained his brisk pace towards the exit without so much as a glance in her direction.

"I understand that the most likely suspect is still the husband. But if it's not him, there's a high probability that the killer accessed the back door by navigating around the retention pond and hopping the back fence. It's the best way to get to the house without getting videoed by a bunch of doorbell cameras."

As they pushed through the double glass doors together, Vogel gave a little shake of his head and rolled his eyes. "And you think this black hoodie guy is Jessica's lover? He arranged to meet her, and then they either got into a fight, or he showed up planning on killing her in the first place. Is that where you're going with this? And what does this have to do with yellow work gloves?"

"Well, actually, I don't think the guy who ran by the fence was the lover."

Vogel came to an abrupt halt on the sidewalk and finally looked at her. "Then who is the guy in the hoodie supposed to be?"

"The witness thought he might have been Hispanic. He was on the shorter side, and he was wearing yellow work gloves that appeared to be stained. There's an all-Hispanic landscaping crew that maintains the neighborhood, including the area around the retention pond. Perhaps someone on the crew was looking for unlocked doors, found one in the Turners' back door, and stumbled across Jessica while trying to steal something."

Vogel spun away from her, grabbing his head and shaking it in disbelief. Just as quickly, he pivoted back around and threw his hands wide. "Are you kidding me? Not only do you want to throw a mystery lover in the mix, now you want to speculate that a short Hispanic man just happened to wander his way into the backyard of the one house with an unlocked door? And instead of running at the sight of the half-naked woman he finds in the home, this landscaping crew member grabs a knife and stabs our victim forty-seven times?"

Olivia could feel the blood rising into her face and radiating off her cheeks. "I know it seems far-fetched, but don't you think it's an odd coincidence that coarse yellow fibers were found on the knife, and coarse yellow gloves were seen on this man running behind the fence line? Maybe the guy running *was* the lover. The witness didn't get a good look at him. We only know what Jessica's lover looks like from his pictures on the phone. Maybe he's shorter than he looks. All I'm saying is that it might be worthwhile to figure out who was running behind the fence line right around the time Jessica got murdered."

Vogel glanced in the direction of his car in the parking lot and then down at his watch, before giving her one last eye roll and shake of his head. "Look, if you want to track down these crazy leads, then have at it. Chase them down to your little heart's desire. But first, find me the bloody shoes. Turn that house upside down if you have to, but find me those shoes. Got it?"

"Yes, I've got it."

She watched Vogel speed-walk to his car, shaking his head

the entire way. She was beginning to wonder how this guy had closed so many cases with how little time he seemed to spend on investigating them.

CHAPTER TWELVE

The conversation had been every bit as painful as Jonas feared, and included even more tears than he'd expected. His parents had offered to fly out first thing tomorrow morning to be there for him, but he had convinced them to wait. Weekend flights out of Arizona would be expensive for their modest income. He also had no place to put them up. There was no telling how long it would be until the police no longer considered his house an active crime scene and released it back to him. So they'd agreed to wait until he could pin down the funeral arrangements and figure out a place for them to stay.

Thinking about funeral arrangements had given him a mild panic attack—heart fluttering, intestines clenched tight, and body breaking out in a cold sweat. The police had given no indication as to when they would release her body, but once they did, he would be responsible for figuring out how to honor Jessica's life despite never having talked through what she wanted.

Would she prefer to be cremated or put in a casket? What

would she want on her tombstone? And how in the world was he going to pay for all of this?

Stop it. Stop it. Focus on the task at hand.

The only way he had been able to function the last twenty-four hours was by focusing on finding Jessica's killer. This is why he was here, at Jessica's workplace, rather than sitting in his motel room alone.

He watched as a white-haired woman opened the door for an old man gingerly exiting with a walker. It was almost closing time at Elite Physical Therapy. He would have preferred to wait until all the patients were gone, but he didn't want to risk any of the staff leaving before he asked his questions.

As he got out of his car and walked to the door, it occurred to him how displeased Officer Selman would be if she knew he was here asking questions. Technically, he was not breaking his promise. Just kind of skirting around it. He wasn't trying to track down the killer or investigate the case so much as he was trying to understand the personal reasons for why his wife had been forced to leave work unexpectedly.

Yes, that was the only reason he was here.

As soon as he walked through the door, the receptionist audibly gasped. Her eyes were huge behind the big lenses in her gold frames, and the kinky curls of her mountain of yellow-gold hair bounced as she bounded out from behind her desk and gave him a big hug.

He'd tried to catch her name from her nametag, but there had been too much bounding. He knew they had met two or three times over the years, but he was terrible with names, and they'd only exchanged quick pleasantries.

"Oh, Jonas, I am so sorry for your loss. We can't believe she's gone. We are so, *so* heartbroken for you, and for us, and all our patients. Jessica was such an amazing person."

Looking away so her sympathy didn't derail his

composure, Jonas responded as steadily as he could. "Thank you. You're right. She was an amazing person, and I was blessed to have her."

Elite wasn't a huge facility. Just one floor, under three thousand square feet, with ten employees. Most of the other physical therapists had stopped what they were doing and gathered around the front desk.

The receptionist asked, "Are you here to collect Jessica's things?"

He could see her nametag now. Krissy. He looked around at the therapists who had gathered around. There were only two males on staff: a young black man named Eton, and a middle-aged white man named Sam. He didn't want to go there, but he couldn't stop himself from assessing the likelihood of Jessica engaging in an inappropriate office romance with one of them. He hated Detective Vogel for opening that door of possibility in his mind.

"I guess I should go ahead and collect her things while I'm here, but that's not the reason I stopped by. I'm just trying to understand what happened yesterday. I know Jessica left for work, and as far as I knew, she was planning on working her normal hours. I was hoping someone could explain why she decided to go back home."

The staff around the desk exchanged looks and a few of them glanced over their shoulder, but only Krissy spoke up. "I remember her leaving and saying that she would be back after lunch, but I don't think she said why she was leaving. Just that Tamera would be covering her patients the rest of the morning."

"Is Tamera here? She's the one I was most hoping to see. I know Jessica tells her everything."

The group of staff members parted and turned in the direction of the back corner of the room. Tamera was the only therapist still actively working on her patient. It seemed odd to him that Jessica's best friend would be the least affected by his sudden appearance, but as he approached the table where she was massaging an old man's calf, he saw that tears were streaming down her face.

Without a word and without eye contact, she let go of the man's leg and wrapped her arms around him in a rib-crushing bear hug. "Oh, Jonas, I am so sorry. I am so, so sorry. I can't believe she's gone."

Tamera broke down in guttural sobs. It was tempting to open his heart and let out a little of his grief as she poured out hers, but Jonas was uncomfortable exposing that part of himself in public, especially in front of people he barely knew. Instead, he let his mind go numb and held her tight for what felt like ten minutes. He watched as another therapist led the old man off the table and up to the reception desk. He could feel his chest getting damp from where Tamera's tears were pooling on his shirt.

As her sobs grew softer, he gave her one more tight squeeze and then pulled back to make eye contact. "Tamera, is there someplace we can sit down and talk for a few minutes?"

She nodded, looking down and wiping tears away with the back of her hands. "We can go to the back office. Follow me."

The room was tiny—just a desk with a desktop computer, an office chair behind it, and two waiting room chairs in front of it. Tamera sat down in one of those chairs, and Jonas took the other.

After fidgeting with her chair for a few seconds, Tamera looked up, making it only as high as his chest, before speaking in a quiet voice. "What did you want to talk to me about?"

The questions he had were simple, but for some reason he felt the need to explain why he wanted to ask them. He struggled to put his thoughts into words. "Jessica's death...

has been a lot to process. I don't understand *any* of it. The police have no idea who did it. I can't think of any reason why someone would kill her. I don't even understand why she was home. The fact that someone broke into our home and killed her the one time she was home at a time of day when she was never home seems so random and improbable."

He couldn't read Tamera's face, since she was bent over, staring at her hands folded in her lap. Jonas looked around the room, searching for the right words. "I guess I just don't want to believe her death was some horrible, random coincidence. Maybe it's stupid, but if I knew she had a really good reason for going home, that it was unavoidable, it would make me feel better. So, basically, I'm just hoping you'll be able to help me understand why she left work to go home."

The silence in the room felt like it lasted an eternity before Tamera finally mumbled, "I don't know."

Jonas had braced himself for the answer. He hadn't been expecting "I don't know", and confusion filled the void of his deflated expectations. "You don't know why she left work? She didn't tell you why she had to leave unexpectedly?"

Tamera shook her head, never looking up. "She didn't fully explain why she had to leave. Just that she would be back in a couple of hours."

"She didn't *fully* explain? Did she give *any* indication as to why she was leaving? She asked you to cover her patients for her, doubling your workload. Surely she wouldn't ask you to do that unless she had a really good reason. Did she say anything at all that gave you an impression of why she was leaving?"

Tamera slowly shook her head. "Not really. She just said she would be back in a couple of hours."

Recognizing when people are being deceitful is a skill most middle-school teachers develop over time, and Jonas's instincts were screaming at him that she was lying. But why?

To what end?

"Tamera, my wife is dead. She's dead because someone attacked her in our home when she should have been safe at work. If you know why she left work to go home, please, I'm *begging* you, tell me why."

Tamera burst into tears again. Bent nearly double in the chair, her body rocked up and down while she hugged herself tight. "I don't know, I don't know, I don't know. I'm sorry, I'm sorry, I just don't know."

Part of him wanted to get up and comfort her, but his limbs suddenly felt very heavy. He couldn't imagine mustering the energy to stand, let alone console someone else.

They sat there like that a long time, with him staring numbly into space while she cried and repeated "I don't know" and "I'm sorry".

Eventually, he pushed himself out of his chair and stood on legs that felt like cement. "I'm sorry, too. If you remember anything else about why she left, I would really like to hear it. You have my number. Just give me a call."

He left the room without looking back and made his way to the exit. Krissy was there with a box of Jessica's things. He took the box from her with a nod and walked out to his car, feeling like a terminated employee doing the walk of shame.

CHAPTER THIRTEEN

Pulling the sliding glass door closed behind her, Olivia noticed her reflection. She was a hot mess. Her uniform was untucked. Loose strands of hair had pulled free from her ponytail, while little white pieces of fluffy insulation from the attic clung tight throughout it. Dark smudges covered her face from exploring air vents and crawlspaces. She needed a long, hot shower in the worst way.

Two hours of checking every nook and cranny in the house had yielded zero results. She could not imagine a hiding place that she had overlooked. The bloody clothes were simply not in the house.

She walked onto the Bermuda grass and closed her eyes, letting the early evening breeze cool her down and clear her mind. If she was honest with herself, part of her was happy not to find the clothes. Her instincts told her Jonas Turner wasn't their killer, and she wanted to be right.

On the other hand, she really wanted to make Vogel happy and improve her chances of becoming a detective.

She opened her eyes and looked in the direction of the

back fence. Walking up to it, she rested her arms on top and looked up and down the path between the fence line and the forest. She didn't spot anything of interest, but between the tall grass and dense forest, it was hard to see anything from a distance. What if Jonas had simply balled the bloody clothes up and chucked them into the woods?

Olivia backpedaled a few steps, took two quick strides forward, and vaulted over the fence, using the top for leverage. Taking out her flashlight, she used the beam to peer through the brush and trees directly behind the back porch. Nothing but leaves and branches.

She glanced in the direction of the setting sun. Within thirty minutes, she would be thrashing around in the dark. Heading back to the precinct and putting in a request to the K-9 unit crossed her mind, but she decided to do a quick scan of the tree line before she left. Starting at the far edge of the next-door neighbor's fence on the right, since she couldn't imagine anyone tossing clothes further than that, she began scanning the edge of the forest.

A couple of crushed aluminum cans and a white plastic grocery bag were the only items to give her momentary pause the first forty feet, but then her beam landed on something that looked like dingy white fabric. She used her left foot to carefully press down on a tangle of briars and hopped over to a clear section near the fabric.

Shining her light up and down as she did a slow 360-degree spin, she confirmed there was nothing else to see nearby. Turning back to the item, she used her flashlight to beat back the briars on top of it and grabbed one of the many branches lying around. Squatting down low, she used the branch to dig under the fabric and lift it out of the debris.

It was a sock. A nasty old sock. Judging by the deep imprint left when she pulled it free from the dirt and debris, it had probably been out here for months, if not years.

She stomped her way back over the briars and continued her search. Nothing else of interest appeared as she made her way to where the forest met the clearing around the retention pond. She was about to head back to her patrol car when she spotted something leaning against the bottom of the fence around the pond.

Turning sideways and shuffling down the steep slope one step at a time, she made her way to the object. The closer she got, the faster her heart started pumping. It was clearly a shoe, a big shoe, propped against the fence upside down. As she came within a few feet of it, she nearly stepped on a second shoe submerged in tall grass.

Squatting down, she parted the grass to reveal a pointed, abstract symbol resembling a bird. She had only seen this symbol once before—on Jonas Turner's confiscated running shoes.

She pulled out a latex glove and slipped it on. Carefully grabbing the shoe by its tongue, she lifted it out of the grass and held it above her head. The tread on the sole was worn nearly bald around the edges, and there was a big tear in the heel. Most of the sole was a faded black, but the creases were white, and most of those creases were stained with a rusty red residue.

So much for her instincts.

"I know, Mom, I know. I heard you the first time, geez."

Blake slammed his bedroom door shut. She was always nagging him about his homework. It was nothing but stupid busy work, and he was making Bs and Cs despite a number of missing homework assignments, so what was the big deal? He couldn't believe Ms. Agnew had ratted him out on a Friday.

He grabbed the remote off his nightstand and flopped down on the bed. Without even thinking about it, he found himself streaming another episode of *Cold Case Files*. It was his current comfort show. Much like his other favorite true crime shows, *Forensic Files* and *Homicide Hunter*, he was fascinated by the science and detective work. And they always ended with the bad guy getting caught, so they were great shows to fall asleep to.

But they reminded him of Ari.

She was much more into horror movies, but she would humor him when she came over. Sometimes they would even watch the same episode and text late into the night, each trying to predict the killer and the motive. Their ongoing joke was to text "It's the spouse!" as soon as a victim was revealed to be married. It was almost always the spouse, and the motive was almost always sex or money.

He looked down at his phone and checked it for messages. Ari was still giving him the cold shoulder. Friday nights were their nights. It was rare for them not to hang out, or at least spend the night texting. He didn't want to come across like a desperate loser, but he couldn't help himself.

He texted, *Hey what are u up to?*

He tried to pay attention to the show rather than his phone, but he was so focused on willing it to vibrate that when it did, he jolted like he had been electrocuted.

Blake read the text eagerly.

Ari: Heading to the movies

The movies? Who with? She hated going alone. Whenever the newest horror movie came out, she always dragged him along with her.

Blake: Cool what r u going to see?

Ari: The new fast and furious

What? The new *Fast and Furious* movie? She always made fun of people who watched those movies. What was going on here? He couldn't stop himself from asking.

Blake: U going with anyone?

Ari: Ya im going with Cameron

Blake: R u serious? R u going on a date with him?

Ari: What do u care?

Blake: Come on don't be like that. Why would u go out with a loser jock like Cameron?

Ari: Maybe I want to spend time with someone who isn't repulsed by my touch

Blake dropped his phone and grabbed two big fistfuls of hair. He knew he'd messed up the other night, but he hadn't anticipated this level of spite. A little cold shoulder was one thing, but going out with Cameron? That was beyond cold-blooded. That guy had only one thing on his mind. How far was she willing to take her revenge?

He snatched his phone back up.

Blake: Come on Ari it's not like that. U know it's not. U caught me by surprise. Can't we talk about it?

Ari: We'll see. Maybe we can hang out next week if you can stomach being around me. I gotta go. Cameron's waiting on me.

Blake read the message three times before slamming his phone down on his bed. If that slimeball Cameron touched her... he didn't know what he would do, but he would be pissed.

Reaching into his book bag, he pulled out his earbuds and put them in. A little bit of Solence, his favorite Swedish heavy metal band, was what he needed right now. Nothing like some heavy guitar riffs and drums to pound his problems into oblivion.

CHAPTER FOURTEEN

The parking lot was slammed. There were even cars parked all over the grass around the lot. The only open spots Olivia could see were a couple that had a sign saying "First Time Guest Parking". Well, that certainly applied to her, so she eased into one of the two open spots left.

She pulled down her visor to check her makeup one last time. Then she leaned back in her seat and stared out the window, shaking her head. How had she let herself get talked into this situation?

Vogel had been thrilled with her discovery of the shoes. She was back to being his favorite person. They had arranged for the K-9 unit to meet them back at the Turner residence early Saturday morning to hunt down the rest of the bloody clothes, but the search had come up empty.

One of the dogs had taken her handler all the way to the pool parking lot, but not a single item of interest to the investigation was found. This hadn't seemed to bother Vogel, but it bothered Olivia. What reasonable explanation was there for finding the shoes, but not the clothes? If you found a way to conceal bloody clothes, why would you leave bloody shoes out in the open?

When she had expressed this concern to Vogel, he'd shrugged her off and told her to go home and get some rest. She went home, but she couldn't rest. There were too many aspects to this case that weren't adding up, and she could not shake the desire to track down Jessica Turner's lover. She knew she would never be satisfied until she interviewed him.

Unfortunately, she was hesitant to go into the precinct and use her computer for fear of running into Grady. There was no telling what that idiot would do after she'd embarrassed him in front of everybody. It would be better to give him a few days to cool down before they ran into each other again. So she had to be content with reaching out to the two people from Jessica's contact list she had already researched.

Jessica's most frequent contact, Tamera Lewis, hadn't answered her calls or respond to her voice message. Olivia had considered going to her home and pressing the issue, but she'd decided to wait until Monday so she could also interview Jessica's other coworkers.

The second person on the list, Brittany Childress, had answered the phone but said she wasn't available to meet that evening. She'd suggested that they meet up at church the next morning, where she could introduce Olivia to the Turners' other close friends.

So here she was. Wearing a dress for the first time in years. Walking into a church for the first time in over a decade. She desperately wanted a new lead in her investigation, but this was a gigantic leap outside her comfort zone.

The moment she stepped outside her car, a man directing traffic in the parking lot greeted her. "Welcome to Restoration Church! Are you a first-time guest?"

"Uh, yes, this is my first time."

"Wonderful, we are so glad you decided to join us this morning. What's your name?"

"Olivia."

Holding up traffic, he walked her across the parking lot to the sidewalk, where a woman in a flowery blouse and brown capris was greeting people. "Hey, Nicole, could you show Olivia here where to go and make sure she gets one of our First Time Guest gift bags?"

"I would be happy to. It's a pleasure to meet you, Olivia. We love having guests. How did you find out about us?"

"Well, actually, I'm here to meet with Brittany Childress."

"Oh, you know Brittany? That's wonderful! She has such an amazing voice. I just love when she sings for our worship team."

As they approached the main entrance, two people standing at the doors opened them wide and greeted her with big smiles and a cheerful "Good morning!" Nicole led Olivia to a desk in the lobby, grabbed a blue gift bag from behind it, and handed it to her.

"This is just a small thank you for joining us today. You'll find some information about our church in there, too, but if you have any questions, please don't hesitate to ask. Our sanctuary is right through either of those two double doors. We really hope you enjoy your time with us."

"Thank you." Olivia held the bag awkwardly, not knowing what to think of it. She wasn't supposed to meet with Brittany until after the service, but she had decided to attend the whole service to get a feel for the place and make sure she didn't miss out on meeting any of Jessica's other friends.

As she walked through the sanctuary doors and looked for a seat near the back, several more people greeted her. These people were weirdly friendly.

There were no spots open on the back two rows or any aisle seats available, so she squeezed past a middle-aged couple three rows from the back and sat down. After an hour of internet stalking last night she knew what Brittany looked like, and she wasn't hard to spot. She was on the stage behind a mic stand. A guy with a beard and an acoustic guitar strode to the center stage mic and said, "Let's all stand up and worship the Lord this morning."

Olivia wasn't used to seeing electric guitars and drums on stage. When she'd gone to church growing up, it was always a piano and an organ. Every once in a while there might be a special number with a brass ensemble, but this was something else altogether. A rich, full sound filled the sanctuary.

The singers on stage were good. Really good. But she was even more amazed by the singing of the congregation. These people were singing loud, and about a third of them had their hands lifted above their head. There was an energy in the room that gave her arms goosebumps.

She wasn't familiar with the song, but the lyrics were moving. They reminded her of another song she'd grown up with, something about an "old rugged cross". The second song was even more beautiful than the first, and she found herself hanging on every line projected on the screen.

As the congregation was led into the chorus again, Olivia felt her eyes well up with tears. What was going on? She never cried unless she was really angry or embarrassed. Where was this coming from? She stared up at the vaulted wooden ceilings and tried to blink the tears back in, but they trickled down the sides of her face anyway.

As surreptitiously as possible, she crossed her arms and snuck a hand up to wipe the tears from each cheek. Apparently she wasn't subtle enough, because a man leaned forward from the row behind her and handed her a tissue. She nodded in appreciation and then bit down hard on her lip.

What was wrong with her?

JONAS PULLED THE pillow off his head and peeked at the clock on the nightstand. 10:07. He rolled over onto his back and stared at the ceiling. He should be in the middle of his Sunday school lesson right now. Teaching through the book of Hebrews sounded much better than flopping around on this bed, obsessing over questions he had no answers for. But he'd been unable to bring himself to go to church this morning and face the sea of sympathy from his friends and acquaintances. He'd like to think that he was all cried out from last night's breakdown, but he knew he would crumble again the moment he registered their looks of love and concern. It was better to go crazy in a hotel room than make a public spectacle of himself by weeping like a baby.

He threw off the covers and reached down for his laptop bag. Maybe working on his lesson plans would take his mind off Jessica's murder. He wasn't sure going into school tomorrow was a good idea, but he also wasn't sure he could maintain his sanity spending all day in a hotel room doing nothing.

Pulling up his lesson plan template, he started typing out the daily activities he had planned for the week. His students were working their way through *Fahrenheit 451* while also honing their persuasive writing skills. The entire weekly plan was fleshed out in less than twenty minutes.

After staring at the screen mindlessly for five minutes, he clicked on his Internet browser and found himself scrolling through Facebook. His notifications were full of posts and messages expressing things like "I'm so sorry for your loss" or "You are in our thoughts and prayers" or "Let us know if there's anything we can do to help." On some level he appreciated the expressions of concern, but right now the words seemed empty and meaningless, and he scrolled right by them.

He stopped scrolling when he saw the familiar face of Detective Vogel. One of Jessica's friends from the gym had posted a video from WYFF News Channel 4 that showed Detective Vogel speaking into a microphone. Jonas clicked the link and started watching.

Long after the video stopped playing, he sat stone still on the bed. It wasn't until a sharp pain in the front part of his skull began to develop that he unclenched his jaw and slammed his laptop closed. He hopped up from the bed and began pacing the room, mulling over his options.

He didn't know what he was going to do, but he knew one thing for certain. He was no longer going to sit around and trust the cops to solve this case.

CHAPTER FIFTEEN

After the closing prayer, most of the people around her began mingling or heading for the exit, but Olivia remained in her seat. The sermon had been nothing like the ones she remembered hearing as a girl growing up in a small Episcopalian church. The pastor had been funny and engaging, sharing stories about his life growing up on the mission field in Cochabamba, Bolivia. But it was his portrayal of God that had her rooted to her seat in deep contemplation. She had always viewed God as more of a strict judge who demanded perfection rather than a doting father or loyal friend. It was hard to believe that this great big cosmic being really cared about her thoughts and feelings. It was a nice thought, but hard to believe. Especially with the things she had seen and experienced.

Seeing Brittany enter the sanctuary from a door to the left of the stage broke her out of her reverie. She hurried to intersect her. "Hey, Brittany, would now be a good time to talk?"

"Oh, hey, are you Officer Selman? Yeah, now works for me.

Do you want me to introduce you to Pastor Joshua? He knows the Turners well, too. He might be worth talking to."

"Um, sure, we can do that."

Brittany glided over to Pastor Joshua, who appeared to be wrapping up a conversation with a young couple.

"Hey, Pastor Joshua, do you have a second? This is Officer Selman. She's working the investigation into Jessica's murder."

Pastor Joshua turned to her with a face that registered both friendliness and sadness as he extended his hand. "Thank you for the work that you do. We are heartbroken over Jessica's death and hope you are able to bring the killer to justice. It's hard to believe that this could happen to someone like Jessica."

Olivia nodded along. "How well do you know the Turners? Did you ever spend time with them outside of a church setting?"

"Yes, I know them pretty well. I did their marriage counseling. We didn't hang out frequently, but my wife and I would have them over for dinner a few times a year, at least. I've been trying to get Jonas to leave the teaching profession and come join my staff for a couple of years now."

"As a pastor?" Olivia heard the surprise in her own voice.

"Yeah, that guy knows the Bible inside and out, and he's a phenomenal teacher. I would love to have him on our team."

"Even now?"

A slight smile tugged at the corners of his mouth as Pastor Joshua fixed her with a knowing look. "Yes, even now. I saw the press conference that your detective gave the other day insinuating Jonas's involvement in the murder, but he's got it wrong. There is no way Jonas would do something like this. I never believed it in the first place, but after talking to him for over an hour last night, I'm even more convinced. He's completely innocent."

Olivia mulled that statement over for a few moments before deciding on her next question. "You seem to have a very high level of trust for Jonas. Did you trust Jessica to the same extent?"

Pastor Joshua opened his mouth as if to speak, but then closed it. He glanced at Brittany as he opened his mouth a second time, only to close it once again. He gave an embarrassed smile before offering, "I don't know that I would trust her to quite the same extent as I would Jonas, but that's not to say she wasn't trustworthy."

"What made you trust Jessica less than Jonas?"

Pastor Joshua looked at his shoes for a moment, rubbing the side of his face with his right hand, before meeting her eyes. "Jessica struggled with her faith at times. There were certain aspects of the Bible that bothered her, and it kept her from engaging here at Restoration Church to the same extent as Jonas. But she was a wonderful person who was well loved by those who knew her."

Olivia acknowledged his words of praise with a gentle nod but kept the questions coming. "Were you aware of any marital problems between Jessica and Jonas?"

Pastor Joshua shook his head. "No, not that I'm aware of. Every marriage has issues at times, but they seemed to be doing well to me."

"So it would come as a complete surprise to you if you found out that Jessica was having an affair?"

The wide-eyed and open-mouthed shock on Pastor Joshua's face appeared genuine. He looked at Brittany again before stuttering, "Jessica—she—you, you found proof she was having an affair?"

"I'm not saying that. I'm just asking the question. Would her having an affair come as a complete shock to you?"

"Yes, yes, certainly it would." Pastor Joshua's head went from an emphatic bob up and down to a gentle shake from side to side. "I would hope she was above something like that. Jonas would be crushed."

"As unlikely as it may seem, if you found out she was having an affair with someone at church, who would come to mind?"

"At church? Wow, what an awful thought." Pastor Joshua continued shaking his head, contemplating the question. "No one. Really, I can't imagine her having an affair with anyone from church. I've never seen so much as flirtatious behavior between her and another man. I think you're barking up the wrong tree with this theory."

Olivia extended her hand. "Just trying to be thorough. I really appreciate your time. I'm sure you're a very busy man, so I won't take up any more of it."

"I'm happy to help. If there's anything else I can do, please don't hesitate to ask."

There were three other people mingling in the vicinity, obviously waiting their turn to speak to the pastor. He pivoted in their direction; Olivia turned to Brittany. "Do you just want to sit down on one of these pews and talk here, or what did you have in mind?"

Brittany glanced past her at Pastor Joshua, then casually scanned the room at large. "Why don't we go sit down on the back patio? It's a beautiful day today, and we'll have some privacy."

She led the way down the center aisle and out the left side of the lobby to a large, covered patio. Its only occupants were an old man and a young child in the far corner. The old man was watching what was likely his grandchild run around the patio furniture. Brittany chose a table on the opposite end to them.

"What else would you like to know, Officer Selman?"

"Well, first, I'm curious if you agree with Pastor Joshua's assessment. Do you think it's beyond the realm of possibility that Jessica would have an affair?"

Brittany looked down at the cast-iron table. "I can't imagine her having an affair with anyone at church. All her friends here were women. I can't think of a single guy she spoke to on a regular basis." It sounded like she was choosing her words carefully.

"But could you imagine her having an affair with someone outside the church?"

It took a while, but Brittany eventually met her eyes and said, "It wouldn't shock me as much as it would Pastor Joshua."

"Why do you say that?"

Brittany let out a big sigh and shook her head slightly. "Part of it has to do with her general attitude towards Jonas the last six months or so. She was always complaining about something he did, and it was always something really trivial. And if anyone talked about what a great guy he was, she would roll her eyes or say something dismissive. A year ago she would never have responded that way. Jonas was her world."

Brittany went quiet. Olivia let the silence soak for a few moments before prompting, "You said that was part of it. What's the other part?"

"There were a couple of weird things that happened recently. Two months ago I planned a girls' night out with some of the girls here at church. We were going to grab some dinner and do some karaoke afterwards. Jessica came, but she only ate dinner with us. She even left early, probably thirty minutes before the rest of us. The next day at church, Jonas asked how the girls' night went—just kind of making small talk, you know? After I told him it was a lot of fun, he responded, 'Yeah, I could tell. It's not easy convincing Jessica to stay out past midnight.'

"I didn't know what to say. Jessica left us by 7:30. I asked

Jessica about it later, and she kind of gave me that 'deer in the headlights' look. After waffling a few seconds, she told me she had driven up to the mountains for some fresh air and alone time, but that seemed weird and unlike her.

"Then, about two weeks later, while we were grabbing lunch together, she gave me her phone so I could read a crazy post from one of her friends on Facebook. While I was reading it, she got a text from someone named Dee. It said something like 'Hey baby girl you free to meet up so I can lay it down?'

"I felt bad for reading it, but it just popped up as I was looking at the screen. It was hard not to. I gave her back the phone and told her she got a text from Dee. You should have seen her face. It went white as a ghost's. Even more so after she read the text. I asked her who Dee was, and she told me Dee was an old girl friend from high school. I was like, 'Really?' but she was like, 'Yeah, she has a quirky sense of humor and texts crazy stuff like that all the time.' I didn't know what else to say, so I just let it go."

Olivia was tempted to reveal what she knew about Dee, but she was afraid the news would get back to Jonas Turner. She wanted to be in the room when he was told about the affair to see his reaction. She was confident she would be able to tell if he was truly surprised by the news or not. "Hypothetically, if Jessica was having an affair, who would be the most likely candidate?"

"I really don't know. I gave it some thought when these things happened, but no one I know seems like a likely candidate. I just kind of dismissed my fears as crazy misunderstandings until I listened to you question Pastor Joshua. If she did have an affair, it was probably someone from work or the gym, but I don't really know her coworkers, and we don't go to the same gym."

"I plan on going by her work in the next few days. I'll see

what I can find out. Do you know what gym she used?"

"Yeah, it's the YMCA in Travelers Rest. I know she had several gym friends who always did the 5:30 kettlebell class. I would try asking the ladies in that class."

"Thank you, this has been very helpful. Before I go, I've got to ask. If Jonas found out about an affair, do you think he would be capable of murder?"

Brittany didn't hesitate. "No, I really don't think so. He would be devastated, but I've never seen him out of control, let alone crazy enough to stab his wife to death. I agree with Pastor Joshua. I think you're barking up the wrong tree with him."

"Okay, well, if you can think of anyone else who would have a motive to kill Jessica, please let me know. We're pretty short on other suspects right now."

"Well, if you're going to stop by her gym, you might want to ask about her stalker. That's the only guy I could come up with who could do something like this to her."

Olivia did a double take and responded much louder than she'd intended. "What?"

"Did Jonas not mention her stalker? Yeah, she had some weirdo at the gym who became obsessed with her. He wouldn't leave her alone and followed her around like a puppy dog. The creep even followed her home one night. That was the last straw. She filed for a restraining order against him. This was maybe a little over a year ago. I haven't heard anything about it since, but it's probably worth looking into."

CHAPTER SIXTEEN

Jonas put the cap back on the dry erase marker and made his way back to his desk. As he settled into his cheap office swivel chair, he scanned the room one more time. The student desks were impeccably straight. The day's instructions were neatly printed on the white board—at least, as neatly as his handwriting allowed. And the stack of graded paperwork was arranged on his desk, separated by class, ready to be handed out.

He was feeling first-day-of-school-like jitters this morning. It was naïve to hope his students wouldn't ask about his absence Friday or already know about his wife's murder. They would pepper him with a million questions, and he wasn't sure he could handle it. Coming in early and setting up for class, keeping busy, had felt good. Much better than sitting around a hotel room all day with his thoughts. But he was still an emotional wreck, as his ten-minute cry-fest in the shower this morning had demonstrated.

He sighed and laid his forehead straight down on his old wooden desk.

"What are you doing here, Jonas?"

Jonas popped his head up at the sound of the deep, gravelly voice and found Assistant Principal Bryant filling up the doorframe with his broad shoulders.

He tried to play off the question with a lighthearted laugh. "I still work here, don't I? How's a teacher going to teach his students without showing up to class?"

Principal Bryant folded his big arms and leaned against the doorframe, never taking his dark brown eyes off Jonas's face. It was obvious he wasn't going anywhere until he got a better answer to his question.

"What do you want from me?" Jonas asked.

"I want to know why you're already back at work when your wife was murdered just a few days ago?"

Jonas broke off eye contact and stared at the paperwork on his desk. "I was sick of sitting around all day with nothing to do but think. I wanted to get back to work so I could focus on something other than what happened to Jessica. Why don't you want me here? Are you worried that I had something to do with her death?"

Principal Bryant snorted. "Please, I've looked killers in the eyes before. You're not one. I'm just worried about you and your mental health. If someone had killed my Jeanie, I would be a basket case. You wouldn't see me in these halls the rest of the year. I would be too afraid of either breaking down and crying like a little baby or bashing in the skull of the next student who mouthed off to me."

Jonas couldn't help but respond with an amused smile. "I have a hard time picturing you crying like a baby. You bashing in the skull of a student, on the other hand, I have no trouble picturing." He looked up at Principal Bryant and spoke with quiet seriousness this time. "I appreciate you checking in on me. I really do. But I think I can do this, and I would like to try."

Principal Bryant nodded and shouldered his bulky build away from the doorframe. "If you need anything, you know where to find me."

"Hood off, Blake, and lose those earbuds, too."

Geez, Ms. Agnew was always on his case. He wasn't even in the classroom yet. *Just chill, you frizzy-haired old woman.*

The moment he took his earbuds out, he heard the name "Ari". He looked over at the lockers across the hall, and sure enough, Cameron was there surrounded by some of his idiot basketball buddies.

Blake turned his back to them, pretending to mess with a locker that wasn't his, listening to what they were saying.

"Come on, man, give us some details. Did you hit that?"

Cameron laughed his cocky laugh. "Naw, naw, it wasn't like that. At least not yet. We just watched a movie."

"Just watched a movie? You mean to tell me you didn't even get a kiss?"

"Well, I didn't say all that."

"Yeah, that's what I'm talking about. I knew that girl would give you a little something."

A few more comments were made, followed by laughter, but Blake couldn't hear them over the buzzing in his head. Before he realized what he was doing, he cocked his arm back and slammed his fist into the lockers.

The hall around him went quiet. He could feel everyone looking at him, but he ignored them and walked into his first-period class.

Olivia was eager to get over to Elite Physical Therapy and talk to Jessica's coworkers, but she wanted to find out more about this stalker she'd heard of yesterday. Hopefully, she could find what she needed and get out of the precinct before she ran into Grady.

Not much came up when she did a records search for Jessica Lynn Turner. Just two speeding tickets, a parking ticket, and the restraining order she'd filed against a Eugene Fitzpatrick.

The document was short on details. It was a temporary order for protection against "stalking, aggravated stalking, or harassment" signed by Judge Harvey Reynolds on February 12th of last year. The explanation given for granting the order was that the accused had a pattern of following the plaintiff around her gym that had escalated to following her home.

Olivia was disappointed there wasn't more to the report, but the adrenaline rush of uncovering another major development in the case put a smile on her face. Jessica had had a stalker.

Stalkers made great murder suspects. They were second only to husbands and boyfriends when it came to being responsible for brutal homicides of attractive females. How had this not come up in their interrogation with Jonas? She would call him and harass him about it later for sure, but right now all she wanted to do was pull Eugene Fitzpatrick's address and get out of this precinct.

There was only one Eugene Fitzpatrick in South Carolina, and it was the one with a restraining order on his record. Olivia typed his address into her phone, locked her computer screen, and spun out of her seat.

As soon as she stood up and looked towards the exit, she spotted Grady heading her way. The whole room seemed to freeze with her, going quiet with a sudden absence of typing. She watched him walk with a casual ease, looking in her general direction, but not quite at her.

Some part of her subconscious screamed, "Grab your gun!" but she resisted the urge to move her hands in the direction of her belt. She tensed as he came within ten feet of her, but that was as close as he came. Without a word, he sat at his desk and began opening tabs on his computer.

Olivia looked around the room and made eye contact with some of her fellow officers, who all responded in a similar way, with raised eyebrows and shrugs. Senses still on hyperdrive, she slowly made her way to the exit, walking right past his desk. Grady never once glanced in her direction or acknowledged her presence.

Was he really willing to move on from their altercation the other day? Everything she had seen up to that point indicated that he would be the retaliation type, but maybe she had misjudged him. Maybe he was a big enough man to let it go after all. It surprised her, but she wasn't about to look a gift horse in the mouth.

There was too much to do to worry about office drama. She was hot on the trail of Jessica's lover *and* Jessica's stalker.

CHAPTER SEVENTEEN

Who do you think did it?"

Jonas took a deep breath and looked to the ceiling for the tenth time that period. "I have no idea, Frankie."

"Do you think it was someone you know or some crazy stranger?"

"What part of 'I have no idea' do you not understand? No more questions. Finish up your writing assignment."

"Do you have any enemies?"

"Am I going to have to put your desk in the hallway? I said no more questions. Get back to work."

Frankie held his hands up. "Fine, fine, I'm just trying to help."

Coming in today had been a mistake. If he wasn't getting awkward questions, then Jonas was on the receiving end of wide-eyed stares or fearful avoidance. He had done his best to keep his students busy, but it wasn't working. He found himself watching the clock in anticipation of the lunch bell more than his students.

Mercifully, it rang.

"If you didn't finish your writing prompt today, make sure you get it done by the end of the week. I'll be collecting journals on Friday. See you guys tomorrow."

"See you tomorrow, Mr. T."

"See you tomorrow, Frankie."

Other than Frankie, the class was unusually quiet streaming out. He felt the urge to fill the awkwardness with some banter. Seeing Hoi nearing the exit reminded him about the volleyball match he'd missed as a result of everything. "Hey, Hoi, did you guys win your match last Thursday?"

Hoi flinched and refused to look his way. A barely audible "No" escaped her lips before she bolted through the door.

Well, I guess that's one crush I don't have to fend off anymore, Jonas thought. Cynical humor was his go-to defense mechanism, but he had to admit he was hurt by his students' response to his tragedy. Even Blake, one of his more sensible students, had avoided eye contact all period and now appeared to be trying to keep other students between him and his teacher on the way out the door.

Did these kids really think he was capable of murdering his wife? It made him sad that anyone who had spent considerable time with him could think so. The idea of sitting down to eat at the teachers' table, where he was bound to receive more questions, expressions of sympathy, and judgmental looks, made him lose what little appetite he had.

He decided to go for a walk to clear his head instead. Plainview Middle only used about half of the facilities at this former high school. There were two whole wings at the back end of the property that were only half-heartedly maintained. He headed in that direction in an effort to avoid any teachers or students.

Head down, hands in pockets, he walked the broken sidewalk and considered his options. He didn't think he was up for working any more this week. He had been naïve to think that teaching would take his mind off Jessica's death. It had taken every bit of strength he had to keep it together through three periods, and he felt the cracks widening.

Jonas wasn't sure his sense of duty would allow it, but he mulled over the idea of taking a leave of absence for the rest of the school year. Since he had only called in sick twice in his first six years of teaching, he had accrued enough sick leave to cover the remaining weeks. No one would blame him for taking the time off. The thought of returning after the summer for a fresh start was tempting.

As he came around to the back side of the last building on the property, something red in his peripheral vision caught his attention. He looked up and over to his right, where someone in a red hoodie was sitting on the back steps, smoking a cigarette.

"Hey, what are you doing back here?"

The person jumped at the sound of his voice and looked up. It was a girl, obviously a student, with blonde hair. She looked familiar, but Jonas couldn't quite place her. The look on her face was one of complete terror. She threw the cigarette down and bolted in the opposite direction.

"Hey, stop, get back here right now. Don't make this worse than it already is."

He began jogging in her direction, but pulled up after just a few steps. He had no doubts about being able to catch her, but then what? Was he going to tackle her? Pick her up and carry her back to the principal's office? Chasing after and grabbing a young girl behind some dilapidated buildings sounded like a recipe for disaster. It was better to just write up a report and give her description to the principals.

The sound of a baby's rattle made him look down and notice he was standing in shin-high grass. He took a couple of steps back to return to the sidewalk. The rattling stopped.

A few seconds later, a small snake slithered across the

sidewalk not more than ten feet from him. Its muddy gray body had a distinct diamond pattern down its back.

Jonas shuddered. He had come that close to getting bitten by an eastern diamondback rattlesnake. Sitting around in a hotel room all day was sounding pretty good about now.

Olivia's morning had not gone as planned.

Vogel had arranged for her to help him with the murder investigation full time, but that didn't mean she could just ignore traffic violations. Some idiot in a Camaro had blown through a red light right in front of her, and when she'd turned on her lights, he had tried to run.

The high-speed chase was a brief one; the Camaro had clipped a dump truck as it tried to weave through traffic and ended up hitting a telephone pole. No one got hurt, thankfully, but Olivia had to write up several citations, ask a fellow officer to run the guy to lockup, and wait around for a tow truck.

She was hungry and annoyed. Jessica Turner's coworkers better not give her the run-around today.

When she opened the door, a perky woman with a head full of golden curls and big-framed glasses greeted her with wide eyes. "Good afternoon, officer. Are you here for a therapy appointment... or something else?"

"Something else. I would like to speak with Tamera Lewis. Can you point me in her direction?"

"Well, uh, she's with a patient right now. Are you okay waiting about fifteen minutes until she wraps up with him?"

Olivia responded with a look that made the receptionist recoil into her swivel office chair. A young black man in scrubs approached from the right side of the front desk.

"Hi there. If you're here for therapy, I would be more than happy to work with you. My name is Eton, what's yours?" He stretched out his hand with what she assumed was his best attempt at a charming smile.

Olivia kept her hands on her utility belt. "I'm not here for therapy. The only people I need help from are those who can help me understand why Jessica Turner was murdered. Are you one of those people?"

Eton's smile faded immediately. He lowered his hand and scanned the room as if looking for help or an escape plan. "I, uh, don't know anything about that. I'm guessing you're here for Tamera. I'll go relieve her so you two can talk."

"That would be great, thank you."

She watched as Eton made his way back to a black woman in her late twenties or early thirties with straight hair that came to the top of her shoulders. She gave Eton a few instructions before grabbing a sanitation wipe and making her way to the front. As she walked, she kept her focus on scrubbing her hands with the wipe, not once looking up. When she spoke, she looked at the receptionist. "Is there some kind of problem?"

"My name is Officer Selman. I'm investigating the murder of Jessica Turner, and I would like to ask you a few questions. Is there somewhere we can go to talk privately?"

Tamera's eyes flitted in Olivia's general direction this time, but settled on a spot closer to her thighs than her eyes. "Why do you want to talk to me?"

Olivia let out an audible sigh. "Because you're her best friend and this is a murder investigation where we exhaust every lead. Not to mention that you are one of the last people to see her alive."

Tamera's eyes went wide, and her voice came out shaky. "Oh, okay, well, I guess we can go into the back office and talk for a few minutes. I need to get back to my patients soon, though."

Olivia scanned the room, picking out the other therapists

on the floor. Everyone was noticeably avoiding eye contact, but that was fairly typical behavior for when a cop was around, even for innocent people.

The office was tiny, with just a small desk and a few chairs. Olivia adjusted hers to face Tamera directly. "Do you know who killed Jessica?"

Tamera almost made eye contact in her surprise. "No, no, I have no idea."

"If you were forced to choose one suspect, who would it be?"

"Oh, I really don't know. I can't imagine anyone she knew doing something so violent."

"Not her husband?"

"Jonas? No way. He would never do something like this. He's trying to figure out who did it himself."

"What do you mean?"

"Well, he came by here last Friday asking a bunch of questions. He was trying to figure out why she left work Thursday and if it had anything to do with her death."

"What did you tell him?"

"Nothing, really. I'm not exactly sure why she left, but I don't think it had anything to do with why she was killed."

Tamera glanced to her right halfway through her last answer. The obvious tell for untruthfulness increased Olivia's optimism about finding Jessica's lover.

"You have no idea why Jessica left work a couple of hours into her work day?"

"I, uh, no, she didn't really say."

"Who covered her therapy sessions?"

"I did."

"So you're telling me that Jessica left in the middle of her morning appointments, dumping them on you, her best friend, and you have no clue as to why she left?"

Tamera shrugged while staring down at the fingernail

from which she was picking off the polish. "She didn't really say."

"She didn't *really* say, huh? Well, that's okay. I don't *really* need you to tell me why she left, because I already know. We have access to every text message she sent or received from this past year, so let me ask you a different question."

The fingernail picking paused as Tamera's wide eyes finally met Olivia's.

"Who is Dee?"

The recognition in her eyes gave her away, but that didn't stop Tamera from stuttering her way to a denial. "I, uh, Dee? I don't think I know anyone named Dee."

Olivia sat there quietly for almost a minute, boring a hole through Tamera with her eyes and letting the silence suffocate her. Then she leaned forward and spoke in a low voice with just a hint of malice. "I don't know why you're trying to obstruct a murder investigation, but if it continues, we're going to be having this conversation downtown in an interrogation room. So I'm going to ask you again. Who is Dee?"

She watched Tamera's face crack and then crumble before she buried it in her hands and started sobbing. "I can't, I can't. I can't do that to my best friend. She trusted me with her secrets, and I can't be a part of anything that would hurt her."

Olivia leaned back and let her cry for a minute before continuing in a calm voice. "Do you believe in God?"

"Yes, I'm a Christian."

"So, you believe in a God of love, and truth, and justice? That's what Christians believe, right?"

"Yeah." Tamera said it almost like a question, as if she was waiting for the other shoe to drop.

"Do you think your God would prefer you to lie to cover up your friend's lies, or tell the truth so you could help bring a murderer to justice?"

Tamera doubled over as if she had a violent stomach cramp. "Oh, I can't. She was my best friend. I don't want to air out her dirty laundry."

"Do you think Jessica's in heaven?"

Tamera's head shot back up. "Of course she's in heaven. How can you ask that? Just because she made a few mistakes doesn't mean she isn't in heaven. She was a good person."

"Okay then. Don't you think Jessica, who's now looking down from heaven, would prefer to have her killer brought to justice rather than have her lies remain hidden? Because right now, the person most likely to go to jail for her death is her husband, who you believe is innocent. How do you think Jessica would feel about her killer roaming free as her innocent husband spends the rest of his life in jail?"

A horrified look spread over Tamera's face. "What do you mean? Why would Jonas go to jail for the murder?"

"Jonas is the only suspect we have right now, and since we know Jessica had a lover, that gives us a motive. There are several pieces of circumstantial evidence that look really bad for him. Like you, I'm inclined to believe that Jonas might be innocent, but I need to track down this Dee guy to prove it. So I'm begging you. Help me bring Jessica's killer to justice."

Silence filled the little office once again, but this time it bothered her more than it did Tamera.

Finally, with a deep breath that came out like a shudder, Tamera leaned forward and spoke in a small voice. "His name is David London."

"David?"

"Yeah. Jessica put him in her phone as 'Dee', but his name is David. It was an inside joke, and if Jonas ever saw a text from him, she could just tell him it was from an old girl friend."

"How did they meet?"

"They met last fall at the APTA conference. It's a conference for physical therapists. Jonas had a volleyball tournament that weekend and a Sunday school class to teach, so she went alone. She met David at an afterhours social, got a little tipsy, and ended up sleeping with him.

"She felt horrible about it. She cried when she told me. But they stayed in contact, and one thing led to another. Before long, she began making excuses to leave work or go out at night to see him. I tried to tell her to break it off, but she was in too deep. She couldn't help herself." Tamera lifted her hands helplessly.

"So David works and lives in town?"

"Yeah, he owns a practice off Cleveland St. called Advanced Physical Therapy. I don't know his home address or anything, but I think he lives somewhere over on the east side of Greenville."

"Do you think he could have killed Jessica?"

Tamera looked down into her lap again. "I don't think so, but I don't know. I only met the guy once, but he seemed pretty normal. A little arrogant maybe, but not a psycho. He owns a practice bigger than ours and is well respected in the physical therapy community. Jessica always raved about what an amazing guy he was. It's hard to imagine him being a crazy psycho slasher."

"Talk to me about the day of her death. We have her texts, but what did she say about them?"

"She was pretty excited about hearing from him that morning. She was beginning to wonder if he was going to break it off because he hadn't been responding the last few days. Or he was really short with her when he did. So when he suggested meeting up, she couldn't resist. She was like, 'Oh, Tamera, I know I'm a jerk for asking, but will you cover my patients until after lunch. Please, please, please!' What was I going to say? I told her, 'Go on, girl, I got you', and that was it. That was the last time I saw my bestie alive." More tears welled in her eyes and spilled down her cheeks. Her lips trembled.

Olivia reached out and patted her on the knee. "Thank you for sharing these details. This David guy might be the key to solving this case. Before I go, one last question. Do you think Eugene Fitzpatrick could have had anything to do with this?"

The confusion on her face appeared genuine. "Who?"

"Eugene Fitzpatrick. Did Jessica not talk to you about her stalker?"

"Oh, was that his name? I don't think she ever mentioned his name. She would always refer to him as the 'little creep from the gym.' You think he might have done it?"

"I don't know. That's why I'm asking you."

"Jessica was definitely bothered by him. She flipped out when he followed her home. I know she served him with a restraining order, and she always carried pepper spray with her after that. Man, I can't believe I forgot about him. He wasn't right in the head, according to Jessica. I would definitely check him out."

Olivia stood. "Thank you, Tamera, you've been very helpful. If you think of anything else that might be helpful, please give me a call." She handed Tamera her card. "Seriously, if you think of anything useful, call me."

"Okay."

Olivia's phone vibrated in her pocket as she exited the office. Pulling it out, she saw Vogel's name on the display.

"What's up, boss?"

"Get your butt downtown. I'll meet you outside the Law Enforcement Center. We've got some major developments to discuss. Things are going to move fast now, Selman. They're going to move fast."

CHAPTER EIGHTEEN

Jonas placed his half-eaten plate of pizza rolls on the nightstand. Typically, he could dust off a twenty-piece bag by himself, but tonight he'd only warmed up half the bag and tapped out after five.

Everything felt wrong.

His wife was gone. Forever. His home was a crime scene. Law enforcement was treating him like their prime suspect. And his time in the classroom today had proved he was nowhere near ready to return to work. His life was going to suck for the foreseeable future.

The only time his mind enjoyed a brief reprieve from the sense of dread and overwhelming grief was when he focused on ways he could help solve Jessica's murder. He was eager to get back to his neighborhood and finish his search for witnesses. There was no telling if Officer Selman would do it herself, like she had said.

He also wanted Jessica's phone back. Surely he could get the phone company to unlock the screen for him. His name was on the account, too. If he could read through her recent messages and look through her apps, then maybe he would get some answers to his questions.

A thunderous three-pound knock on his door startled him out of his musings.

"Police. Open up."

Police? Why would they show up at his motel room rather than calling to arrange a meeting? Jonas looked down at his T-shirt, gym shorts, and bare feet. He considered throwing some jeans on first, but decided to go ahead and open the door before another earth-shattering knock disturbed his fellow motel guests.

The moment he turned the handle, the door was shoved open with such force that he was knocked off-balance. Stumbling backwards, arms flailing, he felt the back of his knees hit the edge of the bed, forcing him into a seated position as a mad rush of black helmets, black vests, and big black guns rushed towards him.

"Show me your hands! Show me your hands!"

Jonas couldn't take his eyes off the gun barrel aimed at his face, but he managed to put his shaking hands up around his head, palms open.

"Get down on the ground! Now!"

Afraid to make any sudden movements, he slowly slid off the bed and down to his knees as rough hands grabbed him by the arms and shoved him the rest of the way down onto his belly. His arms were yanked behind his back, and he felt the chill of metal pressed against his skin. The handcuffs were closed tight enough to feel like they were cutting into his wrists.

All he could see was ugly burnt orange carpet and black boots until a couple of the boots parted, and he heard a familiar voice.

"Mr. Turner, you are under arrest for the murder of Jessica Turner. You have the right to remain silent. Anything you say can and will be used against you in a court of law. You have the right to an attorney."

Vogel kept talking, but the rush of blood in Jonas's ears drowned out the rest. He closed his eyes as the room began to spin. Taking big, slow breaths in and out, he fought a wave of nausea. *God, please help me.*

"Get out of the way, you idiot!"

Olivia yanked the steering wheel to the left and drove up on the raised median, navigating around the Volkswagen Passat in her way. She made sure to point to the ceiling where her lights were flashing and then give a "What's wrong with you?" gesture while passing.

There was no good reason for using her lights and siren, other than because she was pissed-off and in no mood for traffic delays. She wanted to strangle Vogel. How could he send a SWAT team out to arrest Turner? Nothing about his personality or his past indicated he was a threat or a flight risk. It was all for show.

If Jonas Turner was innocent, they'd just made a spectacle of him for no reason. Admittedly, it did not look good for Turner's innocence. The DNA tests had confirmed that the shoes belonged to him, and the blood on the soles belonged to his wife. They now had a motive, proof that he was at the scene of the crime, his fingerprint on the murder weapon, and the victim's blood on his shoes. Thinking about his potential innocence seemed silly at this point, but she couldn't shake the thought.

Which was why she was turning down the street where David London lived. This was a nice part of town. Every home on this street would sell for at least four times as much as her home.

She parked right behind the black Toyota Sequoia in the

driveway. As she walked up the well-manicured walkway to the front door, she noticed two different neighbors—a man walking a dog and a woman sitting on a porch swing—eyeing her with curiosity. She pressed the doorbell and heard pretentious chimes sounding throughout the house.

Waiting approximately thirty seconds between rings, Olivia pressed the doorbell two more times before the door finally opened.

"What do you want?"

It was definitely Dee. His dark hair, blue eyes, and square jaw were unmistakable. Olivia deliberately focused on maintaining eye contact as other pictures on Jessica's phone came to mind.

"Are you David London?"

"Yes, I am."

"Can I come in and ask you a few questions?"

"What is this about?"

"I'm investigating the murder of Jessica Turner."

His lack of response was impressive. Nothing more than a slight, momentary widening of the eyes.

"I don't know anything about that. Why would you think I could help?"

"You do know her, don't you?"

London looked around at the growing number of neighbors who'd found something to do outside. "Look, I might have met her in passing at some physical therapy related events, but I'm sure you can find much better people to interview than me. I'm kind of busy right now, so I'm going to have to ask you to leave."

He took a step back and started to close the door.

Olivia put out a hand to stop it from closing. "'Met her in passing' is an interesting way to describe a torrid love affair."

The door opened back up a few inches. "I don't know who told you that, but it must be some kind of mistake. I barely knew her."

"Oh, it's no mistake. We found concrete proof on her phone. So you can let me in and answer a few questions, or we can take this conversation downtown."

"You can't make me go downtown without a warrant or an arrest. I know my rights. Now if you'll excuse me, I have nothing to say to you."

He began to close the door again, but Olivia's hand, which hadn't left the door, increased its resistance. "You're right. I can't force you to come to the precinct with me, but I'm not leaving until I ask my questions. Now, I can shout them at you through the door or ask my questions to your neighbors, but one way or another, my questions are going to be heard."

London looked around at all the neighbors who weren't even pretending to work on their yards anymore. When his eyes returned to hers, they were smoldering. He spoke through clenched teeth. "Fine. Have it your way."

He spun and stormed through the entryway. Olivia jogged a few steps to catch up with him to make sure he didn't go for a weapon. She was suddenly wishing she had brought a partner along for this interview.

They entered a large living room with high, vaulted ceilings. He sat down on a brown leather sofa, so she took the armchair facing him.

David London looked at her through eyes narrowed to slits as he bit off his first statement. "I don't believe you. I think you're bluffing about the phone."

Olivia pulled out her phone and opened the most damning screenshot she had taken of Jessica and Dee's text thread. London's eyes went wide when he saw himself with Jessica in the barroom selfie.

"We have a number of other pictures that are far less innocent, but hopefully that one will suffice."

"That stupid *whore*. I told her to delete everything.

Always. I never should have trusted her."

"Well, you did, and now she's dead, so let's talk about that rather than speaking ill of her. What happened when you guys last got together?"

"The last time? I don't know. There was nothing unusual about the last time. We both worked it out to take a long lunch and met up at the Quality Inn on Woodruff Road."

Olivia frowned in confusion. "When was this?"

"I don't know, maybe a week and a half ago."

Olivia gave him a withering look for several seconds. "Need I remind you that we have all of Jessica's texts? I'm not interested in hearing about your hook-up from a week and a half ago. I want to know about Thursday's meet-up. Tell me about the day she died."

London's eyebrows knitted together as his eyes narrowed once again. "I don't know anything about the day she died. I didn't contact her the last few days prior to her death."

Olivia couldn't believe the nerve of this guy, boldly lying to her despite the evidence. "Would you like to see the text messages to jog your memory?" She opened her photo app, set up the screenshots, and handed him the phone. "Swipe right to see the whole exchange."

She expected him to glance at the texts before returning her phone and dropping his feigned memory loss, but he appeared to be reading every word. When he swiped left to read them through a second time, she began to suspect he was stalling for time in order to come up with an explanation.

"So, what happened?" she prompted.

He handed the phone back to her and looked up in her direction, but without meeting her eyes. "I texted her that morning, but we never met up."

"Why not?"

"I couldn't get away."

"You couldn't get away? You're the one who arranged the

meeting. What could possibly keep you away from having sex with the woman you were so eager to see? And why no text to let her know you couldn't make it? That seems a bit odd, don't you think?"

"She was dead by the time I was free to text her. Why would I text a dead woman?"

"How did you find out she was dead?"

"It was all over the news."

"The news? You mean the six o'clock news? The news that came out seven hours after your last text?"

London's face went beet-red, and a large vein popped out near the center of his forehead. "Wha—I, I couldn't get away, and then the, the time got away from me. I forgot. I was going to text her back, but then I saw the news report."

"You had plans to meet up with your secret lover, but you forgot about it? What was it, exactly, that kept you so busy during that time?"

London shook his head and looked away. Several seconds passed before he quietly muttered, "I was at the hospital."

"Why were you at the hospital?"

"I was there for my wife."

Olivia hoped her face displayed at least half the disgust she felt. "So you're married. Nice. Why was your wife in the hospital?"

London's eye contact had moved further and further away from her during the conversation. Currently, he was looking down at his left hand as it rubbed the seam on the couch cushion. Olivia was about to repeat her question when he finally responded.

"She was there because of a drug overdose."

"Oh, wow, I'm so sorry. Is she okay?"

"No, she's not. She passed Thursday morning."

"She's dead?" The hair on Olivia's arms stood up. She was suddenly more aware of the gun on her hip. "She died this past Thursday? The same day Jessica was killed?"

London simply nodded.

"So you're telling me that your wife died early Thursday morning. In response, you texted your girlfriend to arrange a hook-up. Your girlfriend then winds up brutally murdered, but you had absolutely nothing to do with it. That's the story you're going with?"

He finally met her eyes with a look of defiance. "That's what happened. There are cameras all over the hospital. I'm sure you can verify my alibi with the footage."

Olivia stood up. "Oh, I intend to. Until then, don't plan any trips in the near future." She took out one of her cards and threw it at him. "And if you see that number calling you, pick it up. I expect you to answer any other questions I have. Otherwise, I'll be back here to ask them."

She backed out of the room, keeping an eye on him, but David London never made a move to stand up.

As she let herself out, the weight of all the investigative work she had to do pressed down on her shoulders. This was beginning to get complicated.

CHAPTER NINETEEN

With each item of clothing Jonas shed, a layer of numbness peeled away, too. Once the cold water hit his back, he was fully awake and back to reality. Quickly lathering up with the soap they'd given him, he hugged himself, gritted his teeth, and turned to face the nozzle.

He couldn't recall anything from his ride to the processing center. Only vague recollections of the past hour surfaced when he tried to think through what had happened. He remembered being patted down and then taken to a desk, where he was asked if he had any personal property needing to be inventoried. Since he had been dragged out of his motel room with nothing but a T-shirt, gym shorts, and underwear on, there wasn't much to process.

After that, he'd been put through a full-body scanner like they had at airports. Then he was taken to a couple of booths where he had his picture taken and his fingerprints processed. Some lady had grabbed each finger and palm and pressed them onto the surface of a digital scanner. Finally, a plastic band with a metal clasp was placed on his wrist, and he was told to go into a changing area and strip down for his shower.

How can this be happening?

A gruff voice pulled him out of his musings. "All right, that's good enough. Here's your towel. Put on your jumpsuit and shoes and follow me."

Jonas dried off furiously, happy to be out of the frigid water but eyeing his new clothes in disbelief. It was an orange jumpsuit, just like you saw on TV. The shoes were made of a rubbery material and looked a lot like Crocs. He put them on and followed the officer down a corridor.

He expected to see cells with iron bars, but he was taken to a room with a large metal door and big Plexiglass windows on either side. Through the glass he could see several other prisoners milling about or sitting against the wall. As the door was opened and Jonas was pushed through, every eye in the room turned his way. Most eye contact registered simple curiosity, but there were also several smirks and a couple of derisive laughs as he shuffled into the room.

He was suddenly painfully aware of his clean-cut look and tattoo-less skin. The room had a concrete bench built into three of the walls. In front of the wall without a bench was a four-foot privacy wall that hid the communal toilet. Without making any more eye contact, Jonas found an open spot along the wall opposite the toilet, sat down, propped his head in his hands, and stared at the floor.

He tried to ignore his surroundings and make sense of this sudden turn of events. What had changed? Why the SWAT team? It seemed like an extremely heavy-handed move unless they were convinced he was the killer. What could have possibly made them so sure today as opposed to yesterday?

A pair of rubber shoes appeared in his view of the floor. "You're in my seat."

Jonas looked up into the face of a Hispanic man with a

shaved head and tattoos dotting his face and neck. Glancing around, Jonas spotted several other open seats in the room. His eyes returned to the man hovering over him.

"Are you deaf, *ese*? I said, 'You're in my seat'."

Part of him wanted to punch the guy in the face, but that didn't seem like a very Jesus thing to do. Not to mention that it would probably cause a lot more trouble than it was worth. Jonas slowly got to his feet, pausing just a moment so the guy had to look straight up into his 6'4" frame, before ambling over to another spot along a different wall.

He resumed mulling over his predicament. He was supposed to appear before a judge tomorrow to be formally charged and have the judge set his bail bond. Surely they would have to present their key pieces of evidence at that time. Hopefully, the hearing would provide him with some answers.

Rubber shoes once again obstructed his view of the floor.

"You're in my seat."

Jonas could feel the veins in his neck pulse as blood rushed to his head. It took every ounce of self-control he had not to react to the guy's voice. He continued staring at the floor, pretending he hadn't heard the man.

"Hey, *estúpido*, I told you to move."

Jonas remained seated like a stone statue.

"Oh, okay, pretty boy thinks he has a pair of *cajones* on him. He don't know who he's messing with. I'll cut those balls off and shove them down his throat."

Jonas watched the man take a step forward and felt his upper body violently shoved against the wall. Without a moment's hesitation, he sprang off the wall and powered up with his legs to shove the man back.

The man was knocked clean off his feet and onto his back. The room burst into laughter as he scrambled back to his feet.

Launching himself at Jonas in a psychotic rage, the

Hispanic man began throwing wild haymakers. Jonas danced out of the way while blocking the blows with his arms and shoulders. The guy kept coming, so he ducked under a right hook, stepped in, and planted a straight-armed punch right to the middle of the guy's face.

"Ahgh, my nowth! *Estúpido pendejo*!"

Blood streamed down the guy's mouth and chin. His nose looked like a child had shaped it with Play-Doh.

The large metal door opened up behind him.

"All right, break it up, break it up. Ah geez, look at this guy. Don, take this one to the infirmary. That nose is going to need some work. And you, sit your butt back down."

Jonas quickly sat down in the nearest open spot and watched them walk the guy out. Before he passed through the door, he turned in Jonas's direction and called out, "I'll be seein' you soon, pretty boy. Real soon."

Blake was scrolling through dumb prank videos, trying to get his mind off crap so he could fall asleep, when his screen notified him of an incoming call. Frankie.

Why the heck would he be calling this late? Why the heck was he calling at all? The only person who ever called Blake was his mom. Or Ari, if it was something urgent or too complicated to explain over text.

He was tempted to ignore it and text him back later, but a phone call from a classmate was so unusual that curiosity got the better of him. "What's up?"

"Dude, Blake, have you seen the video of Mr. T?"

"What are you talking about? What video?"

"Oh man, you're not going to believe it. They arrested Mr. T. They brought the SWAT team down on him and everything. It's crazy. You've got to check it out."

"Why would they do that?"

"Because he murdered his wife, numbnuts. They got proof. They had some detective dude on TV talking about it."

"Mr. T didn't do it. The cops don't know what they're talking about."

"Sorry, Blake, I know you like Mr. T and all, but he's guilty as sin. You don't leave in the middle of the school day and just happen to find your woman murdered at the same time. He definitely diced that ho."

"Whatever, Frankie. I got to go. I'll see you tomorrow."

"Sure, later, Blake."

Blake stared at his phone, trying to process what he just heard. Opening his Internet browser, he typed in various prompts until he found the video of Mr. Turner's arrest. Several black-clad SWAT team members with assault rifles could be seen dragging him from what looked like a motel room. It was surreal seeing his teacher in handcuffs, perp-walked to the backseat of a police car. He continued watching as the News 4 reporter interviewed a detective named Vogel. He seemed very confident about the arrest, but he didn't offer much in the way of proof.

For the hundredth time that day, Blake thought about Ari. He wondered if she knew about this video. She hadn't stuck around after lunch like he had hoped, and she was nowhere to be found during after-school dismissal, either. Apparently, they were back to not texting one another, since his texts had been ignored all afternoon and evening.

Everything felt wrong. He just wanted things to go back to the way they used to be.

Cameron's smiling face floated into his mind's eye. Blake rolled over and soothed his troubled mind by imagining various scenarios where he ended up punching Cameron in the face.

CHAPTER TWENTY

What's your problem, Selman?" Vogel leaned back in his chair, throwing his arms wide.

"Are you worried this will be your last chance to work a murder investigation? Is that why you won't let this one go? We don't need to track down any more suspects. We've caught the bad guy."

"Great, then let me help you prove it. If you get me a warrant for the hospital's security footage, then I can prove this David London guy didn't do it. We can then use him as a witness. We have to submit Jessica's phone into evidence to show Turner had a motive. The defense will have a field day with those text messages if we don't prove London couldn't have committed the crime."

Vogel put his hands on his head and leaned back even further, looking at the ceiling while shaking his head. "You're killing me, Selman. Killing me. Fine. Have it your way. I will place a call to a judge and request a warrant. You better not be throwing a monkey wrench into my investigation. Bring me proof that this guy's alibi is airtight."

"I'll have a report on your desk within an hour of reviewing the footage."

Vogel snorted and rolled his eyes.

"Have they set a time for Turner's hearing yet?" Olivia asked.

"Yeah, it's scheduled for two o'clock today."

"Are you going to mention motive in the hearing?"

"Yes, Selman, judges like to be given a motive in a murder case. Why are you asking?"

"I don't know. I guess I would be interested in seeing Turner's reaction to finding out about the text messages."

"Well, you're welcome to come down to the courthouse and see for yourself, but I can go ahead and tell you what his reaction is going to be. It's going be, 'Oh crap, they know why I killed her'."

"If he did it, then I'm sure that's the face he'll make. But if he's innocent, that's going to be one brutal way to find out your wife was cheating on you."

Another eye-roll greeted her response, followed by a long, exaggerated sigh. "All right, Selman, get out of here. I've got work to do. You'll have your search warrant within the hour. I'll text you when it's ready."

JONAS GRABBED HIS plate of food and turned to face the seating area. It felt like high school all over again, even down to the natural segregation between predominantly black tables, white tables, and Hispanic tables. Like the new, weird kid, he sat by himself at the end of the least populated table.

Nothing on his plate looked particularly inviting, especially with all the nervous energy killing his appetite, but he picked up a carrot stick and took a bite. After choking down a second stick, he noticed a man walking towards him from one of the Hispanic tables.

It was the guy he had punched in the face. He had two black and purple eyes and some kind of guard over his nose. The guy appeared to be taking his tray to the drop-off location, but he was walking unnecessarily close to the seating area. Jonas tensed, preparing to spring out of his seat as the man came within two feet of his table.

The guy never made eye contact and walked right on by. Jonas turned in his seat and watched him a few more strides before turning back to his plate and releasing a long-held breath.

Picking up another carrot stick, he brought it halfway to his mouth before sensing movement behind him. He turned his head just in time to see the bottom of a lunch tray slamming into his face. A punch landed to the back of his head as he threw his hands up to ward off his assailant. He tried pushing up out of his seat, but the guy used his left arm and body weight to keep him down as he continued to throw rapid punches to his head and ribcage.

Jonas made a sudden lunge towards the floor in an effort to squirm out of the man's grasp. He was surprised by the success of the move. He made it all the way to the floor, and he could no longer feel the guy punching him. Looking up, he was startled to see the Hispanic man on his back getting pummeled by a young Black man.

Half the lunchroom was on its feet now as opposing groups of black and Hispanic inmates formed two semicircles around the men on the ground.

Several prison guards rushed in at the same time. "All right, break it up, break it up. All of you, sit back down. There will be no dinner for any of you if you don't return to your tables immediately."

By the time they'd made their way to the inside of the circle, the young black guy had blended back into his group. The Hispanic guy was still on his back, holding his face.

"What happened to this guy?"

The guard might as well have spoken to a wall. The inmates shuffled back to their tables without so much as a little eye contact.

"Let's take this guy back to the infirmary. That nose is definitely going to need more work."

As everyone watched the guards lead the guy to the exit, the young black guy put his arm around Jonas and shouted to the room. "This guy is with me. If you have a problem with him, you have a problem with 2-5. Believe that."

He kept his arm around Jonas and guided him to a seat in the middle of his table. The whole table sat back down and resumed eating.

The back of Jonas's head and ribs were sore, but the right side of his face was on fire. Gently tracing his cheek, he felt a large lump that didn't belong.

"You're gonna want to put ice on that."

Jonas nodded his acknowledgment of the young man's advice. He wasn't sure how to go about getting ice for his face, but he would figure it out later. There were more pressing questions on his mind. "Don't get me wrong, I am extremely grateful for what you just did, but I don't understand it. Why would you help me?"

The young man took a big bite of his bread roll and looked over with an amused grin. "You're a teacher at Plainview, right?"

"Yeah, were you a student there? I'm not always great with names, but I don't usually forget a face."

"Nah, I was there before you arrived. But you taught my little brother, Langdon."

"Langdon Mitchell?"

"Yep."

"No way! Wow, it's been a few years since I taught him. What is he now, a junior or a senior?"

"Senior. He'll graduate next month, with honors. He's gonna be the first one in our family to go to college."

"Man, that's awesome. That is so great to hear. I'm glad he's doing so well." Jonas went quiet for a few moments as he recalled a few of his interactions with Langdon. Another question brought him back to the present. "If I didn't get to Plainview until after you left, how did you recognize me?"

The young man chuckled. "You probably don't remember me because we only met for a second when you came over, but there was no forgetting you. It's not every day that a teacher shows up at your house, especially one that comes over and murders your little brother at basketball."

Jonas let out a laugh and clapped his hands together. "Oh man, I forgot about that. Your brother was quite the trash-talker. He begged me to play him one-on-one for weeks, guaranteeing that he would crush me. In his mind, he was a surefire NBA superstar in the making, so I thought I would bring him back to reality. If I'm remembering correctly, I beat him down pretty bad."

"You could say that. You beat him 21-1, talking trash the whole time. Me and Momma were watching from the window, laughing our asses off. That boy needed some humbling in the worst way, and you gave it to him."

"21-1, huh. Yikes. My competitive nature gets the best of me sometimes. I probably should have let him score at least four or five."

"Nah, that was the best thing for him. He stopped talking about making the NBA after that and focused more on his schoolwork. You were the one who put him in his first honors class, too. We didn't realize just how smart he was until that eighth-grade year. My momma still compares every teacher to you."

Jonas looked away and opened his eyes wide in an attempt to fight back tears. Too much had happened in the last twenty-four hours on too little sleep. The last thing he wanted to do was get misty-eyed in front of a bunch of hardened inmates.

When he once again felt in control of his emotions, he turned towards the young man. "What's your name?"

"Brandon."

Jonas reached out his hand. "Nice to meet you, Brandon. My name is Jonas. Thank you again for looking out for me today. I won't forget it."

Brandon nodded once and held up his fist. Jonas pounded it with his own.

"Now, let me ask you a question," Brandon said.

"Sure, shoot."

"What is a good man like you doing in a place like this?"

"That's a good question, Brandon. A very good question."

CHAPTER TWENTY-ONE

This was stupid. So, so stupid. Why was she risking her career like this? If Vogel found out, there was no telling what he would do. Take her off the case, for sure, but probably ask for a suspension and make sure she never worked another homicide.

At least the detention center had agreed to let her use one of the small interrogation rooms, out of sight from jailhouse snitches. Staring at the greyish-beige wall across from her, Olivia debated the best approach. She had so many questions, but how she asked them and how he responded to them was everything.

The door opened and in walked Jonas Turner in an orange jumpsuit, followed by a short guard with close-cropped blond hair and a wispy mustache.

"Would you like me to cuff him to the table, ma'am?"

"No, that won't be necessary. Thank you."

"You sure? Okay, well, I'll be right outside if you need anything."

Jonas shuffled to the table and sat down, fixing her with

curious but guarded eyes. That was when she noticed the lump on the right side of his cheek. "Geez, what happened to your face?"

Jonas put a hand up and gingerly felt the welt on his cheek that contained several angry shades of red. "I had a little altercation with a fellow inmate."

"Less than twenty-four hours into your stay and you're already getting into prison fights. That's not a good sign."

"It's less than ideal, for sure. What can I do for you, Officer Selman?"

She was undecided about which way to steer the conversation until the moment her first question blurted out. "Do you remember what pair of shoes you were wearing the day Jessica was murdered?"

His eyes narrowed slightly as his head tilted to one side. "Yes, the same pair of shoes I wear every day, a pair of Mizuno running shoes."

"Do you remember the exact model?"

Turner, who had his hands in his lap, lifted them slightly, up and out. "I don't know. Sky something, I think. I don't pay close attention to the weird names they give their shoes. I just know they're comfortable."

"Do you own a second pair of that model?"

"Yes, I have an older pair I use for yard work. Why are you asking me about shoes?"

He'd answered the question so nonchalantly. Her heartbeat quickened. "Where do you keep that pair of shoes?"

"Either the garage or the back porch. It just depends on which door I use to come back inside. Jessica didn't want them in the house." Turner leaned forward. "Look, are you going to explain to me why you keep asking about shoes, or are you going to continue to leave me in the dark like you've done this entire investigation?"

Even though his answer was potentially bad for their case,

she couldn't deny it was the answer she had hoped to hear. She broke eye contact with him while debating just how much to reveal. *Screw it*, she thought. *No risk, no reward.* "The number one reason you're wearing that jumpsuit is that we found your old pair of running shoes down by the retention pond behind your house, and they were covered in Jessica's blood."

Turner bolted upright in his seat. "What? How is that possible?"

"I don't know. I was hoping you could tell me."

"Someone must have planted them there. That's the only explanation. Someone is trying to frame me."

"Who?"

"I don't know. My best guess would be your partner. He's convinced himself that I'm the killer. Maybe he took it a step further and planted some evidence."

"No, we found a bloody shoeprint on the far side of your bed. We were sure it was going to match the shoes you were wearing that day. I was there when the crime scene tech told Vogel your shoes didn't match. He was genuinely shocked. I was the one who suggested you might have a second pair, and I'm the one who found them. No one else is working this investigation. No one on the force planted this evidence."

Turner's eyes narrowed again; he seemed to be assessing her in a new way.

Olivia returned his look with an eye roll. "Are you going to accuse me of planting them next? Why would I be here asking you questions, trying to figure out how the shoes got there, if I was the one who put them there? If I wanted to frame you, I wouldn't waste my time talking to you."

Turner folded his arms and looked away. "Were you able to track down the Hispanic guy in the hoodie?"

"No, not yet."

"So what's the theory here? That guy puts on my shoes to

disguise his foot size, commits the murder, and then chucks them down by the retention pond?"

"It does seem a little far-fetched. It still seems much more likely that you were the one who wore them and discarded them."

"Me? You know what shoes I had on. Did you ever get the video footage from my neighbor across the street? You can see what clothes I had on going into the house. The same clothes I was wearing when I called 911 and met you on my front porch. You saw that crime scene—there was blood everywhere. How did I not get any on my clothes if I was the killer? What are you suggesting, that I ran inside, put on my killing clothes, murdered my wife, took a shower, and then put my teaching clothes back on in the span of five minutes? This is a joke."

Olivia remained silent. He just highlighted all the aspects of the case that had given her pause, and she wasn't sure how to respond.

After putting his head in his hands and fuming in silence for the next thirty seconds, Turner looked up and spoke in a much calmer voice. "Did you find bloody clothes with my shoes?"

Olivia shook her head.

"It had to be the guy in the hoodie. The blood wouldn't have shown up on the black hoodie and dark jeans, but remember the gloves? The gloves looked stained. I don't know how he thought to put on my shoes to throw off the police, but he ran right past the retention pond. It would have been easy for him to toss them there. We've got to find that guy."

She simply nodded in agreement.

Jonas continued, "If my outdoor shoes are all you've got on me, then your case must be pretty weak. I can't believe you sent a SWAT team after me over this."

"For what it's worth, I tried to talk Vogel out of the SWAT

team. It wasn't right for him to bring you in like that, but there's more to your case than bloody shoes. Your thumbprint is on the murder weapon—"

"It's my knife! It's probably the one I used that morning."

"I get that, but it's still another piece of circumstantial evidence that doesn't look good. We're also prepared to show that you had a compelling motive to kill your wife."

"Motive? What motive? I'm not profiting a single penny from her death. We didn't have life insurance policies. I don't even know how I'm going to pay for her funeral."

Olivia had been dreading this part of the conversation ever since she'd begun to toy with the idea of today's interrogation. It was difficult to meet his eyes, but it was vital that she observe his reaction.

"Mr. Turner, I ha—"

"Please, call me Jonas. You're not one of my students. It's weird having you call me Mr. Turner."

"Okay. Jonas. I hate to be the one to tell you this, especially with everything else you're going through, but we found concrete evidence on Jessica's phone that she was having an affair."

There wasn't an obvious reaction. Just a room that went so quiet that to exhale would have sounded like a nearby waterfall.

When Jonas finally spoke, there was both skepticism and dread in his hushed voice. "What does that mean? Concrete evidence."

"We found a provocative text thread labeled 'Dee'."

Jonas let out an audible breath, looking relieved. "Dee is her crazy college friend. She's always sending weird messages, but that's just her odd sense of humor. They're not lovers."

"Listen, Jonas, we know that the Dee on Jessica's phone is a man named David London. They have had a hidden, sexual relationship for at least the last six months. The pictures and text messages on her phone leave no doubt."

Jonas shook his head at her words and pressed his lips together in a look of defiance, but his eyes told a different story. He looked to the ceiling and battled to blink back the tears forming there.

"She would never do that to me. Not once did she ever say she was unhappy with our marriage. Not once. There's no way she would do something like that. Six months? That's ridiculous. There's no way she could be sleeping with some guy for six months without me knowing. I don't know what you think you found, but there must be some mistake."

If he was faking, he deserved an Academy Award. "Have you ever met David London?"

"I have never *heard* of a David London. Where did she supposedly meet this guy? Is this someone from her gym?"

"It's not important where she met him. What you need to know is that this evidence we have will be used to prove you had a motive to kill your wife. I shouldn't be here telling you this, but I didn't want you to be blindsided in court with this news. I'm truly sorry, Jonas."

Jonas dropped his head in his hands again and stared at the floor. She checked her watch. There were other questions she wanted to ask, but she didn't have time.

"I have to go. They'll be taking you to the courthouse soon. Do me a favor and keep this conversation between us. It could be very bad for me if Vogel finds out I met with you. If you do me that favor, I promise you, I will do everything in my power to make sure we find the person responsible for Jessica's murder."

Jonas looked up at her with the saddest eyes she had ever seen on a human being, but he nodded his understanding. As she stood up to leave, he asked, "Is David London a short Hispanic man?"

"No."

"No way he was the man in the hoodie?"

"I don't believe so."

"Is he a suspect?"

"Yes."

"So you have at least two suspects, besides me."

At least, she thought. She wanted to ask him about Eugene Fitzpatrick, but there was no time, so she simply nodded and stood to her feet. "I'll be back as soon as I can with information." As she made her way to the door, she looked back one more time to where Jonas sat, unmoving. "No more fights, Jonas. Keep your head down, and don't do anything stupid."

CHAPTER TWENTY-TWO

Waiting in the bus line with his earbuds in, the crunch of Blake's Cheetos sounded even louder than the screeching of AC/DC, but he didn't care. He was starving. Being ghosted by Ari all day had killed his appetite during lunch, and now his body was making him pay with crazy hunger pains.

A shove in the back interrupted his feeding frenzy. He took an earbud out and spun around to find Cameron and three of his cronies staring at him.

He glared back at them. "What is your problem?"

"Where is Ari?"

"How am I supposed to know?"

"We all know you two are tight, so stop messing around. Where has she been the last two days? Why isn't she answering my texts?"

"Maybe she just doesn't want to talk to you. Can't blame her for that."

Cameron took a couple of steps forward, followed by his lackeys. Blake had to look nearly straight up to maintain eye contact.

"Listen, fat boy, I ain't playin' wich you. If you don't start answering my questions, I'm going to shove those Cheetos so far up your ass, you'll be pooping orange for a week."

Blake responded in a much louder voice. "You want to stick your hand up my butt? That's weird. Why would you want to stick your hand up my butt, Cameron? That's gross."

All four of them instinctually took a couple of steps back and looked around at the suddenly curious faces of other students looking their way. One of the seventh-grade teachers on bus duty started moving in their direction.

Cameron continued to step away from Blake, but he locked murderous eyes on him as he did. "You think you're funny, fat boy, but we'll see how funny you are when I catch you outside of school. I better not find out you're badmouthin' me to Ari. It'll be over for you if I do."

Blake gave him a sarcastic thumbs up and turned back to the bus line.

So Cameron hadn't heard from her either. Interesting. The thought of Ari dropping Cameron like a roach-infested burrito brought an airy lightness to his spirit.

But the realization that *no one* had heard back from her spawned a new soul-crushing thought.

What if she had hurt herself? With how she had responded to her mom's death, he wouldn't put anything past her. Even at the best of times, Ari had a morbid fascination with death and was on medication for being bi-polar. What if she was in a hospital somewhere or a mental health facility? How would he know? He refused to consider the worst possibility. There was no way she was dead. Surely the school would already know if that was the case.

He had to find a way to get in touch with Ari.

OLIVIA WAITED IMPATIENTLY for the little old woman to exit the gigantic revolving door so she could slide by. As soon as there was clearance, she darted over to the help desk on the left.

The two middle-aged ladies talking behind the counter did a double-take when they saw her uniform.

"Can we help you, officer?"

"Yes, this is a search warrant giving me permission to review all relevant video surveillance footage for the morning of April 19th. Can you please direct me to the person who can make this happen?"

The woman stared at the warrant with wide eyes, but it was obvious she was trying to wrap her mind around this new development rather than read what was written.

"What is this all about?"

"Just checking on a suspect's alibi."

"This doesn't have anything to do with that stabbing murder that's been all over the news, does it?"

Olivia tried to be stone-faced in her response and only project the frustration and impatience she felt, but her face must have revealed something else, too.

"Oh my, this *is* about that poor girl's murder. Who do you think did it?"

"Ma'am, I can't divulge details about the case I'm working. I'm here to eliminate a potential suspect. That's it. I need you to direct me to someone who can show me last Thursday's video footage."

"Of course, of course, let me call up to our security command center and have them send someone down for you." The woman picked up the phone and pressed one of the extension buttons. "Hey, Brad, we have a police officer here that needs to review some of our video surveillance footage. Could you send someone to meet her at the main entrance help desk? Great, thanks."

"Thank you." Olivia turned to walk away from the desk to discourage any further questions as she waited.

The woman called out to her anyway. "Is the suspect an employee or a patient?"

Olivia kept walking. "I really can't talk about the case."

"I only ask because this is a big hospital with lots of security cameras. If you don't know where to look, it will take you days to review all the footage."

She stopped. The desk lady was right. She needed the room number to narrow down the search, and the help desk would have that information. The desk lady's face lit up in anticipation as Olivia strolled back to the counter.

"I need to know what room Melissa London was in Thursday morning, April 19th."

Two other people were lined up in front of the other front desk lady to be helped, but all eyes were on the binder that Olivia's desk lady had just opened.

"Let's see, London, London—yes, here it is." The woman gasped and put a hand to her chest. "Melissa London passed away that morning. It says right here, time of death, 8:18. She can't be your suspect."

"Ma'am, all I need is the room number. Please."

"She was in the ICU, fourth floor, bed D."

"Thank you."

"Is your suspect one of her family members?"

This time, Olivia walked away without turning back. She wandered over to the row of elevators, hoping to intercept her escort. The third door to open up and spill out passengers included a dark-skinned black man about her age wearing a security guard's uniform. His eyes locked on to her immediately.

"Are you the officer needing to review our surveillance footage?"

"Yes, I am."

He motioned for her to follow him and stepped back on the elevator he had just exited. Pressing the button for the third floor, he stood ramrod straight, hands behind his back, as she turned to stand beside him.

As the elevator moved slowly up, Olivia side-eyed his posture. "You serve?"

He nodded. "Eight years. Marines."

"I thought so. Only a military man stands that straight."

The doors opened and the man led the way to the right, through a large set of double doors. They continued down another hall leading to a different set of doors. This time he pulled out a plastic card and held it up to a black square, and the door popped open.

A couple more strides led to a door on the right side of the hallway. The security guard pulled out a different key card and slipped it into the slot above the door handle. The door opened to reveal two guys watching a gigantic screen with dozens of images on display.

The men swiveled in their direction when they heard the door open, and one of them, a sandy-haired man with a full beard, stood up and extended a hand. "Hi, I'm Brad. I oversee our video surveillance. What can I do for you, officer?"

Olivia pulled out the warrant again and showed it to him. "I need to check on a suspect's alibi. He claims to have been here at the hospital the entire morning of April 19th. If that's the case, I can eliminate him as a suspect. His wife was an ICU patient on the 4th floor in bed D. Can you show me the footage for that room on that morning?"

"Well, there are no cameras in the room, but I can show you the footage of the ICU floor, which should show anyone entering or exiting the room. Give me just a second to pull the feed for that morning."

Brad sat down at a computer with a monitor larger than her TV screen at home. As he furiously scrolled and clicked, she turned back to the security guard who'd escorted her up. His name badge read 'Mike Dunlap'. "We have a lot of former soldiers on our force. What made you decide to go the security guard route rather than becoming an officer?"

"The pay's better, and there are fewer idiots to deal with."

"You don't have many idiots visiting the hospital?"

"Not as many as you find at the bars and strip clubs you're called to."

"Fair enough."

Brad leaned back in his seat and swiveled his seat a quarter turn to face her. "All right, the footage is queued. How early in the morning do you want to start watching?"

Olivia moved in behind Brad to better see the screen. "Let's start at 6 a.m. and go from there. Fast forward it at five times the speed until we see anyone approach the room."

Nurses darted across the screen periodically, but no one approached Melissa London's room the first hour. At 7:09, Brad slowed the footage down to double speed as a doctor and a nurse conversed right outside the room. A few minutes later, both entered the room. Five minutes after that, they both exited, heading in different directions.

Brad resumed the five times speed, but not for long.

"Slow it down," Olivia blurted out when she recognized the figure of David London trailing behind the doctor who had recently left Melissa's room. They reentered the room together, spending a little over six minutes inside before exiting together.

"Do you want me to fast forward it again?" asked Brad.

"Yes, but stop it as soon as you see that man or that doctor again."

Again, it wasn't long before Brad slowed the footage to normal speed. David London entered the screen, followed by an older couple who had their arms wrapped around someone. As they turned slightly to enter Melissa's room, she could see it was a girl, either a young teenager or older preteen.

No one entered or exited the room for about thirty minutes. Brad slowly sped up the footage more and more until they saw the girl burst out of the room.

Olivia motioned towards the screen. "Rewind it just a bit."

They all watched the girl exit at normal speed this time, which still seemed abrupt. She exited at 8:14, followed closely by the older couple. London didn't emerge right away. A couple of nurses entered the room and then left nine minutes later. They fast-forwarded it until they saw a door open at 8:49. Head down, London walked out of the room and off the screen.

"Okay, let's speed it back up and see if he returns to the room."

They watched the next hour of footage closely, only slowing it down once as two men approached the room with a long trolley. They entered the room with the trolley and emerged four minutes later.

"There goes the body," Brad said. "There's no reason for your guy to return now."

"What are you talking about?" Olivia asked. "That trolley had nothing on it."

"They're made to look that way. They have a false top. We transport dead bodies under that false top so people don't freak out."

"So Melissa London was on that trolley."

"Yeah, that's what those are used for. There's no other reason they would enter an ICU room."

Olivia looked at the time stamp. 9:28. That would leave David London plenty of time to drive over to Jessica Turner's house and kill her.

"This footage doesn't clear my suspect. I need to pin down the exact time this man left the hospital. Can you pull up exit footage?"

Brad and Mike exchanged looks. "There are three major exits, not including the emergency ones."

"Let's start with the main exit and go from there."

"That's fine, I can pull up that footage for you, but it's going to be difficult to spot a face at more than double speed. If your guy doesn't exit shortly after he left the ICU, you could be left searching for hours. We can't devote that kind of time to this. We've got jobs to do, so you'll be largely on your own."

"I'm not asking you guys to do my job. Queue it up and move out of the way. I'll take it from here."

CHAPTER TWENTY-THREE

Olivia mindlessly obeyed the commands of her vehicle's navigation system. In her pocket was a copy of the footage that exonerated David London. It had taken her over two hours to spot him exiting the hospital. He'd walked through the big revolving door at 12:47, which was a little after Jonas Turner's 911 call.

Vogel would be thrilled. They had eliminated the only other suspect tied to the evidence. But it didn't put a smile on her face. She felt like she'd just put another nail in the coffin of an innocent man.

She'd spent two additional hours trying to trace London's movements within the hospital. Why had he stuck around for over three hours after his wife's body was taken to the morgue? What had he been doing during that time? What kind of person arranged a rendezvous with a lover mere minutes after his wife died?

She had been able to track him from the fourth floor to the cafeteria, but she couldn't find him on any cameras after that. Not until he could be seen leaving a hallway not far from the cafeteria hours later, shortly before he'd exited through the main entrance at 12:47.

Could he have found a different way out, driven to Jessica's house, killed her, and then returned to the hospital for an alibi? Or was she becoming a crazy conspiracy theorist because she didn't want Jonas Turner to be guilty? The second option seemed much more likely.

If she wanted to prove Jonas Turner's innocence, she needed a more viable suspect—which was why she found herself at 402 Lockwood Drive. Olivia walked up to the red door in the ranch-style brick house and gave it three firm knocks. Thirty seconds later a woman opened the door with wide-eyed surprise.

"Oh my, is everything all right?"

The woman looked to be in her early sixties, with dull blonde hair turning gray. She was still halfway behind the door, but as she shuffled a little more into view, her enormously wide hips were difficult to ignore.

"Does Eugene Fitzpatrick live here?"

"Yes, that's my son. He lives here. Wha—what's this about?"

"I just need to ask him a few questions. Can I come inside?"

"Um, sure, yes, you can come in. I just don't understand what this is all about. Why do you want to talk to Eugene?"

As they walked into the living room, Olivia was transported back to her grandma's house in the '90s. There were two flowery couches filled with square, puffy pillows. Several Thomas Kincaid paintings adorned the walls, and every shelf and mantle space was covered with some kind of knick-knack. Most of them appeared to be some variation of unicorn.

The woman noticed Olivia eyeing her figurines. "I collect unicorns. It's my greatest vice. I just can't stop myself. If I see a unicorn, I just have to have it. I have over a thousand scattered throughout this house. But, please, officer, tell me why you're here. What do you want with my Eugene?"

"Do you watch the news?"

The woman's eyes went wide, and her "Yes" came out strained.

"Then I'm sure you're aware that Jessica Turner was murdered last Thursday."

A hand shot up to the woman's mouth as she waddled a couple of steps closer. "Oh, you don't think Eugene could do something like that, do you? He's a sweet, sweet boy. He would never do something like that."

"Is this the sweet, sweet boy who stalked Jessica last year?"

"Oh no, that was just a big misunderstanding. He never meant her any harm. He just had a little crush and didn't know how to express it. He's a little bit awkward, socially, but he's as harmless as could be."

"Well, if that's the case, then this should be a short visit. I need to ask him a few questions and then I'll be on my way. Is his room down this hall?"

Olivia was startled by how fast the woman moved to intercept her.

"Oh, I, uh, I'll go get him for you. You just make yourself comfortable on the couch, and I'll bring him out for you."

She had been interested in seeing his room before, but now it was nonnegotiable. "Ma'am, I'll take it from here. I need to talk to Eugene alone. Please have a seat on the couch and let me do my job."

"I'm his mother. I have a right to be in the room with him."

"He's twenty years old. Parental rights went out the window at eighteen. I can take him back to the precinct for an official interrogation if I need to, but I think it would be best for everyone if you just let me ask him a few questions now."

The woman appeared to think it over for a few moments before nodding in agreement. She pointed down the hallway to the last door on the left.

Olivia quietly made her way down the hall, checking back over her shoulder twice to make sure the mother wasn't following. At the door, she pounded on it twice and announced her presence by saying "Police" before opening the door suddenly.

A dark-haired boy with a long face covered in acne startled so hard he dropped the handheld gaming device he was holding.

"Are you Eugene?"

The young man nodded, eyes big as saucers. His hair was long enough to reach his eyebrows and flow over his ears, but it wasn't long enough to hide the odd, asymmetrical shape of his head.

He was wearing a black Metallica concert T-shirt and black jeans. Olivia scanned the room—which had the look, feel, and smell of a typical male teenager's room—looking for a black hoodie to match his jeans. Dirty clothes blanketed the floor, making it hard to tell what was what. Spotting a black wad of fabric near his nightstand, Olivia pretended to be interested in the rock band posters covering the walls to get a closer look. As she moved further into the room, the dresser against the wall on the left drew her attention and then stopped her in her tracks.

Keeping one eye on Eugene, she shuffled sideways for a closer look. The hair on the back of her neck stood up as she did. The dresser had a large mirror attached to the top of it, but she couldn't see her reflection; nearly every square inch had been covered in pictures.

Pictures of Jessica Turner.

Some of them were developed photographs. In most of those, Jessica was wearing gym clothes and appeared unaware of the camera pointed in her direction. Most of the other images were pictures printed out on regular computer paper. Olivia was confident that she would find most of these images on Jessica's various social media accounts. On the outer edge of the mirror were several newspaper clippings. They all contained the same headshot: the one plastered all over the local news coverage of Jessica's murder.

Olivia tried to find some saliva in her mouth so she could swallow. Trying her best to sound casual, she turned back to Eugene. "You have quite the crush on Jessica, don't you?"

Eugene dropped his head, looking like a shamed puppy, as he nodded.

"Have you seen her in person recently?"

Eugene emphatically shook his head.

"Not at all? Not even for a little while last Thursday?"

More vigorous head-shaking.

"Do you know what happened to Jessica?"

A slight nod.

"What happened?"

"She was killed." His voice was higher than she'd expected. More childlike.

"How was she killed?"

Eugene raised his right hand, clenched it into a fist, then swung it down violently for three thrusts.

A shiver ran down her spine. "How do you know she was killed like that?"

"I heard them talking about it on my computer."

She hadn't paid much attention to all the media coverage on this case, but surely Vogel hadn't given news outlets enough details to reenact the murder scene. "Were you in the room when Jessica was killed?"

Eugene's eyebrows knitted together, and his mouth twitched. It was hard to tell if he was confused or struggling with what to say. He ended up just giving her a jerky, sideways shake of the head.

"Are you sure? We just want the person who did this. If you saw what happened, that would be a really big help."

Eugene shook his head more decisively this time. "I wasn't there."

"Where were you last Thursday morning?"

Eugene shrugged. "Here, I think."

"Here? In this room? Do you have any proof that you spent the morning in your room?"

"My mom would know."

Of course. Nothing like an alibi from the person who loves you the most. This interview wasn't likely to go anywhere unless she applied some pressure. She needed some kind of recent physical or circumstantial evidence to turn the screws on Eugene and his mom.

Her eyes returned to the Jessica shrine above the dresser. One of the photos near the middle was a close-up picture of the side profile of Jessica's face. She leaned in for a closer look. There was residue in the shape of pressed lips on Jessica's face, and a clear thumbprint on the bottom left-hand corner.

"I'm going to borrow this picture, Eug—"

Olivia stumbled backwards as Eugene jerked the picture from her with one hand and shoved her with the other.

"No, that's mine!"

The speed with which he had shot out of the bed, coupled with the murderous rage in his eyes, left her at a loss for words. She kept a hand on her gun as they stood there, glaring at one another.

Thunderous footsteps could be heard coming down the hall. The mother shrieked, "What's going on? Is everything all right?" as she appeared, breathless, in the doorway.

"Your son is trying to get himself killed."

The woman wedged her way in between Olivia and her

son. "Eugene, what's going on? You need to be nice. No temper tantrums."

Eugene looked down, once again taking on the appearance of a scolded puppy.

"Ma'am, where was Eugene last Thursday, April 19th?"

"He was right here, with me. I don't think we left the house all day."

"Do you have any way to prove that?"

"How would I prove that? We didn't have any visitors. Don't you have access to satellites that can track our movements? Go ahead and check them if you want. We were here all day."

This woman had watched one too many TV crime dramas. "I would like to collect a DNA sample before I leave."

"Then you'll have to show me a warrant. I know our rights, and we're not giving you anything without a warrant."

"Have it your way. I'll be back for a visit soon."

Olivia walked back up the hallway, twisting her torso every few steps to check her blind side. Speeding through the unicorn menagerie and out the front door, she hustled to her car.

As she opened the door to get in, an odd sensation washed over her. Alarm bells rang, and the hair on her arms stood up as her body tried to tell her something extremely dangerous was nearby.

She spun towards the house, scanning each window. Had one of the curtains moved? It was hard to tell. They looked still now. She stepped away from her car and looked up and down the street, scanning for any passengers in the parked vehicles. She did one more slow, three-sixty spin trying to spot whatever it was that had triggered her subconscious, but everything appeared empty and innocent.

The creepy kid must have gotten to her. She was freaking out over nothing. It had been a long day. Time to go home and get some sleep.

"Lights out!"

Jonas had been lying on his cot in the dark for a couple of hours now, but the prison wing plunged into deeper darkness as the few remaining lights switched off.

He had spent the last hour thinking about what he had done to deserve the life he was now living. No doubt, he was a sinner. On some level he knew he deserved hell for all the sins he had committed in his life.

On the other hand, he had accepted Jesus as his savior, and Jesus had already paid for his sins. He was now a child of God. Why was God letting these things happen to him?

Just today, he'd been slammed in the face with a food tray, told that the love of his life had been cheating on him, and then falsely charged with her murder.

If this was God's discipline, it sure seemed harsh. He wouldn't wish the last couple of days on his worst enemy. And if this was some kind of test, well, he was failing it. His mind oscillated between imagining himself violently avenging the wrongs done to him and thinking of ways he could put an end to his misery. God needed to hurry up and rescue him, because he wasn't strong enough to endure much more of this.

His court hearing had gone even worse than he'd expected, and he was no optimist. The prosecution's evidence had sounded convincing, and his court-appointed attorney had done nothing to help him. The guy had barely spoken during the hearing, and looked as worried as Jonas felt after.

Jonas had nearly had a heart attack when the judge set his bail at five hundred thousand. His lawyer, on the other hand, had treated the bail amount as a win. "Often, bail isn't offered for murder cases," he said. "And when it is, five hundred thousand is about as low as you'll see. He must have decided to go easy on you because you have no prior offenses."

Easy. Yeah, right. The likelihood of coming up with half a million was about the same as coming up with half a billion. Even coming up with the ten percent a bail bondsman would charge seem farfetched, and if he went that route, that was fifty thousand dollars down the drain.

Staring at the ceiling, he could feel the dread crawling down his spine and into his gut. Everything he'd had, everything he'd known, was gone. The image of his wife's lifeless eyes floated to the forefront of his mind. This time, they ceased being lifeless and met his. Her red lips curved into a smile. "I never loved you."

A sob escaped his lips before he jammed his fist to his mouth. A chuckle sounded from a nearby cell.

"It'll be all right, pretty boy."

Jonas buried his head under his pillow and bit his lip. Curling up into a ball, he began to hum the song his mom used to sing to him when he was sick.

Blessed assurance, Jesus is mine.
Oh what a foretaste of glory divine.
Heir of salvation, purchase of God
Born of His Spirit, washed in His blood.

This is my story, this is my song
Praising my Savior all the day long.
This is my story, this is my song,
Praising my Savior all the day long.

CHAPTER TWENTY-FOUR

There's my star investigator." Vogel threw his arms out wide and gave Olivia a Cheshire cat grin. His teeth were so big and white she wondered if they were capped. "I read your report on the hospital's video surveillance. Sounds like his alibi is rock solid. You finally convinced Jonas Turner is our killer?"

Olivia directed her attention to the photos on Vogel's wall. He had several of him receiving commendations from various local officials.

"Yeah, I would have to agree that the husband looks like the most promising suspect. Still, I think it would be wise to eliminate all other possibilities. The reason I came by is I wanted to see if you could make another call to your judge friend for me. Turns out that Jessica had a stalker, and I would like to get a search warrant to take a closer look at this guy."

Vogel stared at her like snakes were growing out of her head and hissing at him. "What the hell are you talking about, Selman? Since when does Jessica have a stalker?"

"It came up when I interviewed a couple of her close friends from church. Apparently, some young guy from her gym became infatuated with her and kept following her around. When the guy followed her all the way home one evening, she took out a restraining order on him. His name is Eugene Fitzpatrick. I paid him a visit last night. He lives with his mother, and they're both a bit off. When I went into the creep's room, he had a Jessica shrine taped to the mirror over his dresser. I'm telling you, this kid was obsessed with her. I could see him doing this."

Vogel closed his eyes and put his hands to his face, rubbing his temples. "What do you mean, 'a shrine'?"

"I mean 'a shrine'. He had all kinds of pictures cut out and taped to this mirror. We're talking hundreds of them. Most were probably printed off the internet, but some of them were clearly taken without her knowledge. One of them looked like it had been kissed, repeatedly, and when I tried to grab it, the kid freaked out. He actually shoved me."

Vogel grabbed his head and leaned forward, resting his elbows on his desk. "Why, Selman? Why? Why do you feel the need to complicate this cut-and-dry case? We have the husband dead to rights. A crap-load of evidence points in his direction. On the other hand, we have no physical evidence pointing to this kid."

"Not yet. That's why I need the search warrant. Let me see if I can find some bloody clothing and search his computer to see what kind of activity is on there leading up to Jessica's death. At the very least, we can collect some DNA to compare to samples from the crime scene."

"You need probable cause to get a search warrant. Even a friendly judge wouldn't sign off on something like this."

"But there's a solid motive and circumstantial evidence."

"No, there's a weak motive and evidence of an infatuation, not a murder. You can't ransack a house because someone has a plausible motive. You have to have evidence that ties someone to the crime scene or points to a clear intention to inflict harm. You have neither." Vogel waved an arm at nothing in particular. "Besides, all the samples have come back as a match for either Jessica or Jonas Turner. No other DNA has been found, and we've stopped all further DNA testing."

"Why would we stop testing the samples we collected?"

"Because testing costs money, and we already have our guy. Now, I'm done talking about this. No more investigation. I appreciate all you've done, but no more investigative work is needed. We have our culprit and all the evidence we need to put him away. I'll call Chief Duncan later today to let him know I no longer need your services."

The words jolted Olivia more than any slap to the face could have. She opened her mouth to respond, but no words came out. Returning to traffic work had always been just around the corner, but the sudden end hurt more than she'd expected. When she felt a burning sensation in the corner of her eyes, she spun abruptly and bolted from the office.

"YOUR COLLECT CALL was accepted. Please hold."

After the soothing voice of the operator, Jonas heard a split second of static and then a click.

"Jonas?"

"Hey, Ma."

"Jonas, what is going on? I've been worried sick. You haven't returned my calls for two days. Why are you calling from a detention center?"

The frantic, tumbling words were somehow comforting and brought a brief smile to his face. "I've been arrested."

"Arrested? For what?"

"They think I murdered Jessica."

"What? That's ridiculous. You wouldn't harm anyone, let alone Jessica. How can they think that?"

"I was the one who found her, and they always think the husband did it. I think someone might be trying to frame me, too."

"Oh my goodness. Why would someone try to frame you? Who could do something so evil?"

"I don't know, Ma. We live in a messed-up world."

"Well, your father and I are going to fly out tomorrow and help you through this."

"Mom, I don't think there's anything you and Dad can do for me."

"Nonsense. We can bail you out of jail, for one thing, and then get you a good lawyer."

"It's a murder case, so the bail is crazy high. It'll cost fifty thousand just to use a bail bondsman, and that's money we can never get back."

"I don't care about the money. This is a travesty of justice. My son is not sitting in prison with a bunch of criminals. We'll find a way to come up with fifty thousand, and we'll fly to Greenville as soon as we do."

Jonas sighed. He knew it was pointless arguing with her when she was in mama bear mode. "If you can find a way, I'll pay back every penny."

"Don't worry about that, Jonas."

"Mom, I'm going to pay you back. I won't take no for an answer."

"We'll worry about that later. Right now, we just need to get you out."

"Mom, I hate to ask you another favor, but I could use your help with one other thing."

"Anything. What can we do?"

"With being in prison, I don't know what's going on with Jessica's funeral arrangements. Could you call the Travelers

Rest precinct and find out what's going on with her body? I would like to use the Mackey Mortuary on Pine Knoll if possible. I know you helped make arrangements for Grandma and Grandpa. I could really use some help with Jessica."

"Absolutely. I'll make some calls as soon as I get done securing your bail money and our plane tickets to Greenville."

"Thanks, Mom. You don't know how much this means to me."

He heard a sob on the other end.

"Don't cry, Mom. It'll be okay."

He could hear sudden intakes of breath in between quiet crying for almost a minute, but his mom regained her composure eventually. "God's got this, honey. God's got this. We'll see you soon."

"I know, Ma. I know. I'll see you soon. Love you."

"Love you, son."

"Your call has ended. If you would like to place another—"

Jonas stood up and shuffled to the door in his chains, signaling to the guard that he was ready to return to his cell.

OLIVIA HAD DRIVEN around town for two hours trying to come to terms with the end of her detective work. Ignoring two stop-sign violations and an SUV blowing through a red light on her way, she arrived back at the Greenville Law Enforcement Center.

If she was going to try to get away with this, it was now or never.

Security cleared her without hesitation. She headed directly to the elevators and pushed the button for the basement. *Please don't let Vogel be down here.*

When the doors opened, she headed right until she came to a door labeled "Forensics Lab". She gave the door two quick raps.

"Come in." Cory looked up from some paperwork as she slid inside. He flushed, trying to stifle his goofy grin. "Officer Selman, to what do I owe the pleasure?"

"I've been so busy doing the investigative legwork that I'm behind on analyzing the forensic findings. I was hoping you could catch me up."

"Has Detective Vogel not passed along my reports? They were quite detailed."

"I'm sure he has. I've been so crazy busy that I haven't accessed my inbox in days. I'm more of an audible learner anyway, and I would prefer face-to-face interactions. I was hoping you could humor me and walk me through your findings."

Cory's face turned a shade redder, and the crooked grin got more pronounced. "Sure, I could do that."

He got up from his seat and walked over to the table where he'd first debriefed them with his findings, grabbing a couple of folders on the way. Olivia followed, peeking at the door behind her to make sure Vogel was nowhere to be seen.

"We processed both the victim's vehicle and the husband's vehicle, but we saw no evidence of a struggle or any sign of blood in either. We collected some hair and fibers just in case, but Detective Vogel told us to hold off testing them at this time.

"We lifted samples from several locations inside the house, especially along the path from the bedroom to the back door, but the only fingerprints and DNA we found in the house belonged to Jessica and Jonas Turner. If anyone else was in that house, they were extremely careful."

"How about Jessica's body? No other DNA found on it, either?"

"No DNA, but the coroner did find a couple of black fibers under Jessica's fingernails. They were generic cotton fibers that are found in all kinds of T-shirts and sweatshirts."

Or a black hoodie. "What else did you find?"

"I'm afraid the rest of my report doesn't do your case any favors. There are aspects of the blood spatter and blood trail that don't make sense, and we were unable to come to any concrete conclusions."

"What exactly doesn't make sense?"

"Well, first there's the castoff pattern around the body. It's obvious from the lower half of the victim's body and the unblemished part of the bedspread that the killer straddled the victim while stabbing her. But when we digitally reproduced the scene based on the castoff pattern, we estimated the assailant was between 5'2" to 5'6". Jonas Turner is 6'4". Maybe he could have committed the murder all scrunched up. That might explain why so many of the stab wounds were shallow, but it seems weird.

"Then we have the shoes. It's strange that we only found blood on one of the shoes, and only on the sole. When you straddle someone, your legs and feet are splayed out. The shoes should have been covered in high-velocity blood spatter, but they are spotless other than the one sole. I guess it's possible he tucked them in tight to the victim's body, but that would have made him much more unstable and more likely to be thrown off. It's hard to imagine someone tucking their feet in like that."

Olivia's head was spinning with the implications. It was too much to process right now. She needed to get the rest of the information and go somewhere quiet to work it all out. "Is there anything else?"

"I haven't even gotten to the weirdest part. The blood trail is bizarre. First, right beside the perfect shoe print is an area where blood is smeared all over. It looks purposeful, as if someone was trying to wipe something up. Then, after the clear, full shoe print, there isn't one trace of the tread anywhere else in the house. The only blood we could find between the bed and the back door are these strange oval dots."

Cory held up a picture. "There are twenty-nine of these, all similar in shape and size, but not quite identical, along the murderer's likely exit path."

The ovals were red, but they didn't look like droplets of blood. Droplets pressed down with something, maybe, but not natural ones. These markings were too flat and too big. A quarter was included in the picture for size comparison, and the oval was a little taller than a quarter and quite a bit wider.

"What do you think caused these markings?" Olivia asked.

"Honestly, we have no clue. They appear to be blood droplets that have been pressed with a sponge or a rag, but that makes no sense. Why would someone carefully press each drop of blood into a uniform shape rather than wipe it up? Unless our killer has a soft, oval-shaped peg leg, these markings make no sense."

"It's definitely blood? You've already tested it?"

"Yes and yes. We are sure it's Jessica's blood and not the killer's."

"That's too bad. It would have been really nice to have a DNA profile to put in our system and a wound to keep an eye out for." Olivia pressed her lips together thoughtfully. "This is really great work, though. I appreciate the personal update. If you don't mind, let's keep this conversation between the two of us. I don't want Vogel to think I'm a slacker for not reading the reports."

The big goofy grin overtook Cory's face. "Your secret is safe with me."

Olivia nodded and headed out the door and back towards the elevator, head spinning with the new information. In her single-mindedness, she almost collided with a familiar-looking man.

She side-stepped to the left and then stopped abruptly

as the man passed. "Hey, are you the guy who does the lie-detector tests?" she called after him.

The man stopped and turned her way. "Guilty as charged. Norman Feldstein. Can I help you with something?"

"I'm working with Detective Vogel on the Jessica Turner murder investigation. We didn't get a chance to meet the night you administered Jonas Turner's test, but I saw you leaving the interrogation room. Out of curiosity, what was your impression of Jonas Turner? Do you think he was lying to you that night?"

Norman tilted his head and gave a slight shrug. "I didn't at the time. He appeared to pass the test with flying colors. I was shocked when I heard he had been arrested. It kind of made me question my ability to tell when people are lying, to be perfectly honest."

All of her perspiration points began to tingle. "I thought the results of your test were inconclusive."

"No, they were very clear. There were a couple of questions I asked about his wife having an affair that were hard to read. He adamantly denied knowing about an affair, but I think part of him secretly suspected it. Either that, or the thought of her having an affair sent his pulse racing. But every question about the murder itself and his actions throughout that day, he was calm as a cucumber and very convincing. If he killed his wife, then he's either a well-trained con artist or a sociopath with no conscience."

"Thank you. Your feedback has been very helpful. And if it's any consolation, I don't think you've lost your ability to tell when someone is lying."

Norman locked eyes with her, and they shared an unspoken understanding before Olivia headed back towards the elevators.

As she stepped in, her mind swirled with all the churned-up pieces of information from the last thirty minutes. Not much was clear, but of one thing she was certain. There was no way she was going to stop investigating this case.

CHAPTER TWENTY-FIVE

Unable to secure the smaller interrogation room this time, Olivia sat at one of the four tables provided for family and lawyer visits. She watched Jonas Turner shuffle in with his leg chains, handcuffs, and orange jumpsuit. Despite his circumstances and appearance, he did not project the pathetic demeanor of most first-time inmates. His posture was upright and his head lifted, scanning the room. When he spotted her, his mouth formed an amused grin.

The smile didn't reach his eyes, though. As he sat down in front of her, the sadness in his eyes caused an ache in her chest. She lost her train of thought for a moment, and they sat for a few seconds looking at one another until he spoke.

"I want to thank you for giving me a head's up about the text messages. It would have been difficult hearing that information for the first time in court. No one wants to watch a grown man cry in public." He gave her another sardonic grin, one that almost reached his eyes.

She simply nodded before squashing any further emotional responses by getting down to business. "Why didn't you tell me about Eugene Fitzpatrick?"

Jonas's eyebrows furrowed. "Who?"

"Eugene Fitzpatrick. Are you telling me that name doesn't ring any bells?"

His eyes took on a distant look for a couple of seconds before returning to sharp focus. "Is that the kid from Jessica's gym?"

"Yes, the young man who stalked her. You know, the one you guys got a restraining order for. When the police are trying to track down suspects, it's usually a good idea to let them know the victim had a stalker. Especially if you're currently the number one suspect."

"You think Eugene might have done this?"

"Why not? He was obsessed enough to follow her to her house. Why is it hard for you to believe that he would enter the house, leading to an altercation?"

"I don't know. I kind of thought Jessica overreacted with that whole situation. I took it seriously at first, but when I actually met the kid, he seemed fairly harmless."

"You met Eugene?"

"Yeah, I tracked him down and showed up at his house one day. I wanted to see for myself what we were dealing with and personally warn the guy not to mess with my wife again. But when I knocked on the door, the kid's mom answered. She was super nice and apologetic about the whole thing, and when she brought out Eugene to apologize, it was like we were dealing with a child. The mother had like a thousand unicorn figurines decorating her house. Eugene kept grabbing one from the mantle and giving it to his mom as a gift. It was clear that he was somewhere on the autism spectrum. I got the impression he did what he did more from a lack of social awareness rather than any ill intention."

Jonas had been talking with his hands and making sporadic eye contact as he recounted his experience at

Eugene's house, but now he placed his hands on the table and looked her in the eye. "Jessica still followed through with the restraining order, but I honestly haven't given that guy a second thought since meeting him."

"You may want to give him a second thought now. I visited the guy yesterday, and he made my skin crawl. He had a shrine to Jessica set up in his room. A bunch of pictures of her taped to a large mirror. Pictures that he had obviously kissed and fondled. And when I tried to take one down, he flipped out on me. He actually shoved me away from his precious shrine. I'm telling you, the guy's a creep."

Eyes wide and mouth hanging open, Jonas stammered out, "What are you going to do about this?"

"That's one of the reasons I'm here. Right now, we have nothing to tie him to the crime. I can't get a search warrant without more probable cause. I was hoping you could help me out. Have you seen or heard from him in any way recently?"

"No, not at all. He hasn't been on my radar in any way since the restraining order, which was, what, over a year ago?"

Olivia leaned back in her chair and let out a sigh. "Unless something else turns up, my hands are tied. Maybe if I got him alone I could get him to confess, but I doubt his mom will let him leave the house alone anytime soon."

Jonas leaned forward and his eyes hardened, along with the set of his jaw. "What about Jessica's—" He looked away, and his face contorted in disgust as he searched for the right word. "Friend?"

"I checked his alibi. It looks like he couldn't have committed the murder."

"His alibi is rock solid? No way he could have done it?"

This time she was the one to look away, thinking about the wisest way to put it. "He told us he was at the hospital that morning. We spotted him on several camera feeds throughout that morning, and we spotted him leaving the hospital's main entrance after your 911 call."

"Were you able to follow his movements in the hospital to the point that you're absolutely certain he didn't have time to leave, commit the murder, and come back?"

This guy should have been a lawyer. He saw through every hole in her tactful presentations. "It's highly unlikely that he left and returned without being seen."

He shook his head, keeping his penetrating gaze fixed on her. "I want to see the text messages."

"That's not a good idea."

"Why not?"

"Nothing good will come from it. Whatever use they have from an investigative standpoint, we'll figure out. There's no point in you torturing yourself with them."

"You don't think I've been torturing myself without them? You don't think I've been imagining every worst-case scenario there is? I would much rather know exactly what went on between them than sit around imagining just how bad it could be."

Those eyes were squeezing her heart again, and before she realized what she was doing, Olivia had put a hand out and placed it on his. She pulled it back awkwardly. "I'm sorry. I can only imagine how hard this is for you. But right now, I need you to focus on helping me solve the case so you can get out of here. Getting worked up over a guy who has largely been eliminated as a suspect isn't helping."

"But if I can read her texts, I might be able to pick up on something you're not seeing. I know her and her friends better than you do. I'll be able to tell if something is off."

"Jonas, I don't have access to her messages anymore. I got lucky and was able to access them for a brief time, which is how we got copies of the text thread labeled 'Dee', but the phone is locked again. Last I heard, Vogel was sending it off to some digital forensics company to open it back up."

"But you have copies of the 'Dee' thread. You can show those to me."

"I don't have them with me."

"Email them to me when you leave."

"I can't leave that kind of paper trail between us."

"Fine, show them to me when I get out of here. My parents are hoping to get here with bail money within the next couple of days."

"Okay. When you get out of here, I'll reconsider showing you the text messages."

"Thank you."

"Don't thank me yet." She pushed back her chair and prepared to leave. "If you think of anything that might help me get a search warrant for Eugene, give me a call." She handed him her card, figuring the first one was no longer in his possession.

"Did you ever follow up with the landscaping company to see if any of their employees were running behind the fence line that day?"

Dang it. All these other leads she had been chasing had knocked that one completely off the back-burner. "No, I haven't reached out to them yet. I'll be sure to follow up on that tomorrow."

"You know, now that I think about it, Eugene had kind of a dark complexion, and he wasn't very tall. I could see him being mistaken for Hispanic."

Olivia nodded to herself as she left the common room. *Yes, he could.*

CHAPTER TWENTY-SIX

I'm surrounded! Where are you? They're going to light me up if you don't get over here already."

"I'm trying, I'm trying. Some idiot is trying to snipe me from the tower."

"Come on, man, make a run for it. They're closing in."

"I'm dead."

"What, are you serious?"

"Yeah, I told you there was a sniper pinning me down."

"Great, now *I'm* dead. That's four losses in a row. What is going on with you, Blake? You've played like trash all week."

"Yeah, whatever. I don't see you playing any better. I'm tired of this game. I'm going to call it a night." Blake picked up his phone, where Dillon's curly red 'fro filled the screen.

His gaming buddy pleaded with him. "Come on, man. We can't go out like that. One more game."

"Nah, I'll catch you tomorrow." Before Dillon could protest some more, Blake clicked off the video chat.

He wasn't in the mood. Too worried about Ari, who he still hadn't heard from. A gnawing fear had driven him to visit the attendance office to ask about her earlier that day, but they wouldn't share the reason she was absent.

"Can you at least tell me if she's alive?" he'd asked, but the attendance clerk had looked at him like he was crazy and said, "I'm sure she's alive. Now get back to class."

The lady hadn't sounded like she actually *knew* whether or not Ari was alive, so her words weren't much of a relief. That was why he'd broken down and called her dad's office as soon as he got off the bus at home. The receptionist had put him through to Ari's dad, but as soon as Blake had asked, "Is everything all right with Ari?", he'd hung up.

Who hung up on a kid asking about his friend? Had Cameron done something to Ari on their date that had pissed her dad off, and now all guys were off-limits? Or, even worse, had he found out about Ari sneaking over to Blake's house? That would certainly explain his actions.

There were a couple of other possibilities dancing at the back of Blake's mind which he didn't even want to consider. The worst, by far, began to crawl to the surface and fill him with dread. What if Ari had tried to kill herself? What if she was in the hospital fighting for her life and her dad was so distraught that he'd hung up rather than break down on the phone with a kid?

Blake looked down at his phone as a text came in. It was from an unknown number. Unlocking his screen, he read it.

Hey Blake it's Ari.

Relief flooded his chest and trickled down his arms and legs.

Blake: Where have you been? I've been freaking out over here. He kept his eyes riveted to the screen until the next text appeared.

*Ari: Sorry my dad's gone crazy. He took my phone laptop and credit card. He won't even let me go to school. He's lost his mind. Hopefully after the funeral he'll return to sanity *and chill out.*

He thumbed a quick reply. *Blake: That's messed up. I'm so sorry. I'm glad you found a way to reach me. Whose phone is this?*

Ari: It's that one I found last week. It doesn't have a data plan, so it's basically useless except for calls and texts but at least I have a way to contact you. I just have to be really careful. My dad would kill me if he found me with it.

Blake: You staying in touch with your other friends too?

Ari: I don't have any other friends.

Blake: What about Cameron?

Ari: You're cute when you're jealous.

Blake: I'm not jealous. He's just a loser.

Ari: Don't worry about Cameron. We're done. You know I can't stand jocks. You hurt my feelings and I figured that was the best way to get back at you.

Blake: Dang. You are cold blooded.

Ari: You know this already.

Blake: I'm sorry I hurt your feelings.

Ari: Make it up to me by coming over tomorrow night.

Blake: Your dad will let me?

Ari: No my dad will be gone. He has some social event he's going to.

Blake: I don't think my mom will let me go without your dad there.

Ari: Don't tell her. Sneak out and get an Uber.

Blake: My mom would kill me.

Ari: She won't find out. Come on I need you. I'm going crazy with loneliness over here. I would come over there but he's cut me off in every way. Come over Blake. Pleeeeeeeease.

Blake: Ok. I'll try.

Ari: Yes! I love you! See you tomorrow!

Blake stared at the screen. "I love you"? Was she just

happy she was getting her way, or did she actually mean it like it sounded? Should he say it back? That seemed too awkward and risky. He went with a 'thumbs-up' emoji instead and waited to see if she said anything else. After two minutes with no response, he finally put the phone down and let out the breath he hadn't realized he was holding. His heart was racing, and as he fell back on his bed, the room tilted back and forth.

This girl was going to be the death of him.

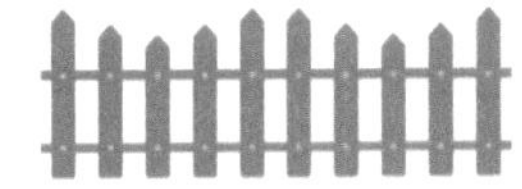

CHAPTER TWENTY-SEVEN

Hey, you've got a phone call. Let's go."

Jonas quickly put his bookmark in the prison library's copy of *The Count of Monte Cristo* and pushed off his bed. He had read the book twice before, but it was no less enthralling the third time around. His current circumstances certainly added texture to its allure. Already seven hundred and forty-four pages into the twelve-hundred page book, Jonas had done little else in prison other than read it.

Following the guard to the phone room, he wondered who he would hear on the other end of the line. His understanding was that incoming calls to inmates weren't allowed, so he guessed it was either Officer Selman or his lawyer. It should be his lawyer, since he hadn't heard from him since the hearing, but he hoped it was Selman with a new development.

The guard directed him to a phone that was blinking. He sat down and picked up the receiver. "Hello?"

"Jonas! Oh, thank God. I was worried they wouldn't put me through to you."

"I don't think they allow incoming calls, Ma. How did you

talk them into it?"

"I told them I'm all the way in Arizona and have no way to reach you, and I guess they felt sorry for me. I may have shed a few tears and mentioned that I didn't think my poor heart could take my only child being locked up without a call from his mother."

"Wow, Ma, you pulled out all the stops."

"Well, it's true. My heart can't take this. I haven't slept a wink since I found out. It's so wrong what they're doing to you. Are you safe in this prison? No one has tried to hurt you, have they?"

"I'm safe. Because it's a murder case, they moved me to the maximum security wing. I know that sounds bad, but I'm actually safer there. I get a cell to myself, and any interaction with inmates is closely supervised."

"Oh good. I've been so worried about you."

"Did you call just to check up on me?"

"No, I wanted to let you know that we will be there tomorrow to bail you out. We're leaving first thing in the morning. With the time difference we won't be able to get to you until the evening, but Lord willing, we'll have you out of there before nightfall."

"How were you able to pull money together so quickly?"

"Don't you worry about that."

"Come on, Ma. I want to know. How'd you do it?"

"Your dad pulled some money out of his retirement. It's not a big deal."

"But that transfer process usually takes seven to ten business days. How do you have the money already?"

"It doesn't matter, Jonas. All—"

"It does matter, Mom. Seriously, tell me how you got the money."

"You are so stubborn. Just like your father. Look, we took out a couple of title loans."

Jonas groaned loudly into the phone.

His mother rushed to reassure him. "It's not a big deal. We'll pay them off as soon as the retirement money comes in."

"It *is* a big deal. Those places are evil. I hope you read the fine print. Whatever it costs you, though, I will pay you back. No matter how long it takes, I will pay you back."

"Don't worry about it. It's just money."

"Yeah, well, I'm going to pay you back every penny of it. I really appreciate this, Mom. I need to get out of here. The cops are bungling Jessica's case. They may need some help coming to the obvious conclusion that someone else killed her."

"I just can't believe they could ever think you would kill Jessica. You're such a great husband, not to mention a teacher and a Sunday school leader. How can they think someone like you could be capable of murder? They've lost their minds."

"Yeah, well, they don't know me like you do."

"Well, they should get to know you then. Certainly before they lock you up." There was silence on the line for a couple of seconds before his mom continued, in a much lighter tone, "I heard Pastor Joshua came by to see you."

"Yeah, he came by yesterday for a little bit. How did you find out about that?"

"He called us last night to see how we were doing. He's such a nice man. I can't believe a pastor would take time out of his busy schedule to call a member's parents who live out of state. Did he tell you about the fundraising account the church set up for you?"

"Yeah, he mentioned some people at the church setting up a fundraising site for me and sharing it on social media. I doubt many people will be inspired to give to a suspected murderer, but it was a very thoughtful gesture."

"Oh, you might be surprised by how highly people think of

you. Guess how much has already been raised."

"I don't know. Five hundred dollars?"

"Hah, not even close. They've already raised over nineteen thousand."

Nineteen thousand? The amount shocked him. He wondered if the number reflected the generous donation of one wealthy church member or if there were a number of people contributing. It took him a while to respond, as his throat constricted and his eyes started stinging.

"Wow, that's a lot more than I would've expected. That money should go a long way in covering Jessica's funeral expenses."

There were a couple of seconds of silence and then an audible intake of breath on the other end of the line. "The other reason I called is to tell you what I found out about Jessica. I called the precinct like you asked, but they told me they released the body to Jessica's aunt."

"Aunt Sharon?"

"Yes, they wouldn't give me the name, but I remembered she only had the one. I found her on Jessica's Facebook page and sent her a message asking her to call me. She called last night. Apparently, she already had Jessica cremated and took her back to Indiana with her. They are planning on having a memorial service for her Saturday at their home church."

"What? In Indiana? How can they set up a memorial service without me? Why was she even given Jessica's body in the first place? They weren't close. Jessica hasn't seen her since our wedding. What is Aunt Sharon thinking? Jessica's friends aren't going to drive to Indiana to offer condolences to people they don't know. Who's going to be at this funeral? This is crazy."

A hint of anger crept into his mom's voice. "Sharon was polite with me, but I got the impression that she believes you killed Jessica. I'm guessing she doesn't want you at the funeral."

Closing his eyes and squeezing the receiver tight, Jonas fought to maintain control as his body trembled with rage. *How can this be happening?*

The voice of the guard who brought him down snapped Jonas out of his righteous indignation. "Wrap it up. You've got two minutes."

"Mom, I've got to go. Thank you for checking on Jessica, and thank you for coming up with the bail money. I owe you big time."

"You owe us nothing. Just stay safe, and we'll see you soon."

"See you soon, Ma. I love you."

"I love you even more."

OLIVIA SLOWED DOWN as she approached the Thornberry Shoals subdivision. Rhododendron bushes with purple blooms lined the entrance, with a large bed of multicolored flowers in front of the wooden Thornberry Shoals sign. She counted seven men trimming bushes, mowing grass, or tending to the flowerbed.

When she pulled off the main road and onto the grass, several members of the landscaping crew looked over and immediately dropped into a crouch as if ready to bolt.

She had spent all morning and afternoon patrolling the north side of Travelers Rest, as her chief of police had ordered. Patrol work was often boring, but the north side was unbearably so. Today had cemented in her mind that she could no longer do regular police work. If she didn't make detective soon, she would have to quit and become a private investigator. This was the kind of work she was born to do.

Olivia headed towards an older-looking, stocky Hispanic man with salt-and-pepper hair. He and the young man in the ball cap were the only two who hadn't wandered to the far edges of the subdivision's front landscaping upon her approach.

As they noticed her walking in their direction, they began speaking in rapid-fire Spanish. She'd taken Spanish all throughout high school and minored in it in college, so she was close to fluent, which had been a huge boon for her police work. Despite their low voices, she caught the quick exchange.

Old guy: "Why is the police coming to us?"

Young guy: "It's probably about that murder in White Meadow."

Old guy: "We have nothing to do with that. Why would they talk to us?"

Young guy: "They talk to everyone when a white woman is killed."

They shut up once she came within ten feet of them.

"Good evening, gentlemen. My name is Officer Selman. Are you Jose Alvarado?"

The older man nodded. "*Sí.*"

"I was told your landscaping crew, Jose & Sons, does the landscaping for a subdivision called White Meadow. Is that correct?"

"*Sí.*"

"Were any of your crewmembers working that property last Thursday, April 19th?"

Jose shook his head emphatically. "No, White Meadow is third Tuesday of month. No Thursday."

"So your crew was there Tuesday, and they work that subdivision at least once a month? I'm guessing your crew is well acquainted with the ins and outs of that property. I have an eyewitness that says she saw a short Hispanic man wearing a hoodie and yellow landscaping gloves run behind her fence, right past the retention pond, last Thursday. I need to question that man."

"No, *señorita*, my crew no murder no one. We not do that."

"I didn't say anything about a murder. I'm just looking for someone running behind a fence. Maybe he forgot something and came back for it. Maybe he was just walking around, peeking into backyards to see if something valuable was lying around. Do you have anyone on your crew who seems to be more interested in watching the houses, garages, or backyards you work than doing the landscaping itself?"

"No, I no hire thieves. They take, I fire."

The younger man spoke to Jose in Spanish. "What about Pepe? We should tell her about him. He could do something like this."

Jose turned away in disgust and spat on the ground.

"Who is Pepe?" Olivia asked.

Jose looked up at her, startled. "You Latina?"

"No, but I speak Spanish."

Jose lifted his hands to the sky and proceeded to speak in Spanish. "Why are you making me talk in my broken English, then?"

"Better than me talking to you in my broken Spanish," she replied, still in English. "Now, who is this Pepe who's capable of stealing or murdering?"

He gave the younger man, whom she suspected was one of his sons, a dirty look before answering her in Spanish. "Pepe is my younger sister's loser boyfriend's nephew. She begged me to give him a job. He only worked for me a couple of months. Like you said, always looking around. We started receiving complaints about things being stolen. When I caught him red-handed, I fired him."

"Is he capable of breaking into a house and killing someone if he got caught?"

Jose took a deep breath and let it out, his shoulders slumping. "Yes. He has shown a violent temper. I think he did bad stuff back home. That's why he came to America. He was in big trouble. He's no good."

Olivia put a hand to her mouth and bit her inner cheek to cover the smile forming there. She had found a genuine lead for the Hispanic man running behind the fence line. "Anybody else on your crew I should talk to?"

"No, everyone else has been working for me for years. We've never had a complaint about stealing until Pepe."

"What is Pepe's last name, and where can I find him?"

Jose sighed again. He looked like he had just been told he needed a root canal. "Pepe Delgado. He stays with my sister in Berea. 427 Montis Drive."

"Thank you, Jose. You've been very helpful. How can I reach you if I have any more questions?"

Jose pulled out a fat wallet from his back pocket and extracted a card. "This number has my cell phone. You can reach me any time."

Olivia nodded her thanks and then turned to each of them, making sure to make eye contact as she spoke. "Don't tell anyone about this conversation. That includes your sister or anyone on your crew. If I find out that Pepe received advance warning of my arrival, I'll know it came from you, and I won't be happy. Do you understand?"

In unison, they nodded and replied, "*Sí, señorita.*"

Olivia made her way back to her patrol car. By the time she was behind the wheel, the crew had resumed working on the bushes near Jose. Heading towards Berea, she considered calling in for backup. She was familiar with Montis Drive, and that was a rough area. On the other hand, she didn't want to explain to anyone what she was doing.

As she turned onto Duncan Chapel Road, she glanced in her rear-view mirror and spotted a dark-colored SUV two cars back. It was the third time she had noticed a similar-looking car behind her in the last hour. Dark SUVs were ubiquitous, so it probably wasn't the same one, but something about it made her senses shift into high alert. She took a right onto Old Buncombe Road, keeping her eyes on her rear-view mirror.

The SUV turned right.

She put on her blinker to get in the left lane. The SUV slowed. After letting two cars pass it, creating a buffer, it shifted into the left-hand lane, too. Olivia slowed way down, but the two cars between her and the SUV refused to go around her. Too afraid to pass a cop, she assumed. She took a left on New Perry, a two-lane road. The SUV nearly came to a stop, but just before she went around a small bend, she saw it turn to follow her.

A few yards from her turn onto Montis Drive, she came to a complete stop and waited for the SUV to approach. It was moving at a brisk pace when it first appeared in her rear-view, but then it slowed down dramatically. She half expected it to stop and do a three-point turn to reverse direction, but it kept crawling forward. Her hand went to her gun as she prepared for a good, long look at the driver going by, but the vehicle sped up while passing, and she could barely make out the silhouette of the man through the darkly tinted windows. All she could tell was that he was wearing a baseball cap and looking away from her.

Olivia sat forward and tried to make out the license plate, but it appeared to be splattered in mud. She couldn't be sure of a single letter. Gripping the wheel, she braced herself to pursue the SUV. At the very least, she could cite the driver for a concealed license plate.

As she prepared to step on the gas, indecision gripped her. Was she being paranoid? What if it wasn't the same vehicle she'd spotted earlier? What if the guy had simply slowed down because he saw a cop car stopped on the side of the street with its brake lights on?

The sun was going down, and she didn't want to waste

time on a wild-goose chase. This Pepe Delgado was a real lead, and she was eager to chase it down.

The SUV had taken a left at the stop sign and was nearly out of sight now. Olivia took her foot off the brake, drove to the stop sign, and took a right.

She found number 427 a quarter of a mile later on the left side of the street. It was a small, rundown house with dingy white vinyl siding chipped and cracked in several places. She gave the front door three quick, firm raps.

A round-faced, middle-aged Hispanic woman cracked the door and stuck her head out. "Yes?"

"I need to speak to Pepe."

The woman pulled her head back inside and spoke quietly in Spanish. It sounded something like, "The police are here for Pepe." When her head reappeared she said, "There no Pepe here."

"I know he stays here. I just need to talk to him. It would be better if we talked here and now rather than making me haul him down to the station."

The woman opened her mouth to speak, but Olivia held up her hand to silence her as she heard the unmistakable sound of a screen door opening and banging shut. She raced around the corner of the house and arrived at a six-foot, warped wooden fence enclosing the backyard just in time to see a short Hispanic man leaping the back of it.

Olivia grabbed the top of the fence and used it to catapult herself high enough to swing a leg over, and then the other. At a dead sprint she jumped up and mounted the back fence like a pommel horse, swinging one leg over and then the other.

A wooded area backed up to the yard. Pepe was already out of sight, but she could hear him crashing through the woods. She took off after him. Navigating the trees, brambles, and cobwebs while listening for footsteps was difficult. Every thirty seconds or so she stopped to listen so she could reorient her pursuit. Each time she stopped, the footsteps sounded farther away.

After another minute of chasing, the sound of distant crashing was barely audible. The sun had dipped below the tree line, casting the woods in deep shadows. If she didn't turn back soon, she might struggle to find her way back. For the first time, she thought about snakes.

Pulling out her flashlight, she listened carefully for the sound of creature movement. She didn't hear anything, but the mere thought of something slithering her way sent her jogging back in the direction she'd come.

"Honey, do you want us to stop to get groceries first?"

Jonas pulled his gaze from the view outside his backseat window. "No, I'll pick some things up tomorrow. I just want to go straight home if that's all right."

"Of course, dear, we'll head straight there."

His parents had made it to the detention center earlier than expected, and the bailout process had been relatively quick and easy. The only hiccup of the day had been picking up his stuff at the motel. The cash in his wallet had managed to disappear, and his car had been broken into. He wasn't sure what was missing because he didn't keep anything valuable in there, but the thieves must have turned the overhead light on because his battery was dead.

He'd arranged to have his car towed to a local body shop to fix the broken driver's-side glass and replace the battery. It was another gut-punch, but all he was focused on was sleeping in his own bed.

While in prison, he'd been told that his house had been cleared and it was in his best interest to have a biohazard team professionally clean it as soon as possible. He'd nearly had a heart attack when he received the quote from the company recommended to him, but what choice did he have but to pay it? It wasn't like he could live in a house where Jessica's blood was spattered across the walls. He prayed that the company had done the job well and his house didn't still look or smell like a crime scene.

As his parents neared his driveway, Jonas hit the garage opener he had snagged from his car before it had been towed away. The noise seemed to startle his neighbor Billy, who was in his front yard throwing the football with his two boys in the last rays of dusk. They stopped and stared as Jonas waved at them sheepishly from the back seat.

"If I park here, will you still have enough room to get out?"

Jonas looked at his dad in the driver's seat and then followed his eyes to the car sitting in the garage. He had completely forgotten about Jessica's car. Seeing it there in the garage tightened the muscles in his chest and poured acid into his stomach. He had already been mentally preparing to pick up a rental car tomorrow until his got fixed, but that made no sense with Jessica's available to him. The thought of driving her car weirded him out, though.

"Yeah, you're fine here. Thanks, Dad."

He glanced back across the street as he stepped out of his parents' rental car. Billy and his kids were no longer in their front yard. Now that the neighborhood pariah had returned, he expected most of his neighbors would respond in a similar fashion and avoid him at all costs. Jonas shook his head as he hit the button to close the garage door.

When he walked into the house, a pungent odor of disinfectant punched him in the face. He stepped over to the first hallway and lowered the thermostat so the fan would kick on.

He turned back to his parents. "You know where everything is. Just help yourself to whatever. I think I'm going to turn in early. It's been a long day."

"Yes, go get some sleep, honey. Don't worry about us. We have everything we need."

"Thanks, Mom. I can't thank you guys enough for getting me out of there and back home."

They came together for a group hug, which was awkward because they weren't a hugging family. Jonas broke away and headed to his room before his eyes got too moist.

The disinfectant smell was even stronger there, but he was pleasantly surprised to find the walls absent of any sign of blood. From what he could tell, the only indication that his room used to be a crime scene was a faint pink stain on his bare mattress. As he stared at the spot, the image of Jessica's lifeless face floated into his mind.

He shut his eyes tight and sat down on the bed, facing away from the stain. This wasn't going to work. It wasn't just the mattress. How could he stay in the same room where his wife had been killed? How could he stay in the same house? Everything would remind him of her.

An image of Jessica with a lover popped into his mind, uninvited. Had she had sex with someone else on this bed? He shot up off the mattress and bolted into the master bathroom, closing the door behind him.

Sitting on the edge of the tub, he put his head in his hands. He couldn't afford to be a basket case. There was too much to do. Too much to figure out. He pulled out the slip of paper with the phone number his mom had given him and keyed it into his phone.

She answered on the fifth ring. "Hello?"

"Hey, Aunt Sharon, it's Jonas."

A long pause. "Are you calling me from prison?"

"No, I'm out. This has all been a big misunderstanding. It's getting worked out, though. I heard you were having a memorial service for Jessica tomorrow. Is that true?"

There was no answer, so he kept going.

"If that's true, it's going to be really difficult for me and my parents to make it there by two. Is there any way we can push it back, or even move it to another day?"

"Jonas, we don't want you at her service. If you drive up here, you'll be wasting your time. We'll have a cop here to escort you off the premises."

Jonas's blood ran cold; his mouth went dry. When he finally responded, he emphasized each word. *"Sharon, I did not kill Jessica."*

"The police are sure you did, which is why they released her body to me. So, you'll have to excuse me if I don't trust the word of a murderer."

"They had no right to release her body to you."

"She belongs with her family."

"I'm her family!"

His mother rushed to his bedroom door at his yell. "Honey, is everything all right?"

Jonas covered his phone with a hand and held it away from him. "Everything's fine, Mom. I'm just on the phone and got a little too upset. Sorry to worry you."

He glanced at the screen as he was putting it back up to his ear and saw that Aunt Sharon had ended the call.

Great. Now what? Aunt Sharon was being completely unreasonable, but what could he do? He was going to miss his own wife's funeral. When was this nightmare going to stop getting worse?

CHAPTER TWENTY-EIGHT

Blake couldn't believe what he had gotten himself into. If his mom ever found out he'd slipped out his window and ordered an Uber after she went to bed, she would have a stroke. And if she ever recovered enough to leave the hospital, she would beat him until he needed one.

His Uber driver looked like a frat boy and kept trying to start a conversation with him to show how cool he was. Blake was too preoccupied to pay him much attention. He kept looking down at his phone, where he had Ari's last text pulled up.

Ari: Have the driver drop you off at the end of the street. Don't come to the front door. Head straight for the backyard. I'll meet you there.

So much cloak-and-dagger stuff. It was really freaking him out. The driver slowed to turn onto Ari's street.

"This is good. You can drop me off here," Blake blurted out.

"Right here? At the stop sign?"

"Yes, thanks." Blake leapt out of the car and shut the door

before the man could get another word in.

Flipping the hood up on his big, black Megadeath hoodie, he jammed his hands in his pockets and made his way to Ari's house.

Her back yard was surrounded by wrought-iron fencing with spikes at the top. He began stressing about how he was going to get over it until he noticed the padlock on the gate was hanging loose. He unhooked it and walked right in. There was a fire pit lit in the center of the yard with two camping-style chairs sitting behind it, facing back towards the house.

As Blake approached the fire pit, a red blur appeared from the shadows of the house. He turned in that direction, knees buckling, but recognized Ari a moment before she jumped up and swung her arms around his neck, clamping her legs around his waist.

"You came! I was worried you would chicken out. It has sucked not getting to hang out with you."

She kept squeezing harder and harder. Blake was so taken aback he just stood there and took it, like an animal in shock being crushed by a boa constrictor. What was this? Ari wasn't exactly the hugging type.

He eventually returned the hug in hopes that she would let go before he embarrassed himself. While the half of him that had a brain was weirded out, the other half was loving a hot girl engulfing him in an embrace.

Ari finally released him and stared into his eyes. "I've really missed you. It sucks not having anyone to talk to. You're the only person who really knows who I am. My mom knew me, but she's gone now."

Her gaze shifted to the flickering of the fire pit, and they stood there staring into the flames without speaking. He noticed that she pulled out her heart-shaped locket from the neck hole of her hoodie and began rubbing it with her thumb and forefinger. The locket her mother had given her for her tenth birthday.

Blake tried to think of something to say. "What about your dad? I know he's being a hard-ass now, but isn't he someone you can talk to?"

Ari's face took on a hard look as she shook her head. "Not anymore. If we talk at all it's only to scream at each other."

"That sucks. Is there anything I can do?"

Ari pulled her eyes from the flames and met his. "Will you come with me to my mom's funeral?"

"Of course. I'll be there. Do you think your dad will let me sit with you?"

"He won't make a stink at the funeral. He's all about appearances. We're having a visitation before the funeral. It would be great to have you there with me in the receiving line. I'm dreading having to greet a bunch of stupid people I don't know."

"Yeah, for sure. I'll have my mom drop me off at the start of the visitation."

"Thanks." Ari's eyes shimmered in the firelight as they filled. She turned back to the fire pit and leaned forward, propping her arms on her legs so her hands covered the tears leaking out.

Blake felt pressure to fill the silence. "Hopefully, after the funeral, your dad will let you come back to school so you have people to talk to. I mean, he's got to. Parents can't keep their kids out of school. It's against the law."

"I told him the same thing. He told me he would enroll me in a private school if anyone tried to force his hand. He's even talked about moving out of the state."

Blake's mind swirled with the implications of this news. "So, I'm guessing he—"

Ari bolted upright, looking in the direction of her house. A light on the first floor had been switched on. She turned the knob on the gas fire pit, dousing the flames and plunging the backyard into darkness. "Quick, Blake, hide."

Blake was frozen in place as she made her way back towards the house, but when he saw the back door begin to open, he dove down behind the fire pit.

He heard the angry sound of her dad's voice. "What are you doing out here?"

"I wanted some fresh air."

"If you want some fresh air, open a window. I told you not to step foot outside this house."

"You can't keep me trapped inside forever. Even prisoners get to go outside for an hour. Why are you acting like this?"

Her dad's voice sounded even closer and more venomous when it answered. "I don't trust you."

"You don't *trust* me? You don't trust *me*? That's hilarious. You've got to be the world's biggest hypocrite."

Blake flinched as he heard the unmistakable sound of skin being slapped.

"Don't you ever talk to me that way. Go back to your room—*now*."

There was a long silence. Blake badly wanted to peek around the fire pit and make sure Ari was all right, but he knew any movement might give him away and make matters worse. It seemed like forever before he heard her whisper something he couldn't make out, followed by the sound of a door closing.

He stayed in the same position for at least ten minutes before daring to pop his head up. Seeing no one, he crept to the gate and eased his way out. Once he got to the end of the street, he pulled out his phone to access the Uber app, but his hands were still shaking too badly to use it.

OLIVIA STEPPED OUT of Maria Alvarado's house almost two hours after arriving. She didn't have much to show from her time there other than a good photograph of Pepe to help with identification, which she had found on her own while rummaging through his stuff.

There were four other people living in the house, and all of them had tried to use the "I no speak English" card until she started speaking to them in Spanish. Even then, they were incredibly evasive. They were unaware of any criminal activity. They had no idea where he would go when in trouble. They claimed he only stayed there occasionally and probably wouldn't be back.

Olivia was worried that the last part might be true. Now that he knew the police were after him, he might not ever return to the house. Heck, he might even leave the state or return to Mexico.

The two closest streetlights to the house were out, so it was an unusually dark path back to her patrol car. It forced her to pay more attention to her other senses, which must have included her sixth sense, because a tingling sensation crept up her spine. She stood still and strained to listen for any atypical sounds.

Something, she wasn't sure what, drew her attention to the right. She pulled out her flashlight and shone it on two cars parked along the street: a little white Honda Accord and a baby-blue Ford pickup truck. Directing the beam further down the street, Olivia found two more vehicles parked along the road. A white panel van and some kind of SUV.

She walked towards the vehicles, keeping her beam trained on the SUV. As she got closer, she could see it was the same color as the one she'd seen earlier. Her beam bounced as she began to jog towards it.

There was a commotion in the front seat right before the SUV's high beams flipped on and it began to go in reverse.

Olivia took off in a sprint after it. Distant headlights appeared down the street behind the SUV, which forced it to slow down and allowed her to close the gap.

Running in the middle of the road now, Olivia pulled her gun and yelled, "Police! Stop where you are."

The SUV stopped, but only for a moment. It revved its engine and accelerated forward.

Olivia gripped the gun tighter for a moment as she considered emptying a clip into the windshield, but she chose to take two quick steps to her right and dive over the drainage ditch instead.

In a single motion she tumbled back to her feet and ran after the SUV to get a glimpse of the license plate. All she was able to see was a confirmation that it was the same mud-smeared plate from before.

By the time she made it back to her car, the SUV was out of sight. She grabbed her radio. "Dispatch, do you copy? I need an APB put out for a newer model Chevy Traverse, dark gray. The bastard just tried to run me over."

Jonas stared at the ceiling, though it was too dark to see anything. He had created a makeshift bed on the thick carpet of his walk-in closet with a pillow and a bedspread. He'd hoped he could fall asleep as long as his wife's crime scene was no longer in plain view, but the closet had proved to be little improvement.

In the darkness, his sense of smell had taken over, and the aroma of his wife's clothes tormented him. The thought of never smelling her unique scent again had a steady stream of tears running down his temples to his earlobes.

If he could have just lain there and revisited the good times he'd shared with her, then he would have welcomed the pain. But every time he remembered a moment with her in his arms, an unwanted image of her with someone else attacked his mind.

Rolling to his feet, he switched on the light and grabbed the pillow and bedspread.

Leaving his room, he headed for the bonus room. It was sparsely adorned with a TV, two bookshelves, and a couch. He tossed the pillow and bedspread on the couch and lay down. Rather than reminiscing, he focused on Jessica's investigation.

No matter which aspect of the case he tried to analyze, his mind circled around to her texts. Surely, her leaving work early and her death could not be a coincidence.

Jonas pulled out the card that Officer Selman had given him. It was kind of late to call, almost 10 p.m., but maybe she was a night owl. A few moments of indecision gave way to resolution, and he dialed the number.

"Hello?"

"Officer Selman?"

"Jonas? Are you out of prison?"

"Yeah, I just got out a couple of hours ago."

"Good, I'm glad."

There was a moment of awkward silence; the warmth in her statement threw him off a bit. After a brief pause, he stammered out, "Did you have any luck tracking down the landscaping crew?"

"Yeah, I was able to talk to the owner today. He gave me a promising lead on a crewmember he recently fired. Pepe Delgado."

Jonas sat up. "That's great. Do you know where he lives? Are you going to bring him in for questioning? Maybe we can put him in a lineup and see if my neighbor can identify him."

"Jonas, take a breath. I just left the house where he's staying. Unfortunately, as soon as I announced my presence, Pepe bolted out the back door and took off into the woods. I wasn't able to track him down."

"Okay. What's the next step? Are you guys going to stake out his house? Are you checking in with his known acquaintances?"

There was a pause long enough to make him look at his display screen to make sure the call hadn't been dropped. "Jonas, I'm the only one investigating your case. Vogel is convinced you're the killer and that he has everything he needs to convict you. Technically, I'm back to working traffic patrol and no longer officially assigned to your case. Everything I've done the last two days to track down other potential suspects has been done in an unofficial capacity. If Vogel finds out I'm still working leads, I will be in some serious hot water. I only tell you this so you understand that we have no resources at our disposal. Until we find some concrete evidence to exonerate you, we are limited in what we can do."

Jonas leaned forward on the couch, head down between his elbows. He felt nauseous. The whole Greenville county police force was focused on sending him to prison for life. All he had was one rogue Travelers Rest cop on his side.

"Why are you risking your career to help me?"

"Because I know you're innocent. I'm not going to be a part of an investigation that sends an innocent man to prison."

"So what do we do next?"

"We keep an eye out for Pepe and Eugene. If we can bring them in for questioning, maybe whichever one of them did it will trip up and give us something to work with. If we're lucky, with enough pressure, they might even confess."

"Do you want me to watch one of their houses while you watch the other?"

"I have to work traffic again tomorrow until evening, and I don't know if I like the idea of a civilian doing a stake-out by himself."

Jonas looked around the room, grasping for inspiration and a solution to their problems. His eyes fell on an old Polaroid camera sitting on the bookshelf for decoration. "What if I go out and get a couple of those motion-sensor cameras and attach them in an inconspicuous spot facing their houses? Then I could monitor them without being anywhere near and let you know if I see anything."

"That's probably illegal and sounds like a bad idea. If you can figure out a way to install them in an inconspicuous spot without being seen then it might help, but I would advise against it."

"I understand," Jonas responded, "but send me their addresses just in case I can figure something out."

Officer Selman let out a sigh on the other end of the phone. "Okay, I'll send you their addresses and a picture of Pepe so you know what he looks like. Please don't make me regret this. Be smart."

"I will. Don't worry about me."

"All right. Well, it's late and I have some things I need to do before I get some much-needed beauty sleep, so I'd better let you go. Unless there was something else you needed?"

"Actually, there is one other thing. I would like you to send me the texts you found on Jessica's phone."

He heard another deep sigh. "Jonas, I think that's a bad idea."

"Officer Selman, ple—"

"Jonas, you don't need to keep calling me Officer Selman. We're just two unofficial investigators trying to help one another out. Please call me Olivia."

"Oh, uh, okay. Olivia, will you please send me the texts? I need to know what they say. For my sanity. And I may see something in them that you wouldn't recognize as important."

After another pregnant pause, he heard resignation in her

tone. "Look, I'm starving, and I need a shower, but before I go to bed I will text you the screenshots I took of her texts."

"Thank you."

"Just don't do anything stupid after you read them."

"I won't. I promise. Goodnight, Olivia."

"Goodnight, Jonas."

With a million thoughts tumbling around his brain, Jonas stared at a fixed point on the wall, unmoving. He sat that way a long time before rising to his feet. There was so much to figure out, and the only thing he was certain of was that he would never be able to fall asleep before Off— Olivia sent him those texts. Might as well do something productive in the meantime.

He tiptoed to the door of his guest bedroom and gave it a couple of gentle knocks.

His mother responded. "Jonas, is that you?"

"Hey, is it okay if I borrow the rental car? I can't sleep, so I'm going to go to the 24-hour Walmart and pick up a few essentials."

"Sure, the keys are on the island in the kitchen. Do you want us to come with you?"

"No, no, you guys go back to sleep. I'll be back in a couple of hours."

"Okay, honey, be careful."

He would have to face driving Jessica's car at some point, but not tonight. Besides, he knew he would be back late and didn't want to open and close the loud garage door.

Jonas darted back to his bedroom to throw on some jeans and a long-sleeved black T-shirt, grabbed the keys off the island, and headed out into the night.

CHAPTER TWENTY-NINE

Blake had underestimated how painful this funeral business would be. Yesterday his mom had gone out and bought him a suit coat from Goodwill. It was two sizes too big and smelled like mothballs, but at least he wasn't "disgracing himself", according to his mom.

He felt like an idiot walking through the funeral home's doors, where a bunch of old people in dark suits milled about and spoke in hushed tones. One of them noticed him standing there like a big doofus and asked him who he was there to see.

He led Blake to a room where Ari and her dad were standing side by side, looking awkward. The face Ari's dad made when he spotted Blake almost made Blake pee his pants. It literally contorted in rage—almost like the face Arnold Schwarzenegger made in *Total Recall* when he was choking to death from a lack of oxygen.

He made a move towards Blake, but Ari stepped between them, tilted her right cheek towards her dad, and said, "Would you like to add a little rouge to this side of my face, too?"

Her dad freaked at that, looking around like a cornered cat burglar to see who might have overheard the comment, and then stormed to another corner of the room.

Ari looked at Blake with grateful eyes. "Thanks for coming."

"Sure. Glad I could be here," he lied.

"My grandparents want me to stand beside them. Will you stand with me?"

"Sure. Whatever you want."

She led him right past the open casket. You could tell it was Ari's mom, but she didn't look right. It was like a bloated version of her with a weird skin texture. Ari wedged herself and Blake into a spot between her grandparents and some other couple he had never seen before.

Within a few minutes, the few people meandering through the room had formed an organized line that grew longer every time he looked up.

Standing in the receiving line with Ari was a nightmare. A sea of people he didn't know introducing themselves, offering their condolences, and wondering who he was. Most of them said something to the effect of, "Oh, is this your boyfriend, Ari?"

She answered them differently every time.

"Actually, I don't even know this kid. What was your name again? Jake?"

"No, just a good friend from school."

"Yes, this is my new boyfriend, Blake."

"No, we're just friends with benefits."

"Yes, this is my longtime boyfriend, Blake. We've been dating since elementary school and became lovers this year."

Ari had always been a bit crazy, but now she seemed unhinged, like whatever had kept her from drawing outside the lines was gone. She kept grabbing his hand, and every time she did, he felt a thrill shoot through his body as it begged for more—while at the same time, terror trickled down his spine and the rational side of his mind screamed, "Run!"

In the brief lulls caused by someone holding up the line with a hug or conversation, Blake found his attention drawn to Ari's father. He had taken up a spot near the front of the line. Not once did he glance in their direction. Apparently, he was too preoccupied by the attention he was getting in the receiving line, or the lack thereof. Blake couldn't help but notice that at least twenty percent of the people offering their condolences skipped right past Ari's dad without so much as a nod or a handshake.

Ari's dad tried to play it off with a smile, like he didn't even notice, but Blake caught the flash of anger in his eyes every time it happened. Blake found it hilarious.

Serves you right, you jerk.

THE SUN WAS unbearable. The sidewalk was blindingly white as Jonas forced himself to put one foot in front of the other, his head pounding from lack of sleep. He was paying for his late-night escapade, but he didn't care. Having two live video feeds was worth it.

The installation at Eugene's place had been a breeze. There was a big, leafy tree with easy-to-climb branches in the yard directly across the street. The neighborhood had been motionless at one in the morning, and he was able to zip-tie the camera into place facing Eugene's front door in under ten minutes.

Pepe's neighborhood had been a different ballgame. Even after two in the morning four or five cars had passed by, forcing Jonas to duck and cover. None of the trees in the neighboring yards had branches he could climb; half the houses on the street had dogs that erupted in a barking frenzy whenever he walked nearby. One such frenzy brought a homeowner with a shotgun to the front porch, but Jonas had managed to dive into the drainage ditch before he could be seen.

Ultimately, he'd decided on attaching the camera to the ivy-covered awning of a dilapidated house two doors up and across the street. This meant he had to actually step up onto someone's front porch, but by the appearance of the trash-covered veranda, it wasn't a homeowner that paid attention to detail. With any luck, the camera wouldn't be noticed until Christmas.

It was after 3:00 a.m. by the time he arrived home. After slipping through the front door and tiptoeing to the bonus room, he should have gone to sleep immediately.

But he hadn't.

He couldn't.

There had been an email in his inbox that was impossible to ignore with a brief message from Officer Selman: *Here you go. Don't do anything stupid.* Attached to the email were fourteen images.

For the next two hours, Jonas had tortured himself with a thousand cuts by reading and rereading every text between Jessica and "Dee". He'd cried. He'd punched the couch over and over again. He'd even run to his bathroom and thrown up once.

By the end of the two hours, he had a fairly clear picture of how they had conducted their affair. All the excuses, the odd behaviors, and the last-second plans made sense now.

The sexting and graphic pictures had been especially hard to stomach. Jessica had never done anything like that with him. She'd always said it was too risky. "What if someone hacked our phones? Can you imagine how embarrassing that would be?"

You were right, Jess. It is embarrassing.

He'd tried to put those texts out of his mind and focus on the ones that mattered. The ones at the beginning and end of the thread were of particular interest.

About a month into their relationship, a particular text from Jessica had caught his eye.

Jessica: I'll meet you in the pool parking lot and show you the way.

And another one from a couple of weeks later.

Jessica: Don't forget to park in the same place. Look for the flamingo.

It was obvious to him that these were texts arranging rendezvous in their home. The flamingo referred to the lawn ornament Jessica kept in the garden behind their house. She'd showed this guy how to park in the pool parking lot and get to their house the back way to avoid cameras.

Jonas had the urge to set his mattress on fire, but he squashed those feelings for the time being. He had too much to do. Maybe later.

The last texts Jessica had sent were to arrange a similar meet-up with this guy. That was why she'd left work early. This guy explicitly stated his intention of coming over to her house shortly before she was killed. *How is this guy not the prime suspect? Even if he didn't do it himself, he's got to be the one who orchestrated it.* It seemed too far-fetched that Jessica's stalker, or some landscaping crew thief, had just happened to be there to walk through the door left open for this guy.

Jonas just needed to prove it—which was why he was walking uphill, facing the sun with a piercing headache, to interview his neighbors living near the pool parking lot.

The pool was located at the end of a short cul-de-sac near the front entrance. Standing in the middle of the cul-de-sac, Jonas did a slow ninety-degree turn, taking in the parking lot and adjoining homes. He was immediately drawn to the two homes without a fence. The space between them was on an almost direct line from the parking lot entrance to the retention pond that backed up to the homes on that side of the cul-de-sac.

He decided to start with the house on the right, since the garage door was open. Once he bypassed the Suburban in the driveway, he found a middle-aged man bent over a lawn mower.

"Is it that time already?"

The man looked up, startled, but put on a friendly enough smile. "I'm afraid so. My Bermuda grass is still dormant, but the weeds didn't get the memo. They need cutting before the HOA police start sending me notices."

"Yeah, no one wants that," Jonas agreed. "This may seem like an odd question, but were you by any chance home a week ago Thursday, April 19th?"

"You mean the day that girl down the street got killed? No, I'm afraid not. I work nine to five Monday through Friday. Why do you ask?"

"We're trying to track down a potential murder suspect. We believe someone in a black hoodie and dark jeans parked in the pool parking lot, walked between your house and your neighbor's, and murdered the woman down the street. Then escaped back the same way."

"Are you serious? I saw that guy."

Jonas's mouth went dry. It was all he could do to choke out his follow-up question. "How?"

"With my front door camera. I didn't know there was a murder until a couple of days after it happened. We're not in the loop with all the neighborhood gossip. But once I found out, I read about the details online and then checked my door camera videos from that morning. Around 11:15, this guy parks his SUV in the pool parking lot and walks right by my house, wearing a black hoodie and looking all suspicious.”

“Did you see his face? Did he look Hispanic?”

“No, I couldn't see his face. He kept his head down and the hood up. That's why I say he looked suspicious, not to mention the fact that he walked directly through my yard.”

“Was he wearing yellow gloves?”

“I don't know. He had his hands in the pockets of the hoodie the whole time. Even on the way back to his car.”

“Can I take a look at these videos? Do you still have them?”

“Sure, they come directly to an app on my phone.”

The man pulled a phone from his back pocket and used both hands to hold it as he navigated the screen. He swiped upwards a couple of times and then stopped. Jonas's heart sank when he saw the look on his face.

“Shoot, I forgot the app only keeps footage for the last seven days. The videos from that day were deleted two days ago.”

“There's no way to retrieve them?”

“Not that I know of. I've tried before and couldn't figure a way to do it. Once they're gone, they're gone. Sorry, man.”

Suppressing the sudden rage Jonas felt was like trying to put a lid on a volcano. If the cops had done their job rather than focusing all their resources on him, then they would've had video evidence of the killer coming and going. He squatted and placed a hand on the pavement to steady himself.

Don't take your frustration out on this guy. Stay calm.

He stood back up and made his face appear as calm as possible. “Why didn't you report what you saw to the police?”

The man shrugged. “I thought about it, but I figured if the cops aren't asking around, they must already know who did it. Then I saw that they arrested the husband, so I figured it was a done deal.”

Jonas nodded. "Seems like a reasonable assumption. Unfortunately, the cops have made a mess of this case. I know for certain that the husband didn't do it. What can you tell me about the SUV?"

The man rubbed his chin. "I don't know. It was just your typical SUV. I remember it being a dark color. Either black or a dark gray, like charcoal. It struck me as a nicer, newer one, but I don't recall the brand. Sorry, I'm not a big car guy, and I was more focused on the man walking through my yard."

"Any chance you got a glimpse of the license plate and can recall any of the letters or numbers?"

"No, I'm afraid not. The picture quality on these cameras is pretty good, but you can't make out license plates with them. At least not from here to the pool. But you might be able to get that information from the old guy that lives right next to the parking lot." He pointed to a blue house with white trim to the right of the parking lot. "I was telling him about the man who parked by the pool and walked right through my yard, and he went on a tirade about the guy. He said he's seen him park in the pool parking lot several times over the past couple of months even though the pool is closed, and he said the guy's always walking through someone's yard."

This time, Jonas didn't have to fake the smile on his face as he extended his hand. "Thank you. You have been a tremendous help."

"Sure, any time. My name's Derrick, by the way. What's yours?"

"Jonas. Jonas Turner."

Watching the blood drain from the man's face as his eyes grew as big as saucers amused him more than it should have, but reflection and repentance would have to wait. He jogged across the cul-de-sac to the blue and white house.

Before he even got to the top step, the door opened. An older black man with thick grayish-white hair on the sides and a few wisps on top stared him down. "Whatchu want?"

"I was told you might have seen a dark-colored SUV in the pool parking lot last Thursday, April 19th."

"I didn't see nothin' last Thursday. I was at the doctor's office getting poked and prodded all dagum day. Not that it's any of your business. What's this about?"

"I'm investigating the death of Jessica Turner. Your neighbor across the street, Derrick, said you were familiar with the SUV that parks in the pool parking lot on occasion."

"You the police? You don't look like the police."

"No, I'm more of a private investigator."

"I find it hard to believe that girl needs a private investigator. I bet the whole police force is looking for that white girl's killer. Now, you know who needs a private investigator? A brown girl. Those are the cases that don't get solved."

Jonas grabbed the bridge of his nose, trying to mask his frustration. This was not going as he'd hoped. "Sir, it is extremely important that we track down the owner of that vehicle."

"You think that pretty boy killed that girl?"

"You know what this guy looks like?"

"Of course I know what he looks like. He walks right by my house and through my neighbor's yard at least once a month. One time, I came out here and asked him what's he doing, and he just ignored me, like the words that come out of my mouth meant nothin'."

"What did the guy look like?"

"He looked like you."

"What do you mean?"

"I mean he looked like you. A pretty white boy. He mighta been a little shorter, and his hair mighta been a little darker, but those are the only differences I see."

Jonas's head was killing him. He just wanted this

interview to be over. "Did you by any chance write his license plate down?"

"Of course I did. A man acting all suspicious like that, walking through people's yards and going behind people's fences. I took down his license plate the first time I saw him go back behind the houses in case something went missing. I'll make you a copy of it."

The man disappeared for a minute and a half, reappearing with a turquoise sticky note. Jonas took the note, transfixed on the three letters and three numbers written there.

"Is that it?"

Jonas looked up at the old man, still feeling a bit overwhelmed. "Yes, that's it. Thank you for your time."

His eyes were open on the walk back to his house, but a carnival of clowns could have paraded down the street and he wouldn't have noticed. He actually walked a half a block past his house before he realized it. The unfamiliar car in his driveway had probably sabotaged his subconscious awareness.

The rental car reminded him he needed to pick up his car from the repair shop. It also reminded him to check the video feeds on his phone. He sat down on his front porch steps between the two monster hydrangea bushes and pulled up the app.

There had been no movement at Eugene's the last hour. A car had pulled into Pepe's driveway, but only a woman got out, and only a woman greeted her at the door.

Jonas pulled the sticky note from his pocket. Selman cou—Olivia could look up the license plate and nail down the driver in two seconds, but part of him wanted to find out before she did. He opened a browser on his phone and searched, *How can I find the owner of a license plate?* Several ads popped up for companies who claimed to do what he wanted. He scrolled through the descriptions and selected the most promising-sounding one.

After he'd typed in the license plate, the screen said, *We are compiling your comprehensive report.* Thirty seconds later, it told him, *You can access your report for $1. Enter your payment information below.*

Jonas sighed in frustration. He knew if he gave this site any of his personal information, he could expect to be bombarded by spam emails and would have to remember to cancel the subscription he was no doubt signing up for. Was the hassle really worth it?

Screw it. He was dying to see the name attached to the license plate. He put in his credit card information, agreed to be charged $19.99 after the first month, and opened the report.

The name that popped up wasn't a surprise, but it was surreal seeing his suspicions confirmed. His vision narrowed as darkness crowded the edges of his sight. He put his right hand down on the top step to steady himself. Keeping his eyes closed and taking deep, slow breaths helped the moment pass.

When he finally opened his eyes, he felt somewhat normal. He pulled up the most recent addition to his contact list and pressed call.

She answered immediately. "Hello?"

"Hey, this is Jonas."

"Hey, Jonas, this is Olivia."

There was a playful mocking in her tone that threw him off. For a split second, he forgot why he'd called. "I would like to meet up and touch base. I've uncovered a few things, and I would like to talk them through with you."

"Well, consider me intrigued. I'm going to be starving once I get off this shift. Why don't you take me out to dinner and tell me what's on that mind of yours?"

The suggestion caught him off-guard again. "Oh, um, okay.

Where do you want to meet?"

"How about Shortfields in downtown TR? Say 8 p.m.?"

"Okay, I'll get there a little early and get us a seat. It can be a little busy there on Saturday nights."

"Sounds good. See you tonight, Jonas."

"Okay. See you then."

Jonas remained seated on the steps, staring at the empty street, trying to imagine eating dinner in a restaurant with Olivia. He struggled to picture a scenario where it wasn't all kinds of awkward.

CHAPTER THIRTY

Olivia kept an eye on her hair as she shook her head in the mirror. She wasn't happy with one strand that lacked the bounce of the others. Grabbing her curling iron, she rewrapped the troublesome strand while leaning forward to check her makeup one more time.

Her conscious mind had spent the last hour interrogating her subconscious. *Why are you wearing makeup? You never wear makeup. Why are you doing your hair? You never take the time to do your hair. Why are you wearing that bra? You never wear that bra.*

Olivia stepped back from the mirror and turned sideways. Going from a sports bra to a pushup bra was definitely a game-changer. Couple it with her favorite jeans, and she wasn't hiding any of her curves tonight. Facing the mirror again, she examined the top she was wearing: a form-fitting white button-down top with thin blue vertical pinstripes, top button undone to show just a hint of cleavage.

She stared at the second button, straining not to come undone. Reaching for it, she undid it and reassessed.

Hmm, that might be too much. She buttoned it back up.

You realize this isn't a date, right?

Yes, I realize that.

Then what are you doing? This is unlike you.

Nothing. Is there something wrong with looking good in public for once?

Hands on her hips, Olivia rotated at the waist, analyzing every angle of her face and hair. Taking in her whole reflection one more time, her left hand lifted to the second shirt button, rubbing it between thumb and forefinger. After a moment of reflection, she popped it loose and headed out the door.

A YOUNG, BLONDE-HEADED hostess walked Jonas to his table—a small two-seater near the back. He would have preferred a bigger table that projected less intimacy, but he had already waited forty minutes for this one and wasn't about to wait longer.

It was ten minutes after eight, so Olivia should be walking through the door at any moment. Jonas thumbed through the extensive menu. He was eager to get the ordering out of the way so they could get down to business.

Periodically glancing up towards the entrance where a throng of people stood waiting to be seated, he did a double take as the crowd suddenly parted. Men rushed to make room for someone coming through, nearly trampling their significant others in the process. Initially Jonas was too busy watching the angry expressions of wives and girlfriends to see what caused the disruption, but once the woman passed by the host desk, he understood. A gorgeous woman with scandalous curves was making her way to the back of the restaurant, walking almost directly towards him.

Not wanting to appear like he was checking her out, Jonas

focused on watching everyone watching her. Almost without fail, as she approached a table, the men at the table would look up in her direction, and then turn their heads and check out her backside as she passed. *Guys are such idiots*, he thought. Was a glance at a beautiful woman really worth the next hour of frosty conversation?

The woman was close enough to his table now that he had to stare down at his menu to resist the temptation to become one of those guys.

"Thanks for getting us a table. It's a madhouse tonight."

Jonas flinched at the sound of Olivia's voice, and looked up as she settled into her seat. Her appearance was so dazzling that all he could think was, *Don't look down. Don't look down. Don't look down.*

"What are you going to get?" she asked.

"I, uh, I think I'm going to get the TR jumbo burger."

"Ooh, yeah, that's one of my favorites. I think I'll have the same."

Their waiter sidled up to the table a split-second later and asked what they were drinking. They went ahead and ordered everything: two TR jumbo burgers with fries, a sweet tea for her, and a water for him.

As the waiter left, awkward silence filled the space. Jonas jumped in to counteract it. "You look different out of uniform."

"Yeah, I don't get out much, so I decided to do my hair. It looks a lot different with curls as opposed to being pulled back tight in a bun."

Jonas gave her a sarcastic grin. "Yes, that hair of yours is quite the head-turner. I'm sure that's why every guy was falling out of his seat to get a look at you."

Olivia returned his mischievous grin. "If it's not my hair, then what is it, Jonas?"

Jonas threw up his hands. "Oh, I agree, it must be the hair.

I wouldn't know what else could cause such a reaction."

Olivia rolled her eyes and crossed her arms. "So, what do you have for me? You said you wanted to talk. Let's hear it."

It was difficult to shift gears into case mode, but he gathered his thoughts and laid it out. "I saw something in Jessica's texts. She referenced meeting her guy in the pool parking lot to show him the way. In a later text she references the flamingo lawn decoration we have in our backyard. I think it's safe to conclude that Jessica's lover was familiar with the path from the pool parking lot to the back of our house by way of the retention pond." Jonas looked up to make sure she was following. "So I spent the afternoon talking to neighbors living in the cul-de-sac adjacent to the pool parking lot. I talked to a guy who caught our black hoodie suspect on a doorbell camera leaving and returning to a black SUV in the pool parking lot."

Olivia's bright green eyes sparked with interest, and her ruby-red lips parted in the shape of an 'O'. "He has our suspect on camera? Can you see his face?"

"He *had* our suspect on camera. But his app deleted the video after seven days, so he no longer has it. And he said he couldn't make out the face because the suspect kept his head down the entire time."

"Why didn't he give this evidence to the police?"

"He said he was under the impression that the police had already arrested the killer."

Olivia looked sick, frustrated, and embarrassed all at the same time. "I'm so sorry, Jonas. I should have interviewed those neighbors. We should have that video as evidence."

"I don't blame you. I know you've been busting your butt chasing down all kinds of leads by yourself. The help you've provided means the world to me. Detective Vogel, on the other hand, I do blame. If he hadn't thrown me in prison, I would have retrieved that video in time. But all is not lost.

While we don't have our suspect on video, I know who he is."

"How?"

"An old man who lives right next to the parking lot took down the guy's license plate."

Olivia's eyes narrowed. "You've already looked up the license plate, haven't you?"

"Yep."

"Well, just don't sit there. Who does the vehicle belong to?"

"David London."

There was no attractive 'O' shape when her lips parted this time. Her jaw went slack, and her eyes lost focus as she spoke in a hoarse whisper. "That's not possible."

"It's his car. A black Toyota Sequoia. He must have slipped out of the hospital and then returned to establish his alibi. I don't know how he did it, but I'm sure he did. Not only do we have his text messages arranging the meeting, but we have eyewitnesses spotting his car in the pool parking lot the morning of the murder."

"You're telling me you have two eyewitnesses who spotted David London's Toyota Sequoia in the pool parking lot on the day of the murder?"

Jonas squirmed in his seat. He was tempted to just say yes without any of the qualifiers nagging at his conscience, but his sense of integrity won out. "Technically, the old guy wasn't home at the time of the murder. He didn't see the Toyota Sequoia that day, but he wrote down the license plate from all the other times that vehicle parked in the pool parking lot."

"Was the guy who caught the SUV on his doorbell camera sure it was a Toyota Sequoia?"

"He wasn't sure about the specific model, but he remembered it being a dark-colored SUV."

"I don't know, Jonas. There are a lot of dark-colored SUVs out there. Heck, I was nearly run down by one the other night."

Jonas sat up with alarm. "What? What do you mean 'run down'? By who?"

"I don't know. The license plate was covered with mud, but it was a Chevy Traverse, not a Toyota Sequoia. Somebody in a different 'dark-colored SUV' tried to take me out, and I have to assume it has something to do with this case. No one has tried to run me over prior to this murder investigation."

Jonas leaned back in his seat, his mind swirling with the possibilities. Did London have another SUV? Or was there really someone else trying to prevent this murder from being solved?

Olivia's voice snapped him back to the present. "Listen, Jonas, right now all we have is testimony of a now deleted video who can't recall the make and model of the SUV he saw. Without an eyewitness who spotted the license plate of the SUV in the pool parking lot on the day of the murder, we only have weak circumstantial evidence."

Jonas leaned forward, emphasizing each point with animated hand gestures. "Come on, Olivia. We have David London's texts saying he's coming over to see Jessica. Then we have a dark-colored SUV parking in the pool parking lot the morning of the murder, as we know David London has done in the past. Whether it's enough to convict him or not, he's our guy."

Olivia leaned forward herself, putting her head in her hands and staring at the table, apparently in deep thought. Jonas waited for her to speak.

"I'll go back and review all the video surveillance footage at the hospital, if I can. Let's just hope they store the footage for longer than seven days and that they don't request a new warrant. There's no way Vogel will sign off on another."

"Well, I hope you're given access to the footage, and it's possible that you will be able to track his movements throughout that morning, but I think it's just as likely that he figured out a way to leave the hospital undetected."

Olivia looked up at him. "How would he pull that off?"

"I don't know. He could have found an emergency exit without video surveillance. He could have thrown on a coat and a ball cap to change his appearance. He could fake being deathly ill and keep his head down as an accomplice wheeled him out in a wheelchair. The possibilities are endless."

Olivia shook her head. "I don't know whether to be impressed or concerned by your ability to devise an endless number of plans to avoid detection."

"Yeah, you should be happy I use my intellectual prowess for good. I would make a great supervillain if it wasn't for Jesus."

The waiter swung over to their table with the burgers and fries. Jonas bowed his head and said a three-second thank-you prayer in his head.

"I visited your church last Sunday."

Jonas looked up from his food. "I know. Pastor Joshua told me. He visited me while I was in prison. You made a favorable impression. He said he had a good feeling about you."

"I don't know why he felt that way, but I'm glad. I enjoyed his sermon. It wasn't like any sermon I've ever heard. And the songs were amazing. I was truly moved by them, and I didn't even know the lyrics."

"Yeah, we're blessed with a lot of great vocalists and musicians, and there have been a lot of great worship songs that have come out lately. Have you ever been a church-goer?"

"I went to an Episcopalian church when I was younger, but it's been a while. Last Sunday was probably the first time I stepped foot in a church in thirteen or fourteen years."

"What made you stop attending?"

Olivia looked away and visibly swallowed. "It just became hard to believe that there was a God out there who cared about people."

Jonas paused mid-bite. He was dying to know why a loving God had become hard to believe in, but the vagueness of her statement warned him to proceed with caution. He decided not to press the issue. "I hope you don't find this question offensive, but it's been driving me nuts that I can't place your ethnicity. If you don't mind me asking, what does your ancestry look like?"

The mischievous smile returned to her lips. "Guess."

"No, no, no. I don't want to offend by guessing wrong."

"You've got to give me your best guess, or I won't tell you."

"Ahhh, you're killing me. Okay. I'm going to guess Venezuelan."

"Nope."

"Was I close?"

"Nope."

"Really? Now, you've really got to tell me."

"My dad is half German and half Jamaican, and my mom is full-blooded Cherokee."

"Cherokee. I can see it now. Wow, what a beautiful combination. How did those three bloodlines cross paths?"

"My grandfather's family fled to America when Hitler rose to power, and my grandfather met my grandmother on a vacation getaway to Jamaica. They met at a dance club, fell madly in love, and he brought her back to America. It was a lot easier to do that in those days. My mom and dad met at Furman University. My dad was a brand-new college professor. My mom, the pride and joy of a Principal Chief in the Cherokee nation, was one of his students. They always claimed that they weren't romantically involved while she was still a student, but I have my doubts, along with everyone else. Either way, they got married six months after she graduated, and they had me a year later."

"That is an amazing family legacy. Maybe the most interesting one I've ever heard. Do your parents still live in town?"

"No, my dad accepted a position at Duke University a few years ago. He teaches philosophy up there. My mom is no longer with us."

Jonas put down the fry he had halfway to his mouth. "I'm so sorry. That's so young to lose your mother. I can only imagine how hard that must have been on you and your dad."

Olivia reached over to her sweet tea. Peering at the glass, she drew a vertical line through the condensation with her forefinger. "It was hard. Even more so because of the way she was killed."

She turned the glass a quarter of an inch and drew another line down the side. Jonas felt like a hiker stumbling across a doe in the woods. If he could just be still enough, maybe she wouldn't run away.

When Olivia looked up from her glass to meet his gaze, there was resolve in her eyes. "My mother was raped and murdered when I was twelve. Strangled to death in her own home. They never caught the guy. Happened while I was at school and my dad was at work. When she didn't pick me up from school and wouldn't answer the phone, I called my dad to pick me up. We searched the house for her together. I was the one that found her in the bathtub. At first, we thought it might have been some kind of terrible accident, but the detectives who arrived could tell it was a homicide right away.

"My dad hates what I do. He thinks it's a 'waste of a perfectly good mind.' But I know what it feels like to have your life shattered by a violent crime, and I can't think of a more useful way to live my life than to catch violent criminals and stop them from hurting anyone else. That's why I majored in Criminology in college and why I've spent the last four years as a cop. All in the hopes of one day becoming a detective and actually finding the guys who sexually assault and murder people."

Olivia resumed drawing on her glass of sweet tea.

They sat in silence for a while before Jonas brought up the question weighing on his mind. "Is that why you stopped going to church?"

Olivia gave him a sad smile and slowly nodded. "I woke up the following Sunday and put on a dress as usual, but I found my dad still in bed. He was an early riser, so that was unusual. When he told me we weren't going to church, I put my pajamas back on and went downstairs to watch TV. That was the last time we even talked about it."

Jonas shook his head. He wished he had the words to comfort her. "I can't imagine losing my mom at such a young age. The heartache you and your dad experienced must have been overwhelming. I wish you'd never had to experience something like that."

"If anyone could understand what it was like, it would be you. You're living through it right now. So tell me, are you going to go back to church? Has this experience affected your faith in God?"

"If it's had any effect on my faith, it's only served to make it stronger."

"How is that possible?"

"I believe God is the source of all truth, all hope, and all peace. This mess I'm in has me turning to him now more than ever. I don't think I could get out of bed in the morning if I didn't believe in his promises. God promises that he will work everything out for the good of those who love him and serve him, and I'm clinging to that promise. Maybe it won't come true for me until the next life, but I'm trusting that he still has great things in store for me in this one."

Olivia leaned forward and rested her chin on her clasped hands. "I love your optimism. Your faith and resolve in the midst of this disaster is kind of inspiring. I just don't understand how you can be so sure that there is a God who loves you and cares for you."

Jonas picked up his unused straw and began bending it in random places as he composed his thoughts. "I made the decision to give my heart to Jesus very young. It's hard to explain why you believe at that age. It was like the air I breathed. I couldn't see it, but I knew it filled me up and kept me alive.

"I've always been an analytical person who wants to know everything, so in high school and college, it was very important to me to make sure what I believed was true. I studied every major religion and read book after book on philosophy and theology. Nothing I read compared to the Bible. The wisdom, the insight, the influence—it's so far beyond any other text. There's a reason it's the most read book in history, by an unfathomable margin. Societies flourish when its teachings are followed, and crumble when they are ignored. For so many reasons, I'm convinced that the Bible is God's word and we were meant to follow it.

"Then there's what I have seen and felt with my own eyes. At times, I have felt Him communicating to me. Not audibly, but I know the thoughts that have formed in my mind at times are not my own. And there have been times, like finding Jessica's body, or being tackled by a SWAT team, or sitting alone in a maximum-security cell, where I have prayed for help and experienced an immediate peace and comfort.

"I don't know. I just know he's real. Sorry, I know I'm rambling on and on."

Olivia shook her head. He liked the way her long, wavy curls bounced around her face.

"No, don't apologize. I like listening to you talk about what you believe. I would love to have your faith." She smiled another sad smile that did something to his chest. He wished in that moment that he could transfer some of his faith to her.

CHAPTER THIRTY-ONE

For the second time in the last five minutes, a waitress walked by, giving them the stink-eye. Their waiter had settled the bill with them over an hour ago, and the restaurant had all but cleared out. They had talked for hours about anything and everything, and Jonas found himself wishing it wouldn't end. Feeling normal for the first time since the murder had reawakened something—a desire to live.

Olivia turned her head towards the entrance, scanning the restaurant. "I think we'd better get out of here before the wait staff throws us out."

"I know, but there was one more thought about the case I wanted to share with you."

"All right, let's hear it."

"I've been thinking about the text exchange between Jessica and this David London guy on the morning of the murder. They're sending messages to each other until shortly before her death. To do that, London would have to have the phone with him, and he would likely keep it with him in case something came up. Can't the police track which towers a cell phone pings? If so, we can track where this London guy was during the murder even if he found a way to sneak out of the hospital."

He had trouble reading the look on Olivia's face.

"You know, Jonas, it's really annoying that you keep coming up with ways to crack this case that I haven't thought of."

"Hey, I'm the one sitting around all day with nothing to do but think about the case while life in prison hangs over my head. You've got a life and a full-time job, in addition to your freelance work to help me."

She smiled a playful grin. "I don't have much of a life, but I do have a lot to do tomorrow between reviewing video footage and begging for a warrant to track a cell phone. But before we go, I have one more question for you, too."

"Okay, shoot."

"When the forensic lab shared its findings with me, there was one detail that confused them, and I haven't been able to make heads or tails of it either. All along the blood trail leading from your bedroom to the back door, there are big oval circles of Jessica's blood."

"How big?"

"Pretty big for drops of blood. About this size." Olivia held up both hands in the shape of an oval a little bigger than a golf ball. "It looks like some kind of fabric was pressed down on droplets of blood to spread them out that way. The ovals were relatively uniform in shape and size. The lab supervisor joked that it looked like someone walked in blood with a soft peg leg. I've been racking my brain for a realistic alternative. Do you happen to have a cane or crutches lying around your house?"

"No, I'm not old enough or stylish enough for a cane, and we've never had crutches in our house."

"No pogo stick or stilts, I'm guessing?"

Jonas started to laugh, but something nagging at the back of his mind strangled the laugh in his throat. He stared off into the empty dining room to his left.

When the unformed thought finally crawled its way to the surface, he whipped his head back to Oliva. "I don't have anything like that, but I *have* seen people on stilts in our neighborhood. Our subdivision is relatively new. The builders use a Hispanic crew to paint every new house that goes up. They always have a couple of guys on stilts painting the ceilings and upper trim."

Olivia's mouth dropped open again. "Are you saying I need to chase after another Hispanic work crew?"

"Possibly, but I wonder if that landscaping crew has anyone who has experience on stilts. Maybe Pepe does. We really need to find that guy."

Olivia burst out laughing and slapped her hands together. "Are we really this desperate for leads? Now we're looking for a psycho slasher on stilts? Why would anyone commit murder while wearing stilts?"

Jonas shook his head. "No, I'm not suggesting he stabbed my wife while wearing stilts. I just think it's possible he put them on when he used my shoe to frame me, in order to avoid leaving any of his own shoe prints."

"Huh. That sounds a lot more plausible. Still far-fetched, but plausible. Great, my day tomorrow just got fuller. Check the video surveillance at the hospital, get a warrant for David London's phone, and track down the stilt-wearers on these work crews. You're going to be the death of me, Jonas. Now let's get out of this restaurant before they throw us out."

Dodging a waiter who had started mopping the floor, they hustled towards the exit. Once outside, Jonas pointed his thumb down the street. "I'm parked this way. Where are you?"

Olivia pointed in the opposite direction. "I'm up this way.

That's why I was late. I couldn't find parking anywhere. I ended up parking on the grass behind that outdoor sports store."

"Sunrift Adventures? It's not very well lit behind there. I'll walk you to your car."

"That's very sweet of you, but I can take care of myself." Oliva held up her little purse. "If any bad guys jump out at me, my Glock will have something to say about it."

"Are you sure? I would be happy to walk you to your car."

"Goodnight, Jonas. Thank you for dinner."

Jonas watched as she began walking up the street with a little more sway than he had noticed before. Once again, he found himself thinking, *Don't look down. Don't look down. Don't look down.*

OLIVIA COULD FEEL Jonas's eyes still on her. She was aware of the movement of her hips and couldn't resist making her movements a little more pronounced than usual. The conversation had been riveting; three hours had felt like thirty minutes. Her cheeks were sore from smiling so much.

Jessica was an idiot for sleeping around on this guy.

And *she* was an idiot for not thinking about tracking David London's phone. There was no way she could have come up with the landscaper-or-painter-on-stilts theory, but she should have come up with the phone-tracking idea on her own. If she could place London's phone at the scene of the crime, backed up by the eyewitnesses who'd seen his vehicle in the pool parking lot, she would have enough to arrest him. The problem was getting the warrant to force London's cell service provider to hand over the report of his movements. Vogel would probably flip his lid if she even suggested it to him, and she didn't have any judge friends like he did. She thought about asking Chief Duncan, but he was usually hesitant to cross jurisdictional lines.

After scuttling across the little side street, she began speedwalking through the Sunrift Adventures parking lot. Jonas was right; it wasn't very well lit. She unzipped her purse just in case.

The parking lot had emptied out by this time of night. There were only two other vehicles in the lot: a pickup truck near the store and an SUV parked way in the back, on the grass, about twenty yards down from her patrol car.

The closer she got to her car, the more her eyes were drawn to the SUV. It was dark gray. It was a Chevy. It looked like the same model as the one from the other night. She walked right past her car, eyes laser-focused on the driver's side window of the Chevy, hand near the opening of her purse.

She sensed, more than heard, movement from behind her, but before she could turn her head, she saw a flash of black dart below her chin. Dropping her purse as instinct drove her to use both hands, she desperately clawed at the arm that was cutting off her air supply. It was like a steel vise.

With the assailant's other arm pressed into the back of her neck, she was losing consciousness fast. Dropping to her knees, she tried to flip him over the top of her, but he held on tight, letting his full bodyweight pin her down.

Her vision narrowed to a pinprick. *This is how I'm going to die.*

Thwack! The weight on her back and the arm around her neck were suddenly gone. Gasping for breath, Olivia looked up and saw Jonas wrestling with a man dressed in all black, wearing a ski mask.

She crawled over to her purse and pulled out her service piece. "Get away from him, Jonas, so I can shoot him."

It hurt to talk and her voice sounded like a lifelong smoker's, but at the sound of it, Jonas pushed off the man, who put up his hands.

"Jonas, could you grab my keys from the purse and go get a pair of handcuffs from my car. You'll find some in the door."

Jonas grabbed the keys and sprinted to her car.

She moved a little closer to the man in black. "Please, I'm begging you, give me a reason to shoot you."

His eyes were darting around, but the rest of him remained perfectly still, on his knees with his hands up.

Jonas returned with the handcuffs.

Eyes never leaving the ski mask, Olivia barked out an order. "Lie face down, hands behind your back. Jonas, go ahead and put the cuffs on him. I'll make sure they're secure after."

Once Jonas had both hands cuffed, she reached down and made the cuffs even tighter while keeping her gun pointed at the back of the ski mask. She gave the man a thorough pat down and then emptied the contents of his pockets. The only items she found on him were several long, black zip ties and three condoms.

No weapon. No ID. Just zip ties and condoms. Olivia stood up and moved towards the man's head, struggling to hold her gun steady. The man rolled onto his side as she reached down and snatched the ski mask off his face.

It was Grady.

"You sick bastard. I'm going to kill you!"

She reared back to kick him in the face when she felt herself lifted off the ground as a calming voice spoke in her ear.

"Easy, easy. Don't give this guy a reason to get you suspended or fired. He's not worth it."

Soothing words weren't enough to quell her rage. She screamed at Grady from Jonas's arms. "You came here to rape me? You get knocked down at work, and your revenge is to stalk me and rape me? I'm going to end your stupid, miserable life."

Jonas spun her around, letting her go but putting himself between her and Grady. "Olivia, I know he deserves it, but you can't strike this man while he's in handcuffs. Let's think this through rationally."

"The rational thing to do would be to kick him until his sick, twisted brains fall out!" Olivia closed the distance, forcing Jonas to give up more of the ground between him and Grady.

He held up his hands as he continued to inch backwards. "I know, I know, but this guy isn't worth all the trouble that would put you in. How about we just arrest him and let him get the crap kicked out of him in prison?"

As Jonas spoke, he continued to shuffle backwards, eventually backing right into Grady. When he made contact, he stumbled, waved his arms wildly as his left foot lifted into the air. Olivia reached out to steady him as he cried out, "Whoa, whoa!"—and his foot suddenly swung back down and landed squarely in the center of Grady's face.

Grady screamed.

"Oh, I am so sorry," Jonas exclaimed. "I didn't realize how close I was to you and tripped. Are you okay?"

"You broke my nowth, you athhole!"

"I am so sorry. I can be so clumsy sometimes. Hopefully the doctors will be able to reset that. It looks like it really hurts."

Olivia kept looking back and forth from Grady to Jonas. It had all happened so quickly and naturally, she still wasn't sure whether it was an accident or if Jonas had done it on purpose.

Until he turned his back to Grady and gave her a wink.

That's when the thought of killing Grady was replaced by another. *I think I love this man.*

CHAPTER THIRTY-TWO

The sun was just now peeking over the tree line, blinding Olivia with its rays. It was way too early for her to be up, considering how late she'd gotten to bed last night. She felt like the roadkill she carefully veered around to keep her car's tires clean—some poor opossum that had crossed at the wrong time.

By the time her fellow cops had hauled Grady away last night, and she had answered all their questions and filled out her report, it had been after two in the morning. She would have happily slept until noon, but a dream had forced her awake at 7:04 a.m. Her right hand went to her throat just thinking about it. She rarely remembered her dreams, but this one—a boa constrictor wrapped around her neck, squeezing tighter and tighter—wouldn't leave her mind.

She pulled into the Travelers Rest precinct's tiny lot and parked in the only empty spot she could find. It was busy for a Sunday morning, no doubt due to last night's incident. Chief Duncan was rarely in the office on the weekends, but she had hoped he would be in today, trying to stay on top of the potential public relations crisis, and she wasn't disappointed. His new Chevy Tahoe was parked in his reserved spot. Olivia walked through the doors of the front entrance with a determined stride and headed straight for his office.

As she entered the general office area, the early morning bustle in the place died down and all heads turned in her direction. Not wanting to talk about last night, she was careful to avoid eye contact, but a loud commotion to her left made her look that way.

Jumping quickly out of his seat, Roger had knocked over a desk-organizing tray and then tripped over its contents, sending another office chair crashing onto its side. Ignoring the mess he'd made, Roger jogged over to where she stood. "Olivia, are you all right?"

"Yes, I'm fine."

"Is it true what they're saying? Did Grady really try to, um, uh, did he—"

"Yes, he assaulted me with foul intentions. Now if you'll excuse me, I need to talk to Chief Duncan."

She didn't wait for Roger to respond. Six long strides took her to the Chief's closed door, which she gave three light raps.

"Come in."

When Chief Duncan saw who opened the door, he looked startled. And worried. Olivia wondered if he was more worried about her well-being or about the PR nightmare last night's incident could spawn.

"Selman, what are you doing here? You should take the day off, or even the week, if you need it."

"I'm okay. I couldn't sleep anyway. What's the story with Grady?"

"He's over in county lockup right now. His hearing won't happen until tomorrow afternoon. We've got a judge who doesn't go easy on this kind of stuff. We're going to throw the book at Grady. Stalking. First degree assault. Attempted kidnapping. Attempted murder. Hopefully, we can convince the judge that he's an imminent threat to you so he'll be denied bail. With any luck, Grady won't see the outside of a prison for at least ten years."

"That would be nice. If he's released, there's no telling what he might do."

"Well, we're going to do everything in our power to make sure that no more harm comes to you." Chief Duncan leaned forward and rested his chin on his clasped hands. "Has anyone from the press reached out to you for comment about last night?"

"No."

"They will. There's no doubt about that. Do you plan on talking to them when they do?"

"I'll tell you what. If you do everything you can to keep Grady behind bars, then I'll do everything I can to keep last night as low-profile as possible."

Chief Duncan broke out into a big grin. Olivia had to stifle a laugh at the look of relief on his face. "You can count on that."

This time she was the one who leaned forward and rested her head on her hands. "I do have one additional favor to ask of you."

Chief Duncan threw his hands out wide. "Anything."

"I have a suspect who has been spotted at the scene of a crime. We know he used a cell phone leading up to the crime, so I would like to get a warrant to retrieve his cell phone data from the service provider. If we can prove his cell phone was in the vicinity of the crime, we can blow apart this guy's alibi."

"That sounds reasonable. Which case is this for?"

"The Turner case."

Chief Duncan's eyebrows shot up. "The Turner murder case? The one you're no longer working? Does Detective Vogel know about this?"

Olivia maintained fierce eye contact, fighting the temptation to look away sheepishly. "Vogel has convinced himself that Jonas Turner murdered his wife. The same Jonas Turner who saved my life last night. This is despite mounting evidence pointing in other directions. Vogel took me off the case because I kept uncovering evidence that poked holes in his case. He's willing to send an innocent man to prison just to close the case. We can't let that happen."

"Calling in a warrant for a case outside our jurisdiction could make some serious bureaucratic waves."

"Maybe. But I imagine those waves pale in comparison to the tsunami of bad publicity we could be facing. Just think of what a public relations nightmare it will be when the press finds out we sent a grieving husband to prison for a murder he didn't commit, not to mention everything else that's going on."

Chief Duncan wasn't stupid. Her thinly veiled reference to the Grady situation had hit its mark, and he appeared to be weighing his options.

"You're that confident Jonas Turner isn't the killer?"

"Yes."

"Should I be questioning how Jonas Turner happened to be there to rescue you last night?"

"He asked to meet me because he uncovered new information about the case."

"I've seen the pictures from last night submitted as evidence. You were, hmm, not in uniform."

Olivia felt her face get hot but kept her eyes fixed on Chief Duncan's, hoping he couldn't see her blush under her naturally dark complexion. "No, I was off duty at the time, and it was a last-second meeting."

"So you have not become romantically involved with the prime suspect of a murder case?"

"No, sir. I would not do that."

Chief Duncan stared at her for what felt like minutes but was probably closer to ten seconds.

"Okay, Officer Selman. Send me the cell phone number you want to track, and I'll get you your warrant. You'll have it by tomorrow morning. Just remember our agreement, and tread carefully."

Olivia nodded her understanding and quickly exited the chief's office. Once again avoiding any eye contact, in addition to a couple of "Hey Selman" greetings, she got back in her patrol car and pulled out of the precinct.

She fully intended to be true to her word about not getting romantically involved with a suspect, but her first thought leaving Chief Duncan's office was *I've got to call Jonas*, which she did now.

He answered on the first ring. "Hello?"

"Hey, hero, you rescue a damsel in distress and then leave without saying goodbye? What's up with that?"

She heard a low chuckle. "Yeah, well, when all the other cops showed up, they were pretty adamant about keeping us apart. When they finally told me I could go, I got the impression that getting close enough to you to say goodbye wasn't in the cards."

"Sorry about that. Sounds like they were being a little overly protective. Now that I think about it, I do recall there being a ring of officers around me until I got into my car to leave."

"I'm just glad you're okay."

"I am, thanks to you. In all the chaos, I don't remember thanking you for saving my life."

"No thanks needed. I'm just glad I was there to help."

"Speaking of which, how *did* you happen to be there to help? Were you *stalking* me?"

"Ahhhh, I was hoping you wouldn't think about that."

There was silence on the other end for a beat or two, but then he explained. "After you started walking in the direction of your car, I headed in the opposite direction towards mine. I made it about four steps when, uh, I don't know how to explain it. There was just this sudden dread, stopping me in my tracks. I couldn't shake the thought of needing to make sure you made it safely to your car. So I turned around and followed you at a distance.

"I was so worried you were going to turn around and spot me and think I was some kind of creeper. I almost turned back once you were within a few feet of your patrol car, but, I don't know, something stopped me. I felt compelled to keep watching.

"And sure enough, as soon as you walked past your car and headed towards that SUV, that guy in black slipped out from behind a tree, crouched down behind your patrol car, and then rapidly approached you from your blind side. I took off in a dead sprint at that point. He didn't hear me coming until the last second. When he looked up, I kicked him as hard as I could in the side of the head. The blow seemed to make him woozy, which made it a lot easier to pull him off you and keep him pinned down."

Olivia had pulled over into a median, not trusting herself to drive as she listened to Jonas's description of last night's attack. "Do you think that feeling you got was from God?" she asked earnestly.

"You know what *I* think. I'm just telling you what happened. I promise, I'm not a crazy stalker like this other guy in your life. Am I right in gathering that this Grady guy was a fellow police officer? Is he some kind of ex-boyfriend or something?"

"Fellow police officer, yes. Ex-boyfriend, no. Over my dead body. He's just some perv who has been sexually harassing me at work lately. But enough about that jackass. I have some good news. My chief agreed to get us the warrant for London's phone. He said we should have it by the end of the day."

"Wow, that's huge. Thank you. I really appreciate you figuring all that out."

"It was nothing. I'm heading over to the hospital now to see if I can find Mr. London in any of the other video footage. Has there been any activity on your video feeds?"

"Next to nothing at Eugene's house. I have yet to see him leave the house since installing the camera. People have come and gone from Pepe's house, but no one that looks remotely like Pepe. But you told me he escaped into the woods behind his house. Who's to say he hasn't returned the same way?"

"Yeah, it's going to be difficult to get anything on these guys if they remain hunkered down and out of sight. Unless—" Olivia shook her head at the obvious idea that only now popped into her head. "Unless we can get warrants to track their cell phones, too. If we can get the warrants, we can look to see if either of them was within the vicinity of your house the day of the murder and track down their current location if we want to pick them up for questioning."

"How did I not think of that?" Jonas exclaimed. "That's perfect. Do you think a judge will agree there's enough probable cause?"

"Pepe has a record, was recently fired for theft, worked your neighborhood, and ran when a cop showed up. I think he's a safe bet. Eugene will be a little more difficult, but between the restraining order and the weird shrine in his room, it might be enough. Let's see how this David London situation plays out first, but at least we have a backup plan."

"Sounds good. I'll keep you posted on any movement on my cameras. You let me know what you find out at the hospital."

Olivia wanted to suggest meeting up for dinner again to share their findings, but fought the urge. Better not to press her luck. "Sounds good. Talk to you later, hero."

"Stop it. I was just in the right place at the right time. Talk to you soon."

Soon. She liked the sound of that. Her cheeks were still sore from last night. All this smiling was going to take some getting used to.

CHAPTER THIRTY-THREE

Why did Olivia always crave Chick-fil-A on Sundays, the one day it was unavailable?

She settled into a booth at Zaxby's with a plate full of chicken tenders, the closest substitute for her craving. Pulling out her phone, she checked her messages and mulled over the idea of giving Jonas a call with the latest update. She wished she had better news to share. Her morning of reviewing hospital video footage had been a complete bust. Well, at least as far as pursuing David London as a suspect was concerned. She had been able to piece together enough footage to eliminate him.

It was time to redirect her focus to the two remaining viable suspects. Popping a crinkle fry in her mouth, she formed a plan of attack for getting a warrant for their cell phone data. She could have Roger chase down Eugene's phone number for her; using the search engines at the precinct would retrieve it in no time.

The chances of Pepe having an easy-to-track cell phone, on the other hand, were slim to none. Illegal residents weren't big on leaving paper trails. Her best chance of pinning down his phone number was reaching out to her new friend, Jose.

Clicking on the photo app on her phone, she scrolled down to the picture she had taken of the *Jose & Sons* business card and punched in the number. It was answered on the second ring.

"*Hola.*"

"Hi, this is Officer Selman. Is this Jose?"

"*Si.* Is something wrong, Officer?"

"No, nothing's wrong. I just need a little help. Do you have Pepe Delgado's cell phone number?"

"*Si*, I not know if he still use, but I know the number he use when he work for me."

"Perfect, could you read that number to me?"

"One *momento.*"

Olivia heard Jose fumbling with his phone, and then his voice, a little quieter, reading off the numbers. She typed the number into the notes section of her phone.

"Thank you, Jose. You don't happen to know where Pepe is staying these days, do you?"

"No, I not hear anything. My sister, I think she suspects me. She tell me nothing."

"Okay, I understand. I had to ask. One more question for you. Does anyone on your landscaping crew wear stilts on occasion?"

"Stilts?"

"Yes, *zancos*. Do any of them wear *zancos* sometimes?"

There was no response.

Olivia pulled her phone from her ear and checked the screen to make sure the call hadn't dropped. "Jose? Are you still there?"

His voice sounded strained. "Why you ask about *zancos*?"

Olivia sat up straighter in the booth. "I can't tell you that, Jose, but I need you to answer the question. Who in your crew wears *zancos*?"

"My crew not use *zancos*. We only use ladders. The only one to wear them was Pepe. He like them better than ladders. I tell him he *loco*, but he used to work as house painter. He paint ceilings and wear them all the time."

Crap. Crap, crap, crap, crap. It was Pepe. He was the one who killed Jessica, and she had let him escape. "I've got to go, Jose. Thank you for your help."

JONAS LAY STRETCHED out on his bonus room couch. His parents had just left the house to visit with some old friends. The TV was on, but he wasn't watching. Instead, he stared at nothing in particular out the window. He had just finished rereading the texts between Jessica and David London for the fifth time. Prior to the last week and a half, he wouldn't have considered himself a sadomasochist, but he couldn't stop beating himself up since Jessica's death.

His parents had attended his church without him that morning. He hadn't been able to muster the fortitude to face all the unwanted attention his presence would have attracted. Most of it would have been from well-meaning friends and acquaintances happy to see him, but there would also be plenty of whispers and stares generated by his arrest and the skewed media coverage. So instead, he had spent the morning reading the Bible and praying.

That, and rereading texts that ripped the heart out of his chest.

Jonas shot to his feet. He needed some fresh air. Sitting around with his thoughts wasn't getting him anywhere. Pulling the sliding door wide, he walked across his small back porch and out onto the Bermuda grass. The texture against his bare feet felt good. He tipped his head back, closing his eyes as the sun washed over his face, and took in three deep breaths.

Much better. Clear your mind. Focus on the positives. The sun feels good. The breeze feels good. The grass feels good.

He spun in a slow circle with his arms out wide, embracing the sensation of nature against his skin. When he opened his eyes, he found himself facing Jessica's garden. The one she'd spent hours in, weeding and planting flowers. The one he had been told to stay out of and not let his soccer ball hit. He looked down at the big pink flamingo inside it, a two-dimensional wooden lawn decoration his wife had painted.

He snatched it up, snapped it over his knee, and sent the pieces flying over the back of the fence. Falling to his knees, Jonas let out a guttural scream.

How could she do this to me? Why did she do it? What did I do to deserve this?

He stayed that way for several minutes, hands and knees on the grass, staring at the ground. "Pull yourself together, man," he muttered to himself at last. "There's no sense in scaring the neighbors."

He pushed himself back to his feet and turned towards the back porch. As his vision crossed over the garden, he did a double take. Something white was sticking out of the dirt where the flamingo had been.

Kneeling at the edge of the garden, he saw what appeared to be the hind end of a hard plastic toy horse. Jonas reached out and grabbed a back leg, pulling it free from the soil.

As soon as it came fully into view, he froze, blood turning to ice in his veins. It wasn't a horse. It was a unicorn.

Jonas released it from his fingers, letting it drop to the rich brown soil. The stalker had been in his backyard. That little creep had killed Jessica. He hadn't taken the kid seriously, and now Jessica's blood was on his hands.

He couldn't think. He couldn't breathe. A vibration in his pocket drew his attention. His hand felt like it was moving through Jell-O as it fumbled the phone out of his pocket.

It was Olivia.

"Hello?"

"Hey, it's Olivia. I have some good news and some bad news. Which one do you want first?"

"You pick." His voice sounded shaky in his own ears, but Olivia didn't seem to notice in her excitement.

"Okay, let's get the bad news out of the way first. The hospital gave me access to their video surveillance again, but all it did was confirm London's alibi. I spotted him at the food court around 10:30. He can be seen entering a hallway that leads to public restrooms a little after 11:15, and he exits that hallway shortly before noon. There's no way he's our guy."

Jonas tried to take in this new information, but the white plastic unicorn filled his vision and dominated his thoughts.

"But now for the good news. Pepe might be a better suspect than we thought. You were right about the stilts. Pepe used to be one of those ceiling painters who wore them all the time. He would even wear them landscaping on occasion. I really think he might be our guy. I got his cell phone number from the landscaping company, and I'm going to ask Chief Duncan for another warrant."

There was a pause on the other end of the line. Jonas tried to pull his thoughts together.

"Are you listening to what I'm saying, Jonas? Do you care to respond? I think Pepe's our guy."

"It's not Pepe," he croaked. "It's Eugene."

"What are you talking about? Why would you think it's him now?"

"He was here. He was in my backyard. He left a calling card. I found a unicorn behind the flamingo in Jessica's garden."

Olivia's tone changed dramatically. "Did you touch it?"

"Yes. I didn't recognize what it was until I picked it up."

"Okay, leave it wherever it is, and don't touch it again. As soon as you get off the phone with me, call 911 and get them to send out a crime scene tech. Make sure you tell the tech where you found it and where you touched it."

"What if Detective Vogel shows up and tries to bury the evidence? Can't you come over and take care of it?"

"I'm just a traffic cop, Jonas. If I bag it and hand-deliver it to the forensics lab, it will raise all kinds of red flags. We need a crime scene tech to document everything. We've got to do this by the book. That's why it's important for you to be very detailed in your 911 call. Those calls are recorded, and it'll make it difficult for Vogel to keep the unicorn out of evidence."

"Okay, I'll make the call."

"Good. In the meantime, I'm going to work on getting warrants for both Eugene and Pepe's cell phone data. I think it's best that we take a closer look at both their movements leading up to Jessica's murder."

Jonas looked down at the two holes where the prongs of the flamingo ornament had been embedded in the garden. "Are you still going to execute the warrant for David London's cell phone?"

"Yeah, probably. There's still a remote possibility that he had Jessica killed for some reason. The black SUV in the pool parking lot still bothers me. It's possible that Eugene or Pepe has access to a dark-colored SUV that we're unaware of, but David London is the only one connected to this case that we know owns one. So I'll look into where he's been and who he's talked to the last couple of weeks."

"I want to talk to him." Jonas's words came out with more steely resolve than he'd intended.

Olivia's response was delayed and genuinely confused. "Who?"

"London."

"What? Oh, no, no, no. That's a terrible idea."

"I need to talk to him."

"Why? You *just* told me that you think Eugene is the killer. *I* just told you David London can't be the killer. Why would you want to talk to him now?"

"I just do. I need some answers that only he can provide."

"How would that even work? How are you going to arrange a talk with him?"

"Show up at his house."

Olivia's voice neared a shout. "Are you crazy? You can't just show up at your wife's lover's house. That's a recipe for disaster. Please tell me you aren't serious."

"I need to talk to him, Olivia. I need to look him in the eyes and be convinced that he had nothing to do with her death."

"Okay, Jonas, I can hear it in your voice. You're thinking emotionally, not rationally. Why don't we let all this new information marinate for a little while? Call 911. Let's get the unicorn to forensics. And let's sleep on everything else. We can discuss this talk with David London tomorrow, in person. Okay?"

Jonas didn't respond right away, but in the end, he conceded—in part. "Okay. I'll sleep on it. But after that, no promises. I'll talk to you tomorrow."

He hung up before she could reply and dialed 911.

"Hi, I just uncovered evidence connected to a murder investigation. Could you please send a crime scene tech to my house?"

CHAPTER THIRTY-FOUR

He slept on it—assuming the tossing and turning from last night could be called sleep. He also stewed on it all morning and afternoon. Other than monitoring the cameras pointed at Eugene's and Pepe's houses and arranging for a sub to fill in for him at school again this week, he did little else.

He felt bad about missing so much work, but he got the impression that the administration was relieved he wasn't coming back anytime soon. An accused murderer teaching middle school would probably elicit more than a few phone calls from concerned parents.

As things were, he had a ton of time to sit around and imagine a conversation between him and David London. It was becoming an obsession. All he could think about day and night. He had to talk to him.

Jonas grabbed his wallet and keys and headed to his driveway.

Using the information he'd gained from his license plate search, Jonas drove into London's cul-de-sac. Apparently this guy's practice did well. The expansive, two-story white home was one of the nicest in the neighborhood, which was saying something. Jonas parked along the street, next to where London's driveway began. Despite Olivia's reservations and the potential risk, he felt no hesitation walking up to the door and pressing the doorbell.

He was familiar with London's face after hours of internet stalking, so he had no trouble recognizing the man who opened the door. Judging by the widening of the man's eyes, he recognized Jonas, too, despite trying to play it off.

"Can I help you?"

"I was hoping you and I could sit down and talk through a few things."

"I'm not in the habit of inviting strangers into my home. What's this about?"

"You know who I am, and you know what this is about. I mean you no harm. I just have a few questions I need answered."

London's face dropped the mask and twisted into a snarl. "I have nothing to say to you. Get off my property before I call the police."

"I'm not going to stop showing up on your doorstep until you answer my questions. I'll keep knocking here. I'll show up at your practice. Maybe get some work done on my bad knees. I'll get a membership at your gym. You'll see me everywhere you go until you agree to sit down with me and have a little chat. And if you want to call the police, then call them. I've uncovered a few things recently I wouldn't mind sharing with them. You'll save me some time."

London's jaw set and his eyes blazed, but Jonas could tell the gears were turning behind the fire. He appeared to be considering his options and not liking any of them.

"Wait here."

London closed the door and was gone long enough that Jonas considered the possibility that he'd gone inside to call the police and was merely buying time until they arrived. But then the door swung back open, and London stood there holding a revolver pointed at Jonas's waist.

An electric current of shock coursed through his body, but he felt much less fear than he would have expected. The thought of seeing Jesus and being the reason London was charged with murder didn't seem so bad.

"You want to talk, then come in and talk. Just note that if you threaten me in any way, you're a dead man."

Jonas stared right back at him. "Works for me."

London backed up, keeping the gun on Jonas. Once they got to a big, open living room, he waved Jonas over to the couch. Jonas sat on the edge of it while London took the armchair opposite of him.

Loud, angry music played from somewhere above them. When London noticed Jonas looking up, trying to place the sound, he shrugged and offered a one-word answer. "Teenagers."

Jonas wanted to look around the room to get a feel for the man in front of him, but he was afraid to take his eyes off the gun. It was surreal being face to face with the man he had so often imagined over the last few days.

They spent a couple of seconds sizing each other up before London broke the silence. "What is it you want to know?"

"How did you and Jessica meet?"

"We met at that APTA conference last October. We shared a few drinks at one of the after-hours parties. One thing led to another. You know how it goes."

"No, I don't, actually. I'm not one to sleep around."

"Yes, that's right. Jessica mentioned what a choirboy you are. Maybe if you had bothered to go with her to the conference, you could have been her moral compass and none of this would have happened."

Jonas forced himself to show no emotion, maintaining a face of stone, but London's words cut deep. He had committed to a major volleyball tournament that weekend in October months before Jessica mentioned going to the conference, but finding out that was the weekend her affair had begun was almost more than he could take. The what-ifs would haunt his sleep tonight.

"Who pursued who after the conference?"

London laughed. "She pursued me, actually. My occasional dips into foreign waters were almost always one-offs before her. I had no intention of pursuing a relationship, especially with someone in town. But Jessica was an extraordinarily attractive woman, as you well know, so when she began texting me, it was difficult to resist."

Jonas didn't want to believe Jessica was the first one to reach out, but he had no way of knowing if London was lying. Jessica had been better about deleting texts in the first few months of their affair. "Did she talk about why she was unhappy with our relationship?"

London tipped his head back and rolled his eyes. "It had nothing to do with her being unhappy. It's not always about you, you know. She just wanted a little taste of the forbidden fruit. Are you only here to appease your insecurities?"

Jonas closed his eyes and took three deep breaths before locking back onto London's face. "The real reason I'm here is to ask you this. Did you kill Jessica?"

"No."

Jonas waited for more, but no more was offered. London said it simply and easily. Jonas didn't perceive any deceptive tells, but it seemed odd for him not to offer further commentary.

"Do you know who killed Jessica?"

"No."

This "no" was almost identical to the first, but not quite. A small, sudden intake of breath and the slightest of eye flickers separated the two.

"Did you arrange to have Jessica killed?"

London snorted and gave Jonas a patronizing smile. "Are you serious? No, of course not. Why would I do that?"

"I don't know, you tell me. Why would someone give their lover the cold shoulder for days, and then turn around and beg to see her immediately?"

"I don't know what you're talking about."

Jonas leaned forward, lowering his voice but increasing its intensity. "You should know that I've read every single text between you and Jessica. Playing dumb with me won't work. So, I'll ask you again. Why did you refuse to text Jessica back the week she was killed? Did you two get in a fight? Did she threaten to expose your affair?"

London broke off eye contact, fixing his gaze six inches to Jonas's right instead. "It had nothing to do with Jessica. I had a family emergency to attend to."

"You mean the one that sent your wife to the ICU? Seems like it would be easy to text Jessica back while your wife was incapacitated, fighting for her life in a hospital bed. All you had to do was step out of the ICU, and she would never know."

London's eyes shifted back to his, widened now in a look of shock and disgust.

Jonas shook his head in derision. "What, are you going to tell me that you would never do something like that? Are you going to try to convince me you loved your wife and would never disrespect her like that?"

Through clenched teeth, London hissed, "I loved her."

"Right, right. You loved her so much you arranged a hookup with your lover mere minutes after you pulled the plug and watched her die."

London shot up out of his seat and screamed, *"I. Would. Never!"*, punctuating each word with his gun hand.

Jonas stood, too, hands outstretched. "What? What would you never do? I've seen the texts."

London's mouth kept opening to speak, but no words came out. Some kind of internal struggle seemed to be rendering him mute until he closed his eyes and took a deep breath.

When he finally spoke, his voice was almost normal. "I would never send those texts in my right mind. I must have lost my head for a moment in my grief. But I came to my senses eventually, which is why I didn't follow through with meeting Jessica."

"See, there's where we run into another problem. Your texts aren't the only damning evidence we have. We also have an eyewitness who spotted your Toyota Sequoia on his doorbell camera the morning of the murder. As clear as day, he watched it arrive shortly before Jessica's murder and leave shortly after. Tell me, how are you going to explain that?"

Whatever mask London had been wearing fell off completely now. Fear and anger contorted his features. "Get out of my house."

"I guess I'll take that as an admission of guilt."

London stepped forward while lifting the gun to point at Jonas's face. "Get out. Get out. GET OUT!"

Jonas backed up slowly with his hands in the air. "All right, all right, I'm going."

"Dad, what's going on?"

Jonas turned in the direction of the voice. A young blonde teenage girl stood on the stairwell looking down at them. When their eyes met, hers widened to an almost cartoonish extent, and she stumbled to a seated position as she tried to step back up the stairs.

London screamed, "Arianna, get back to your room!"

As Jonas watched the girl turn and sprint up the stairs,

his perception went wonky. It felt like his consciousness had been inserted into an unfamiliar body. The words being yelled at him seemed muffled. Even the gun pointed in his face couldn't speed up his response time faster than a walk through neck-deep water.

He felt himself shoved towards the front door and then pushed out so hard he had to cling to the railing not to faceplant down the steps. The injury he'd narrowly avoided didn't faze him. All he could think about was the girl's face. He had seen that look before, but he couldn't place it.

Jonas slowly made his way back to his car, glancing down at the perfectly manicured lawn. Stupidly, he thought about his own lawn, probably the worst-looking one in his neighborhood after the neglect of the last couple of weeks.

Thinking about uncut grass, an image of the tall grass at the back of Plainview Middle School popped into his brain, bringing him to an abrupt halt. That was where he had seen her face. David London's daughter was the girl in the red hoodie smoking in the back of the school grounds.

How is that possible? Why would a rich white girl from the nice side of town attend Plainview Middle School? Plainview was a poverty-stricken place a good fifteen minutes outside of London's school zone. It didn't make sense.

It was a strange coincidence, but it didn't seem important. Considering his current life circumstances, reporting a student smoking on school grounds was pretty low on his list of priorities. So why was he feeling so unsettled about it?

Jonas felt a vibration in his front pocket. Pulling out his phone, he saw that Olivia was calling.

He answered mechanically. "Hey, what's up?"

"He did it, Jonas."

"Who did what?"

"David London killed her. Or had her killed."

It felt like all the blood in his body stopped moving and

turned to ice. "How do you know?"

"I just left the phone company. London sent those text messages to Jessica from his house. Then the cell phone moves in a direct line straight to your neighborhood the morning Jessica was killed, and it moves back to London's house shortly after her estimated time of death. I don't know how he did it, but he did it. I think we have enough to arrest him at this point. At the very least, we should be able to get a search warrant for his house. I'm on my way to the precinct now to talk to my chief."

The gears in his head whirred, drowning out the last part of what Olivia said. He turned back towards London's house. A face peeked out from behind a curtain on the second floor.

"Jonas, are you still there?"

"Yeah, I'm here. Just thinking. Can we meet up tonight? I want to run a crazy theory by you."

"Sure, why don't we discuss everything over dinner again. I'll text you a time and place after I'm done at the precinct."

"Okay, sounds good. See you then."

Jonas put the phone back in his pocket, never taking his eyes off the second story window. He made the international sign for "I'm watching you" at the disembodied head in the window, chasing it from view.

As he settled back into the driver's seat of his car, he paused before putting the key in the ignition, considering the possibilities. After ten seconds of contemplation, he shook his head and chuckled at the ridiculousness of his new theory. It was a silly thought. Ludicrous, really.

But, he thought, *what could it hurt to shake things up a bit?*

CHAPTER THIRTY-FIVE

Olivia peeled into the precinct parking lot and bounded out of her car to the front entrance. Between the adrenaline rush of placing London's phone at the scene of the crime and her new dinner plans, it was difficult to stifle the smile stretching her face from ear to ear. At least it was until, halfway to Chief Duncan's office, she watched the door open to reveal a red-faced Vogel.

When he spotted her, his face turned a hue closer to purple, and he charged in her direction, shouting and pointing.

"There's the snake who's trying to sabotage my case. Who the hell do you think you are? I'm going to have your badge for this!"

He shouted the last few words directly in her face. Droplets of spittle hit her as he tried to intimidate her with close proximity and aggressive hand gestures, but she refused to back up or look away. Out of the corner of her eye she could see a ring of fellow officers closing in.

Vogel noticed them, too, and took a step back while

lowering his voice. "You have no idea the hornets' nest you've kicked over. You'll be feeling the sting for the rest of your career."

"I'm happy to kick over whatever's in my way as long as it means preventing you from railroading an innocent man," she retorted, staring him down defiantly. "You've got next to nothing on Jonas Turner, and you're not even looking at other possibilities."

"Other possibilities? Like chasing unicorns and tracking the cell phone of a suspect with an airtight alibi? Is that what you think good detective work looks like? This isn't an Agatha Christie novel. We have the *husband* at the scene of the crime, *with* motive, *with* his thumbprint on the murder weapon, *and* the victim's blood on his shoes. What more do you want?"

Olivia countered, "We have Jonas Turner's 911 call on record five minutes after we have him on video arriving home. You saw that room. How could he stab his wife forty-seven times and then walk outside with barely a drop of her blood on him? Did he change clothes, kill her, shower, and then change back into his work clothes in five minutes? And where are his bloody clothes? How could he get rid of them in less than five minutes without us finding them? And those bloody shoes you're so proud of—there's no blood spatter on them. It looks like someone pressed the shoe in a puddle of blood and then tossed it down the hill. The murder weapon was a knife Jonas used for breakfast that morning. Anyone could have grabbed it off the kitchen counter. Your case is a house of cards, and I'm going to bring it tumbling down."

Vogel moved in close once again, his nose almost touching hers. Whatever he was going to say was modified by the sound of officers shuffling forward, tightening the circle around them. His eyes flickered left and right before returning to Olivia's.

Putting his hands behind his back, he leaned forward and whispered in her ear. "As long as I have breath in my lungs, you will never be a detective."

With that, he shouldered past her and pushed through the ring of officers, storming out of the precinct.

Olivia turned to her fellow officers, making eye contact and nodding a thank you to each of them. The circle dissipated, revealing Chief Duncan standing there. His eyes looked worried, but he gave her a paternal smile. "Are you okay?"

"Yeah, I'm fine. I'm not worried about Detective Vogel."

"He has a lot of pull in this county. Maybe you should be. He could make life very difficult for us."

Olivia gave him a grin that was almost a snarl. "Maybe it's time to bring Vogel down a peg or two. He might not have as much influence once we bring his shoddy detective work to the light."

Chief Duncan raised an eyebrow. "I'm listening."

"The search warrant you secured for me was a success. We can now place David London's cell phone at the scene of the crime at the time of the crime. I think we have enough to arrest him and search his home. If we can get him to confess or find any trace of Jessica's blood in his car or home, then we're the ones solving the case and Vogel looks like a complete idiot."

A smile crept onto Chief Duncan's face. "Let's go back to my office and hash this out. I want you to lay out everything you have on this David London, and if I think it's enough, we'll go get this guy tonight."

Jonas was on autopilot, completely unaware of his surroundings until he pulled into his driveway. Even then, he sat in his car for several minutes trying to process his visit to David London's home. The more he thought about his suspicions, the crazier they sounded.

Shaking his head again, he got out of his car and noticed his parents' rental car was gone. He checked his phone and found a text from his mom.

Mom: We're out running a few errands. Let us know if you want us to bring home dinner.

He sent a quick reply.

Jonas: No thanks. Already have dinner plans out. You guys have fun.

As he walked towards the steps of his front porch, he couldn't help but notice his lawn. There were at least twenty islands of crabgrass embedded into the Bermuda in his front yard, and a sea of some type of tall, wispy weed. His yard was by far the least manicured in sight. He figured the only reason he hadn't received an HOA warning yet was that no one was eager to upset the neighborhood murderer.

He looked down at what he was wearing. There was nothing special about the pair of jeans and T-shirt he had on, and the shoes he usually wore to do yard work were locked up in evidence somewhere. This outfit was as good as any.

He retraced his steps back to his car and hit the button on the automatic garage opener attached to his sun visor. After giving it one good long stare, he turned his back on Jessica's SUV and pulled his lawnmower out from the tangle of hoses and landscaping tools covering it. Having checked the lawnmower's gas tank and confirmed it was bone dry, he grabbed the nearby gas can and started to pour. It wasn't until the lawnmower was full that he noticed gasoline dribbling down the front from the bottom of the nozzle. His hands were covered.

Ugh, I better get this off quick. I can't go to dinner reeking of gasoline. Rushing to the door leading inside the house, he used his wrists to twist open the knob. Then he darted towards the kitchen sink, poured a generous portion of Dawn soap all over his hands, and scrubbed like mad.

As he reached for a couple of paper towels from the freestanding dispenser on the island, he felt a sharp pain in his back, like a bee sting but somehow deeper. Frantically, he swatted at the spot, only to find something in the way.

Spinning around, he didn't see anything, but heard the sound of shuffling feet. A cold sweat began to bead at every pore as he looked down between his legs and spotted a small, black canvas shoe.

No, it can't be.

He spun around faster this time and caught a glimpse of blonde hair. For a brief moment the pressure in his back lessened, but just as quickly, a new spot screeched in pain. Holding his arms out wide, Jonas ran backwards into the kitchen counter to try to pin down his assailant. A small figure squeezed out from under his arms at the last second.

Bloody switchblade in hand, there stood Arianna London.

I guess my theory wasn't so crazy after all.

For two forever-long seconds they stared at one another. Then Arianna's wide-eyed, fearful expression turned into a narrow-eyed snarl.

She lunged at Jonas with the knife. He caught her wrist and spun her around, using her own arm to pin her down and into a bear hug.

After kicking wildly to no avail, she sank her teeth into the hand holding her wrist.

Jonas screamed in pain but didn't let go. Instead, he used the pain to squeeze her wrist even harder, feeling the bones begin to grind. Arianna yelped and let go of the knife.

As soon as it hit the floor, he began speaking in a soothing voice. "Okay, it's over. Let's just calm down. I'm going to pull out my phone now and call the cops. I don't want to have to hurt you, but I need you to cooperate. Do you understand?"

He saw her nod and felt her body relax in his arms. Keeping his left hand firmly on her wrist, he slowly dropped the other to pull his phone out of his pocket.

The moment his hand entered his pocket, Arianna lunged to the right and grabbed a kitchen knife from the block on the counter.

Jonas shot his right arm up under her chin, released her wrist and used his left arm to press on the back of her neck, forming a tight sleeper hold. Arianna grabbed at the arm around her neck with one hand while trying to stab him with the other. He felt surface-level cuts strike his shoulders, but he kept his head out of the way.

Within five seconds, she went limp. He was afraid she was playing possum again, so he kept the sleeper hold tight for another ten seconds. When he finally let up, there was no doubt she was unconscious.

At least for the moment.

He laid her down gently and pulled the knife from her loose grasp. His back was on fire, and he was feeling a little woozy. He shuddered to think what would happen if he passed out and Arianna woke up.

He needed to confine her in some way. *But how?* All he could think of was the duct tape he kept in the pantry. Grabbing the roll, he began wrapping it around her ankles as tightly as he could manage in his weakened state. Once he thought they were secure, he grabbed her wrists, wrapping each in several layers before binding them together. Raising her to a sitting position, he used the rest of the roll to bind her arms to her body.

Oh man, oh man, this looks bad. He really needed Olivia to get here first. Arianna's head lolled to the side with no sign of life the entire time he had her in the seated position. He began to worry that he'd overdone it with the sleeper hold. *Please don't be dead.* He mentally prepared to begin CPR, but as he laid her back down, he could see and feel her breathing.

When he stood up, the room spun around him. Steadying himself with one hand on the kitchen island, he reached for the spots on his back that were screaming at him. His shirt was sticky and damp with blood. He stumbled to his bathroom with the duct tape. Under the sink was a first aid kit with a couple of large gauze pads.

He peeled off his shirt, which soaked his hair in blood and sent a wave of nausea rolling over him. Using the mirror to guide him, he pressed one gauze pad firmly on the higher wound, praying the knife hadn't nicked an artery or his lung. Then he tore off a long strip of duct tape and wrapped it tight around his chest to secure the pad in place. After doing the same for the other deep wound, he pulled out his phone and called Olivia.

She spoke in a hurried voice. "Hey, I can't talk right now. I'm in the middle of something. Let me call you back in a few."

His breathing was labored; his words came out one or two at a time. "I need. You now. I've. Been. Stabbed."

"What? Are you being serious?"

"Yes. Please help. My house."

"I'm on my way. Are you hurt bad? Do you need an ambulance?"

"Yes."

"Then why are you calling me? You need to hang up and call 911 as soon as possible."

"I need. You here. First. It looks. Bad. It's the. London girl."

"What London girl? The daughter? The daughter stabbed you?"

"Yes."

"I don't know what's going on, but I'll be there in five minutes. Just hang tight. I'm going to let you go so I can get dispatch to send an ambulance."

"Okay."

Jonas ended the call and stumbled back into the kitchen. His lethargy left him as soon as he did. Arianna was no longer in the kitchen. He stumbled to the back door and looked out. No one in sight. Jonas lumbered to the front of the house, where the door to the garage was still open. He peeked into the garage.

He heard her before he spotted her.

"Help! Help! A psycho is trying to murder me!" Arianna, still bound, was hopping up the sidewalk, screaming at the top of her lungs.

Jonas hurried out to the edge of his driveway before pulling up. Billy was standing in his doorway. As soon as they made eye contact, Billy stepped back inside and slammed the door. Looking up the sidewalk towards Arianna, Jonas spotted several other neighbors on their front porch, staring in horror in his direction.

He looked down at his bare, bloody chest and sighed.

Yep. I'm definitely going to have to move out of this neighborhood now.

His legs began to tremble. Shuffling to the grass, he fell to his knees before flipping over onto his back. He stared at the big puffy white clouds as the sound of shouting and sirens grew louder, until his vision went dark and the sounds faded away.

CHAPTER THIRTY-SIX

His mouth felt funny. He moved his tongue across his teeth; the inside of his mouth felt both sticky and dry. His eyes didn't want to open, but he forced them to open to slits.

"Jonas, can you hear me?"

Jonas turned towards the voice, his mother's, and nodded.

"Oh, thank Jesus you're awake. You had us so worried. Honey, I'm so sorry we weren't there for you."

Jonas's dad was there, too, looking at Jonas with sad eyes as he held his wife's hand.

"I'm glad you guys weren't there." His voice sounded more like a croak. His mom handed him a Styrofoam cup with a straw, and he sucked up a few swigs of water. "I would have never forgiven myself if my mess caused one of you to get hurt or killed."

He looked around the room. It was darker than most hospital rooms he had seen, and there were a lot more machines than he would have expected.

"How are you feeling?" his mom asked.

"Not too bad. I guess I passed out, huh? Is this a regular hospital room?"

Sounding as if she was on the verge of breaking down, his mom blurted out, "No, Jonas, you're in the ICU. You've been here for two and a half days. Those stab wounds almost killed you."

Stunned, Jonas looked down at his chest. "Did they puncture any vital organs?"

"The lower one nicked your liver. The higher one missed your heart by two millimeters. If the knife had hit your heart or the connecting artery, you would have bled out before you got to the hospital." She let go of Jonas's hand and brought it to her face to hide the tears; his dad moved in closer to squeeze her trembling shoulders.

"It's okay, Mom. I'm fine. It's over now."

His mom shook her head. "We don't know that. They've already rushed you back twice for emergency surgery. They keep finding spots where you're bleeding internally. I don't think I can handle seeing you like that again." She burst into tears again.

Jonas turned to his dad, who spoke gravely. "It was pretty scary that first night. We knew something was wrong. You went pale as a ghost and started shaking. These machines started making all kinds of noises, and four or five nurses rushed in yelling orders and telling us to get out. We thought we were going to lose you." He squeezed his wife tighter. "But honey, the doctors said they thought he was out of the woods now. That's why they brought him out of his sedation."

Jonas reached out and patted his mom on the arm. "I'm feeling pretty good, Mom. Don't worry about me."

She looked up with tear-stained cheeks. "I hope you're right, but that's probably the drugs talking. They have you on enough painkillers that you probably can't feel much of anything. It might be a different story once they wear off."

"Well, I guess we'll find out sooner or later." While he couldn't feel much physical pain, a sudden dread crept into his chest as he began recalling the scene on his front lawn. What had the cops thought when they pulled up and found that girl bound with duct tape? He scanned the open doorway to his room to see if one was stationed outside. Trying to sound casual but not quite getting there, he turned to his mom and asked, "What happened with the girl who attacked me?"

"They arrested her and charged her with attempted murder. She's out on bail now, but at least the judge ordered her to wear an ankle monitor so the police can track her movements. The pretty female officer has been keeping us posted. She says they'll probably charge her with Jessica's murder, too. I don't really understand how that's possible, but maybe it'll make sense when she explains it to you."

Jonas let out a long exhalation of sweet relief. "That was nice of Officer Selman to keep you updated on what's happening."

"Well, it hasn't been too hard for her to keep us in the loop, since she's been here at the hospital almost as much as we have." His mother cocked her head and gave him a knowing look that invited more information.

Jonas blushed and looked away. "Yeah, we've been working together to try to solve Jessica's murder. She's probably been waiting around for the opportunity to question me."

His mom reached out and patted his leg. "I doubt that's the only reason she's spent so much time here, but you're right about her wanting to talk to you, so we'll give you two some time to talk."

"She's here?"

"Yep, just outside the room, waiting to get in."

His mother and father rose to their feet and shuffled around their chairs. "We'll come back and visit some more after you two are done."

Less than five seconds after they exited, Olivia walked through the door wearing her uniform. When their eyes met, her face broke into a smile so big and beautiful it hurt Jonas's chest.

"So, you let a little girl beat you up and nearly kill you?"

"Hey, she sneak-attacked me with a knife. What's a guy to do?"

"Maybe try closing and locking the doors to your house. That would be a good place to start."

"Sorry, I'm still getting used to living in a horror movie. Two weeks ago I was living in a nice, safe family sitcom."

"Welcome to the real world, Jonas. People suck, so prepare for the worst."

"I'll keep that in mind. Did Arianna admit to trying to kill me?"

Olivia blew a puff of air through her lips and rolled her eyes. "No. She tried to convince me that you kidnapped her and tried to rape her."

A fluttery sensation in his stomach made it through the dulling of the pain medication. "Oh man, is anyone buying that story?"

"I think a few of your neighbors did, but no one that matters. I'm still mad at you for not calling 911 first. You could have bled out. But I'm glad I was the first to arrive at the scene. You weren't kidding when you said it looked bad. I had her tape off and placed her in the back of my patrol car before any other cops showed up, though. Once I explained the circumstances leading up to the stabbing, everyone saw the situation for what it was."

"So, I'm good?"

"Yeah, you're good. We have tons of evidence to nail her. We found her mother's car in the pool parking lot. We have doorbell camera footage from your neighbor across the street showing her sneaking into your open garage. We have her prints all over the bloody knife. Not to mention all the circumstantial evidence leading up to the attempted murder."

"What about her dad? He had to know about this. I just left his house. Did he really sic his daughter on me? Did he use her to kill Jessica, too?"

Olivia sat down in the seat closest to him and leaned forward. He couldn't tell if the fragrance he detected was from her shampoo or some kind of perfume, but it was intoxicating.

"I don't know. It's hard to say. He wasn't home when we went to arrest him. We couldn't get a hold of him, either. Apparently, the cell phone he used to text Jessica isn't his primary cell phone. No one seemed to know where he was, so we waited until he returned to his house. When he finally arrived home and we told him why we were there, he seemed genuinely horrified and grief-stricken. He literally crumpled to the ground. Maybe he was devastated over getting caught, but he seemed more concerned for his daughter than himself."

"Then where was he? Why would he rush out and leave his daughter at home after I visited?"

"He said he was at his lawyer's house. His lawyer confirmed it. According to them, they were discussing filing a restraining order against you. I don't know what you said while you were at his house, but you clearly touched a nerve. Which reminds me—I'm also mad at you for going to David London's house. They could have stabbed you or shot you there and gotten away with it. That was incredibly stupid."

Jonas decided not to tell her how right she was and offered her a simple shrug instead.

They both sat in silence for a few moments as he pondered the details of the case. "The unicorn still weirds me out," he said at last.

Olivia nodded. "Yeah, I think it's proof that Eugene's stalking wasn't as innocent as it seemed. It could have become something serious. But I asked the forensics lab supervisor for his initial thoughts, and he was confident that the unicorn had been out in the elements for at least a couple of months."

Jonas bobbed his head in acknowledgment before shaking it in disbelief. "I can't believe it turned out to be a teenage girl—a student at *my* school. That's crazy. What was she even doing at Plainview? Her parents lived in a nice neighborhood all the way across town."

"That question got answered since we started tearing her life apart over the last couple of days," Olivia said. "Apparently, Arianna has been kicked out of two other schools already. The first one for excessive out-of-school suspensions from fighting and talking back to teachers. The second one was for threatening a student and carrying a weapon. She was found with a switchblade in her backpack."

Jonas shook his head some more. "Clearly, she's a troubled youth. But she's a middle-school student who's nowhere near old enough to drive. It's hard to believe that she did all of this on her own."

Olivia stood to her feet. "Well, I assure you, we will get to the bottom of David London's involvement and anyone else's—but speaking of students, you have one waiting to see you."

"A student? One of mine?"

"I think so. He came in with his mom today and asked the receptionist if he could visit you. His eyes got as big as dinner plates when I walked up to him and asked him why he wanted to talk to you. I couldn't get much out of him, but I got the impression he had more to share with you than just his condolences. Would you be interested in hearing what he has to say? I can go get him if you want me to."

"Yeah, you've got me curious. Even if he's just here to offer get-well wishes, I wouldn't want to turn him away after he made the effort to get here. Bring him in."

Olivia tipped her head in acknowledgement and swept out the door.

Jonas looked around the room at all the machines and wondered what each of the numbers meant. He watched the drip of the saline bag trickle down the tube stuck in his arm.

Several minutes passed before Olivia popped her head back in. "Okay, he's here. I'll give the two of you some privacy."

As soon as she disappeared, the round face and long brown bangs of Blake Bower from Jonas's third period class peeked around the corner.

"Hey, Blake, this is a pleasant surprise. Come on in."

Blake shuffled in with his baggy, too-long pair of jeans and big black hoodie. He stood at the edge of Jonas's bed, stealing looks periodically but mostly looking at the floor.

"Come sit down beside me, Blake. Did you come by just to see how I was doing?"

Blake edged over to the chair that was a little further from the bed and sat down, keeping his eyes on the ground. "I came here to tell you I'm sorry."

"You're sorry that I got hurt? That's really thoughtful of you, but I don't want you worrying about me. I'll be all right."

Jonas couldn't see Blake's face between the downward tilt of his head and long bangs, but there was a barely perceptible shake of the head.

"I'm sorry I didn't tell you about her sooner. None of this would have happened."

Jonas pushed himself up a little higher in the bed, triggering a searing sensation in the wounds on his back. "Blake, are you friends with Arianna London?"

Blake lifted his head to reveal soulful eyes brimming with

tears. "Ari is my best friend. She's always been a little crazy, but never anything like this. At least, not until a couple of weeks ago, when she jumped off the deep end."

THIS WAS INSANE. What was he thinking? If his mom found out, he was a dead man. And we're talking dead, dead. *Like buried-in-the-back-yard, never-heard-from-again dead. Even during the daytime, his mom made him keep the door open when she was over and would pop in every thirty minutes or so. If she found Ari in his bedroom, without permission, after midnight—well, if he escaped with his life then he would be grounded for the rest of it.*

A light tap on his window startled him out of his run-through of worst-case scenarios. Blake hurried to the window and lifted it as quietly as possible. He held a finger to his lips as Ari crawled inside.

"We have to be really quiet so we don't wake up my mom," he whispered.

Ari nodded her understanding and then lunged at him, wrapping her arms around him in a tight hug.

Neither of them were hugging types, so it caught him off-guard, but he returned the hug after a moment or two. They stayed that way for a weirdly long time. It was a little awkward, but he wasn't exactly complaining. She felt good in his arms.

When they finally let go of one another, Blake asked her the most pressing question on his mind. "Ari, what happened to your mom? Is she really gone?"

Ari nodded and walked over to the bed, sitting on its edge. Blake followed and sat down beside her.

"She committed suicide. Took a big bottle of oxy and never woke up."

"Whoa, I'm so sorry, Ari." His words hung in the air as

the two of them sat in silence for a bit. "Your mom didn't seem like someone who would do that. Did she leave a note or give any reason for why she did it?"

"She didn't leave a note, but I know why. She did it because my dad is a lying, cheating scumbag."

A thousand questions bombarded his mind, but Blake forced himself to stay quiet. He would let her tell him what she wanted to tell him, and do it when she was good and ready.

Ari pulled out a necklace with a heart-shaped locket from the neck of her hoodie and began rubbing it between her finger and thumb. "My dad has an office in our basement that's supposed to be off-limits. He doesn't keep it locked or anything, but he flips out if anyone goes in there. Last weekend I snuck down there after midnight, because I know that's where he stashes the good alcohol. I felt like getting drunk.

"Anyway, while I'm looking through his bottles, I heard a vibration in one of his desk drawers. It took me a few minutes to find the source of the noise I heard, but it turned out to be a phone. A text message came through saying, 'Are you up?' This wasn't my dad's regular phone. It looked like some cheap Walmart version of a smart phone.

"My dad has a passcode he uses for everything. His phone. His gun safe. His laptop password. He acts all secretive about it and wouldn't even tell my mom what it was, but I watched him put it in his phone one time when he wasn't being careful. It's the date he hit a hole-in-one during a golf tournament." Ari snorted in derision. "What a loser. He tells that story to everyone, always showing off the picture—which has the date plastered on the bottom. But sure enough, he used the passcode on this phone, too.

"I was pretty sure what I was going to find, but it was even worse than I expected. He'd been banging some slut for months. I wasn't sure what to do about it at that moment, so I just took the phone with me and headed back to my room."

Ari was quiet for a long time. She was staring in the general direction of Blake's Iron Maiden poster, but he was fairly certain she was seeing beyond his bedroom walls.

"I wish I never went into his office. I wish that whore hadn't texted my dad while I was in there. But, most of all, I wish I never showed my mom the texts."

The sadness in her eyes was stabbing daggers into Blake's chest. Of all the scenarios he'd imagined, this was worse than any he could have cooked up.

"I thought about it for two days. I must have read over the text messages between my dad and his skank a hundred times, and each time I read through them, it made me madder. I figured my mom had a right to be mad too, so I decided to show her the phone.

"But she didn't get mad. She just broke. Crumpled to the floor and wouldn't stop sobbing. For two days, she wouldn't eat. She wouldn't get out of bed. She just lay there and sobbed."

Ari went quiet. Blake started to lift his arm to put it around her shoulders, but he chickened out and let it drop back to the bed.

When she started talking again, her words sounded lifeless. "My dad started sleeping in the guest bedroom. So I was the one who found her that morning. Her sleeping seemed too quiet, so I tried to wake her up and couldn't. When I saw the empty bottle of oxy on the nightstand, I freaked out and started shaking her and screaming."

Ari appeared to be reliving the moment, and her voice slowly grew in intensity the more she became immersed in her retelling. "My dad came running in, and when he checked her vitals, he said she was still breathing and told me to call 911. I said, 'Screw that. We can't wait. We've got *to take her to the hospital right now. We can call 911 on the way.' He didn't want to, but I wouldn't take no for an answer. I screamed at him until he helped me carry her down to the car.*

"He had us put her in the backseat of my mom's car. Probably worried about messing up his precious Toyota Sequoia. We got her to the emergency room in less than seven minutes and they took her straight back, but she was too far gone. They kept her on life support until the next morning, but then they told us she was completely brain-dead and wouldn't recover. So my dad gave them the okay to pull the plug, and we all gathered around to watch her die."

Blake felt the pressure to fill the ensuing silence with some kind of expression of sympathy or acknowledgement of her grief, but words eluded him. Anything he could think to say sounded lame and inadequate for the situation. Instead, he manned up and took one of her hands into his, giving it a squeeze.

When she looked in his direction, there was a fire in her eyes. "I knew what I was going to do before I even left the hospital. I had my grandparents take me home, and as soon as we arrived, I asked them to leave because I needed some time alone. They didn't want to leave me there, but I told them my parents left me home alone all the time. I screamed at them until they left.

"Then I went to my parents' bedroom and got the phone that caused this nightmare. I pretended to be my dad and set up a rendezvous with his skank. I knew from their text messages that my dad would occasionally hook up with her at her house. She would have him park in the neighborhood pool parking lot, sneak over the fence with the big flamingo in the backyard, and enter through her back door.

"Her house was the perfect place to do it. A private place with no ties to me. The slut-bag jumped at the opportunity

to meet up. She promised to race home to unlock the door for me.”

Blake's grip on Ari's hand had loosened more and more as she talked, and now he pulled his hand away altogether. He did not like where this was going.

She didn't seem to notice Blake's discomfort as her face became more and more animated. “I knew exactly how I would do it, too. My dad has a gun, but a gunshot would draw too much attention—not to mention that killers are always getting thrown in jail because of cops matching ballistics to guns. I decided to use the switchblade Derrick got me last semester. I knew it would be messier that way, but I kind of liked the thought of getting my hands dirty for Mom.”

Blake covered his face with his hands. He hadn't wanted to believe she was taking him where he thought she was taking him, but now there was no denying it. Dread crept down his body until it reached his toes.

Ari hopped off the bed and began pacing the room, no longer looking at him. “Of course, I couldn't afford to actually get my hands dirty. I had to make sure not to leave a single trace. First, I needed gloves, and not just any gloves. I remembered how often people cut themselves in knife attacks, so I found a thick pair of my dad's work gloves to use. No accidental wounds and no fingerprints, check.” She mimed a big check mark in the air.

“Next, I changed into my black jeans and my black hoodie. Dark colors to mask the blood spatter and clothes that wouldn't easily tear or leave behind fibers, check. Then I pulled back my hair in a ponytail and used a pair of my mom's pantyhose to wear over my head, providing both a mask when needed and protection from leaving hair at the crime scene.

“I knew there was no getting around having bloody

clothes to get rid of after I did the deed, but the tricky part was getting home without any of it getting in my dad's car."

For the first time in a while, Blake was able to find his voice, even though it came out as little more than a whisper. "You took your dad's car?"

"Yeah, how else did you think I would get there? It's not like I could take an Uber. 'Hey, mister, could you please take me to this address? I'm going to run inside and kill someone really quick. You may want to put down some plastic for the ride back home.'" Ari let out a cackle which had Blake glancing at the door, expecting his mom to walk through any minute.

"You know how to drive?"

Ari waved him off. "Of course. My grandpa lets me drive his truck at the farm all the time. My dad's fancy SUV is a piece of cake. But I had to be careful not to leave any trace of blood in it. In our garage, I found a brand-new blue tarp, not even opened yet, and I spread it out over the driver's seat and floorboard. It was stupid loud to sit on, crinkling nonstop, but it was a small price to pay for an evidence-free getaway car.

"I kept my hood up the whole drive over, and no one seemed to give me a second look. My dad's windows have a dark tint to them anyway, so it would have taken someone really paying attention to notice me. I parked in the pool parking lot, just like my dad would, and waited to make sure no one was around. I thought I might have to jump a fence to get behind the fence line, but there were two houses with no fence right where I needed to go.

"The skank's house was down further than I thought. I almost turned around thinking I must have missed it, but then I spotted the stupid flamingo. I was worried the whore would be watching for me out the window, but after I climbed over the fence, I didn't see her peering out from *any window or the backdoor, which was one of those big sliding glass doors." Ari's eyes got wider and brighter as she recounted the details. "There was a pair of tennis shoes on the back porch, right outside the door. They were huge, and it made me think how small my feet were in comparison and how bad it would be if I left shoe prints. I decided to take off my shoes and do it in my socks, which gave me the added benefit of being able to move without making a sound.*

"I thought the door was going to give me away—there was no way to open it without the sound of it sliding along its track. I braced to run at her if she suddenly appeared, but I didn't see or hear anything. I wish you could have seen me creeping through this house. You would have laughed your face off. There was some room to the right, and I was like a cat peeking my head inside. But there was nothing in that room but a TV and a bunch of stupid books.

"When I turned to walk through the kitchen, I saw this big knife lying on the island. That's when I thought, 'What would be more untraceable than using my switchblade? How about using a knife that belonged to the homeowners?' So I put my knife away and grabbed hers.

"Now I just needed to find her bedroom. The dumb cow made it easy for me. I'm sitting there trying to decide which of the two hallways to go down when I hear—" Ari put her hands to her face and mimicked a shrill voice. "'What are you doing out there? I heard you come in. Now get in here and ravish me, baby boy.'

"It was go time. I pulled my mom's pantyhose down over my face, made sure I had a good grip on the knife through my gloves, and I charged into the room."

Ari clapped her hands together and let out a giggle. "You should have seen the look on her face. I've never seen eyes that big. It was hilarious watching her go from sexy pose to scramble mode, trying to crab-walk backwards to get away from me. I jumped on top of her and got two or three good strikes in before she even thought to fight back."

Ari's face was flushed, and her words were spilling out faster and louder now. Blake thought about putting a finger to his lips and shushing her, but at this point he thought his mom's yelling might be more comforting than what he was listening to.

"She caught hold of my arm for a little while, and I was worried she would be able to throw me off or wrestle the knife free, but the adrenaline rush made me stronger than I've ever been. I felt unstoppable.

"And she was losing blood fast. It was going everywhere. I could tell she was weakening, and when I finally pulled my knife hand free, I started slashing her like crazy. Her hands clawed at me for a bit, which made it hard to land any good blows, but they stopped resisting and dropped to the bed eventually.

"I didn't stop, though. I just kept stabbing her, one blow after another, until my arm was on fire. Then I grabbed the knife with both hands and stabbed her in the heart as hard as I could. It was so far into her chest I probably couldn't have pulled it back out if I tried.

"I rolled off the bed and pulled the pantyhose off my face so I could get a good look at her as I caught my breath. Her eyes were open, almost like she was staring right at me, but there was no light in them. I had snuffed it out.

"After soaking in the scene for a few moments, I looked around the room to make sure I wasn't leaving any evidence behind. I didn't see anything on the bed, but when I looked down at the floor, I saw that I had stepped in blood and left a couple of sock prints. Even though they couldn't be traced back to me, I didn't want them looking for a tiny-footed suspect, so I smeared them with my gloves. Then I got up on my tippy-toes and walked out of the house. For once, all

those years of ballet my parents forced me to do paid off.

"I was going to run back to my dad's car at that point, but then I saw those big old shoes on the back porch again." Ari had a maniacal grin on her face as she spun back in his direction. *"I would have never thought to do it if it wasn't for you, Blake. I would have never thought to do half the things I did to cover my tracks if it wasn't for all those shows you made me watch.* Forensic Files. Cold Case Files. Homicide Hunter. *Every stupid mistake criminals make to get caught has been driven into my brain by those shows, training me how to avoid detection.*

"I knew from those shows that a shoe print was almost as good as a fingerprint, so I grabbed one of those sneakers on the back porch, tiptoed back inside, and pressed the shoe in a big smear of blood. It was perfect. The husband is always the murderer in those shows, and now I had the husband's shoe print encased in blood while his kitchen knife was buried in his wife's chest."

Blake grabbed his face, peering at Ari through his fingers as new horror froze his heart. "You framed Mr. Turner for his wife's murder?"

Ari's smile faded; she seemed to notice Blake's reaction for the first time since hopping off his bed. "Yeah, I guess I did. I didn't know it was his wife at the time, but I don't feel bad about it. He shouldn't have married such a slut."

She gave a slight shake of her head as if to dismiss the unwelcomed interruption to her story. "Anyway, as I left the house, I grabbed the other shoe, hopped the fence, and tossed them down a hill near some fenced-off area. It probably would have been better to make them disappear altogether, but I couldn't afford to be seen carrying them.

"I raced back to my dad's car after that. I don't think anyone saw me, but it's hard to say for sure since I had my hood up and kept my head down.

"The whole drive back, I was terrified my dad would beat me home, but when I didn't see a car in the garage it was like seeing the finish line with no other runners in sight. Other than the insides where I put my bloody socks, my shoes were free and clear of any blood, so I didn't have to worry about leaving a trail in the garage. I hopped out of my dad's SUV, carefully grabbed the corners of the tarp, and walked it out to my backyard. Then I stripped off every piece of clothing I had on and hosed myself down in the grass. Once I scrubbed every inch of my body, I placed my bloody clothes in the tarp, wrapped it up tight, and put it in our big trashcan, under a couple of regular bags. Then I went upstairs to take a long, hot shower.

"I would have preferred to burn the clothes, but it seemed too risky at the time. There was no telling when my dad would show up. He ended up coming home about two hours later, and he hasn't left the house since. It's too late now. He wheeled the garbage can to the road Saturday morning for its weekly collection. Hopefully, the tarp is buried in the middle of a huge pile of trash at this point."

When Ari sat back down on the bed beside him, Blake instinctively scooted over a few inches. She turned to look him in the eye, a small crease of worry between her eyebrows. "Do you think the bloody clothes going to the dump will come back to bite me?"

Overwhelmed by everything he just learned, Blake struggled to clear his brain fog and give her an intelligent response. "Uh, I don't, uh, I'm not sure. They won't just go and randomly search a big landfill. You don't live on the same side of town as the victim, either, so unless they identify you as a suspect, they wouldn't know where to look."

She bit her lip. "If they find out my dad was sleeping with her, then he'll be a suspect, and they might start snooping around."

"Yeah, but if your dad was still at the hospital, he'll have plenty of people who can provide him with an alibi. As long as you don't tell anyone what you did, you're probably safe."

Ari looked at him a long time. He couldn't read her expression. She seemed to be mulling something over, but there was no guessing what.

The heart-shaped locket was back in her hands, and she looked down at it now. "This is the only piece of physical evidence left in my possession. I haven't worn it in years, but I put it on before I left to go to that woman's house. My mom gave it to me for my tenth birthday."

She opened the locket and showed Blake the picture inside, a close-up of her mother nuzzling her as a baby. It looked like it had been processed with a red filter. "It must have come out of my hoodie while I was stabbing that woman. I cleaned it as well as I could, but there was nothing I could do about the photograph."

She closed the locket and tucked it back into her hoodie, and then she stood up and took the hoodie off. There was nothing but a bra on underneath. Blake's breath caught in his throat, and his eyes felt like they had popped out of his skull.

Ari shook her head of blonde hair and sat back down, facing him with an entirely different look on her face. "For a moment, after my mom died, I thought my life was over. But after tasting the sweet nectar of revenge, I realized I had just started living. Why do we always worry about what other people will think? Who are they to judge what is right and what is wrong? I think they want to keep us from truly living. The worst thing I've ever done gave me the best feeling I've ever had. I'm done playing by their rules. I just want to feel good."

She leaned her face into Blake's and placed a hand on his thigh.

Like he had been poked with a cattle prod, Blake shot off the bed and backed into the nearest wall.

Ari's face transformed from shock into anger faster than he could process his own thoughts. "What the hell, Blake? Do you not want me? Does my touch repel you?"

"No, uh, no, I, uh, I don't know why I, uh, freaked out. I guess, uh, you just surprised me."

Ari turned her back on him and threw her hoodie back on. "I didn't realize the thought of kissing me would freak you out. I'm sure there are plenty of other guys out there who wouldn't be repulsed by my touch. Maybe I'll go hang out with one of them."

Blake waved his hands frantically, stumbling through his response. "No, no, it's not like that. You just caught me by surprise. You know I think you're hot. It's cool. Please don't go."

Ari was already halfway out Blake's window. Just before she hopped off the window's ledge, she reached an arm back into the room and gave Blake the one-finger salute, then disappeared into the night.

Blake watched her run across his yard before closing his window and flopping onto his bed face-first. Why was he such a loser? Why had he freaked out so bad? He could have kissed her. And second base was right there.

Regret gnawed at him until he fell asleep, hours later, but it wasn't the only feeling rolling around his mind. There was something else pushing back against the regret. He wasn't sure what to make of it, but there was no denying it. He'd felt it the moment Ari left the room.

Relief.

It wasn't until Blake stopped talking that Jonas noticed a pain in his right wrist. He looked down to see he had a handful of blanket and bedsheet squeezed into a death grip.

Letting go of the sheet, and his breath, Jonas looked back up at Blake, who was finally making eye contact. "Blake, are you willing to testify in court about what you were told?"

The eye contact went away. "I don't know. I really don't want to testify against my friend. She needs help. I don't think she would have done this if she hadn't stopped taking her medication. If the police can find the bloody clothes, they should be able to convict her without my testimony, right?"

Jonas gave Blake a wry grin. In a world where his students were more likely to help bury a body than turn in a friend, he shouldn't expect more. "Yeah, that should be enough. Either way, I understand you not wanting to testify against your friend. It showed a lot of character, you coming up here and telling me what you know. Thank you, Blake."

Blake mumbled, "You're welcome," and said he'd better get back to his mom before she started to worry.

Thirty seconds after Blake shuffled out, Olivia popped back in.

Jonas asked, "Did you hear any of that?"

"Every word."

"What now?"

"We have some dumpster diving to do and a locket to confiscate."

"Once those are located, do you think it'll be over?"

"Well, as far as your charges are concerned and you being a suspect, yes. It'll be over."

With a twinkle in her eye and a sly grin, she added, "But as for everything else, I think we're just getting started."

EPILOGUE

Olivia pulled into a visitor's spot at the Greenville Law Enforcement Center. After putting her car in park, she stared at her dashboard. This could be it. The end of her career aspirations.

Captain Lee Bellwood, head of the Professional Standards Division and Internal Affairs, had called for a meeting. She hoped it was about Officer Grady, but knew in her heart of hearts that this meeting was the proverbial axe coming down on her head for crossing Detective Vogel. ·

Once the media had gotten wind of Arianna London's arrest, the whole thing had turned into a circus. She'd been bombarded by interview requests for two weeks straight. Chief Duncan had eventually held a press conference to confirm that Arianna London had been charged for Jessica Turner's murder and Jonas Turner's attempted murder. He didn't provide them with details concerning the evidence, but someone in the department must have. Whole segments were devoted to the bloody clothes they had found at the landfill and the locket with traces of Jessica's blood.

Even though Olivia was dying to put in her application for a detective's position, she had decided to wait. She'd hoped that if she lay low and kept out of the limelight, Vogel's anger would eventually subside to the point he wouldn't block her promotion. But here she was, meeting with the head of Internal Affairs, despite her best efforts not to rub being right in Vogel's face.

No point in delaying it any longer. Olivia power-walked through the parking lot and made her way to Captain Bellwood's office on the second floor. A receptionist told her to have a seat while she let the captain know Olivia had arrived.

She didn't have to wait long. The office door opened, and the man she knew to be Captain Bellwood from her Google search last night opened the door.

"Officer Selman? Come on in and have a seat."

He waited for her to take a seat in front of his desk before he ventured around his huge, fancy wooden desk and sat down.

"Well, you probably know why I've asked you here."

He seemed to be waiting for a response, so Olivia shook her head.

"Really? You have no clue?"

She was even more confident now that Vogel had filed a complaint, but she wasn't about to admit anything, so she gave him another shake of her head.

"I want to hire you as a detective, of course. What is it going to take to convince you to fill out an application?"

Olivia opened her mouth, but no words would come out. She tried again with no better luck. On her third attempt, she managed to push out, "You want to hire me as a detective?"

"Of course. I've looked into what you did to solve the Turner case. That was incredible detective work. Absolutely brilliant. You have talent and drive, and we need more of that.

Also, I'm not going to lie, it would be a huge benefit to have access to a different point of view. Something other than 'old-white-guy' perspective would be nice. So, what do you say?"

Olivia was at a loss for words again. She left Captain Bellwood hanging for a few seconds before she blurted out, "Yes. Yes, absolutely, yes. I would love to be a detective. It's the reason I joined the police force in the first place. Sorry, this has just caught me by surprise. The last time I saw Detective Vogel, he told me that I would never become a detective."

The grin on Captain Bellwood's face turned into something akin to a child tasting black licorice for the first time. "I wouldn't worry about Detective Vogel. He's retiring at the end of the month anyway."

"Really? I didn't get the impression that he was considering retirement anytime soon."

Captain Bellwood leaned forward and spoke in a faux conspiratorial tone. "Between you and me, his retirement wasn't strictly voluntary. What you don't know is that this isn't the first time Detective Vogel has botched a murder investigation. In the last two years, two different convictions have been overturned by DNA evidence. Civil lawsuits have already been filed, and the county is looking at payouts in the tens of millions of dollars. Suffice it to say that Vogel is not our favorite detective right now."

It was terrible news for the whole department, but Olivia couldn't wrestle the smile off her face.

She was going to be a detective.

Jonas leaned into each curve, going a good fifteen miles over the recommended speed on the yellow signs. It had been years since he had been to the top of Bald Rock, but the muscle memory for every turn of the wheel was still there.

Parking on the makeshift gravel lot, he walked through the shallow, sparse tree line and out onto the massive rock face. Graffiti and broken glass covered every flat surface within sight.

There had been a time, in late high school and early college, when he and his friends were up here at least once a month, playing guitar and singing old Radiohead and Weezer songs.

Jonas walked to the edge of the relatively flat part, just before the rock sloped down steeply enough to make walking hazardous, and sat down. He had come here to do some thinking while enjoying a good sunset.

Everything had changed. Every routine, responsibility, and obligation was either on hold or gone forever. There was still a dull ache in his chest when he thought of Jessica, but the pain was fading faster than he'd expected. He couldn't deny that finding out about her affair had affected his feelings of loss. Knowing he had lost her long before she was killed made it a little easier to move on.

Of course, he would never admit that to anyone.

Returning to single life had been weird. Once he'd finally convinced his parents he was fine on his own and they had flown back to Arizona a few weeks ago, he had experienced a loneliness he had never known.

It didn't help that he had so much time on his hands. He had decided not to return to teaching until the fall; by the time he'd recovered enough from his knife wounds to return to school, there had been only a few weeks left. He figured a return that late in the year would have been more of a nuisance than a blessing to the faculty and staff. So, day and night, he was left to his own devices.

He was getting used to free time, though. Plowing through novel after novel, playing two-on-two sand volleyball for hours on end, and watching sports to his heart's content wasn't half bad.

Paying bills wasn't a problem, either. After the true story came out about Jessica's death and his harrowing adventures, the fundraising site that his church set up had gone viral. There were over four hundred and fifty thousand dollars in the account. After paying his parents back for the bond money, he planned to donate most of it to local nonprofits he believed in, but it was nice not having to stress about his mortgage or paying off the medical expenses his insurance hadn't covered.

His days weren't completely devoid of social gatherings. He still went to church every Sunday and hung out with some of those friends on occasion. There were also the weekly dinners he shared with Olivia so she could keep him updated on the case. The conversational makeup of those dinners tended to be about ten percent case-related and ninety percent "other", but he wasn't complaining. There was no hiding the fact that he enjoyed seeing her, and he was seeing her more and more now that she was a regular at his church.

For the first few weeks after Jessica's death, the nightly refrain in his prayers to God had been "Why?". He must have asked ten different questions a thousand times, but the whys had faded as thankfulness returned.

Jonas leaned back and stretched his arms out wide, twisting from side to side. His back was still a little tight where the scar tissue stretched over his two stab wounds, but the doctors had marveled at how quickly he had healed.

He had a lot to be thankful for.

He was alive. He had a meaningful job. He had good friends and wonderful parents. He was part of a great church. He had a home in a neighborhood with tremendous market value that would hopefully sell quickly so he could move far, far away from the neighbors who still suspected he was a murderer.

God really can turn all things into good things for those who love Him. Even if everything in his life fell apart again, he would always have eternal bliss to look forward to.

God is good.

As the sun began to dip to the top of the distant tree line, Jonas felt his phone vibrate. He was surprised he still had reception up here. He pulled it out to read the text.

Olivia: I've got some big news to share. Dinner tonight?

Jonas looked up at the sun for a few seconds and then back down at his phone. *Screw it. There'll be other sunsets.*

He pushed off the rock and jogged back to his car.

THE END

ACKNOWLEDGMENTS

The author would like to thank everyone who helped make this book a reality. I am especially thankful for the following people:

Amanda Thompson for believing in me and putting up with all the late-night writing.

Jacob Allen Publishing for investing in this book and helping me bring it to an audience.

Emma O'Connell for her fantastic editing job and for making the process so easy.

Nathan Gamble for the killer cover design and promotional graphics, not to mention being an all-around great friend.

Joshua Masters for his tremendous friendship and support throughout the process. All those coffee house brainstorming and feedback sessions paid off.

Clay Keller for his expert feedback and editing advice, making the story better with every read-through.

Anne Miller for her amazing proofreading skills.

Yolanda Pender, Brae Dewalt, Jared Thompson, and Rebecca Coursen for providing some helpful beta reader feedback.

www.ingramcontent.com/pod-product-compliance
Lightning Source LLC
Chambersburg PA
CBHW020239010826
48973CB00006B/1584